Skeletons:

Deceit to the Bone

By: Paris Love

Copyright © 2006 Paris Love
Skeletons, Deceit to the Bone

All rights reserved. No part of this book may be reproduced or transmitted in any form or by any means. Electronic, or mechanical, including photocopying, recording or by any information storage and retrieval system, without permission in writing from the publisher. No abridgement or changes to the text are authorized by the publisher.

ISBN number: 1-59712-064-2

Printed in the United States of America by
Catawba Publishing Company
www.catawbapublishing.com

Skeletons:

Deceit to the bone

Three successful black women, Paris Love, Lucky Blue and Lolita Marcus set out to make it big in a world where money was no object and life was their playground. The road to success wasn't an easy one for neither of the women because they all had skeletons from their past that molded their futures.

Paris came from a world of sexuality and her struggles to find true love took her through many bad relationships. She never thought she could trust a man again then she met her true love, Trevor Tripple. They had a perfect relationship until one unexpected day changed their lives forever.

Lucky a successful lawyer with her own law firm made the wrong choice in a relationship that cost her a lot more than she had bargained for, betrayal and deceit has found Lucky and she is not prepared to pay the price.

Lolita had committed murder at a young age and as a teen struggled to free her and her baby brother Leland from a life of poverty. Now with success of several businesses, what is the one thing still missing from Lolita's life?

Edited by: Chelse Marie Weaver – website: chelsemarie@hotmail.com

Book Cover Design by: Silvio Suarez – website: Silviosuarezphotography.com

Models: Baby Girl
TreLesa
TaLisa

Acknowledgments

I would like to thank God for bringing the gift of creativity to life that was deep inside of me and for His many blessings in my life. I am truly thankful! To my mother, Pauline Love and my children, Aaron and Danielle I love you guys, thanks for your love and support; and sincere gratitude to all of my friends who have encouraged me to write this book. Special thanks to Brenda Nance for the vision and the pep talk, girl it really helped push me to finish the book. Kimberly Breckenridge thanks for reading the draft and for your honest opinion. I want to thank Keli Gillenwater. In addition, a special, special thanks to my cousin Chelse for editing my book and getting it print ready. Silvo, you know I appreciate your artistic/photo skills and your work on the cover of the book, Gracias mi amigo! For everyone whoever helped me with the printing and getting this book on the shelf, I say THANK YOU, let this be the beginning of a great year for us all.

Contents

Introduction	i
Skeletons, Deceit to the Bone	1
Lolita	9
Paris	11
Lucky	18
Chapter One	21
Chapter Two	42
Chapter Three	49
Chapter Four	55
Lolita	60
Paris	72
Chapter Five	79
Chapter Six	92
Club Dubai	96
Chapter Seven	114
Chapter Eight	121
Chapter Nine	129

Chapter Ten	139
Chapter Eleven	146
Chapter Twelve	152
Chapter Thirteen	161
Chapter Fourteen	167
Chapter Fifteen	184
Chapter Sixteen	199
Chapter Seventeen	210
Chapter Eighteen	223
Chapter Nineteen	236
Chapter Twenty	242
Chapter Twenty-One	247
Chapter Twenty-Two	265
Chapter Twenty-Three	269

Coming Soon!

Skeletons, Part 2	278
Queen Pin	281
Navy Seals: The New Breed	285

The Fear of Falling In Love	289
RAIN DROPS	290

Paris Love

Introduction

    I first met Lucky at the Charles Grayson Spa in South Park. We were getting "The Works" as they call it—pedicure, manicure and the Swedish body massage. Lucky Blue stood there in her dark blue, Jones of New York pants suit with the white button down blouse to match. She was 5'7" without heels and had big beautiful brown eyes with the longest lashes I had ever seen; they looked like the fake ones. Lucky had long curly hair that came to the middle of her back and her skin tone was the color of caramel candy, smooth and creamy. She had a small nose, small lips, and built like a Barbie Doll with the big boobs, no ass or hips. She was a very beautiful girl, with the exception of one obvious flaw—she had big corn dog feet. I could not believe all the knots and bumps on that girl's feet. No wonder she didn't wear many sandals.

    "Dayam!" I said, "Girl what size shoe do you wear?"
    "A size 10, bitch, why?" Lucky responded in a slick tone.

I just shook my head. "I just haven't seen feet that big on a woman before. I know it must be hard for you to wear open-toed shoes because those long ass toes would be hanging over your sandals like a crow gripping a branch!" I said, laughing my head off at my own little jokie joke.

Lucky did not think the shit was funny. She was starting to get mad at me, but I told her I was just playing and 'quit tripping.'

I eased in the chair next to her. Being the outgoing person that I was, I said, "Girl, your feet look so good. I like that nail polish color you have on your toes," thinking all the time that her feet were ugly as hell. However, I did not tell her that. "Oh by the way, my name is Paris Love, what's yours?"

Lucky looked at me with those big brown eyes of hers and said, "Hey, my name is Lucky Blue."

I told her that I knew she was tripping on me because I just had such an outgoing personality that it sometimes took a little time getting used to me.

We sat there and sipped on a glass of wine. I think we may have finished two bottles before we realized it. I was laughing and telling her about my man Trevor Tripple, the *one* at the time; he was some kind of fine, and Lord knows he was. He was a defense attorney and had a private practice uptown on the top floor of the Bank of America building.

"Lucky, girl, we used to meet there for lunch. I used to go to his office where he had a huge marble top desk. I would slide my fine ass up on that desk and open my legs so he could have his lunch!"

Lucky looked at me and said, "Trevor, girl I know him. I represented one of his boys out in LA last year. I have my own law firm as well."

She told me that she was an entertainment lawyer and many of her clients lived in LA.

"Get the fuck out of here! It is a small world! So how long have you known Trevor?" I enquired, prying a little. I wanted to know just how well she knew him.

She told me that they went to Law school at Duke together and that all the women wanted that fine chocolate-ass man. I just started laughing and said, "Girl I know".

By that time, we were done with our manicures and pedicures, and James, the spa's masseur, came to get us for our Swedish body massage.

The room where we got our massage had dim lighting and the music was that nature music. I could have listened to some smooth R&B myself, but this was cool. There were two dressing rooms, where we changed our clothes and put on these nice soft robes. We each lay on the two massage tables in front of the two handsome, strong men waiting to take care of us.

"Which one do you want?" Lucky said, with that look on her face as if she had already made her choice.

It did not matter to me because they were both fine as hell.

As we lay there listening to the music playing, the men went to work on our bodies. Now I did not know about Lucky, but the wine and the music were making me more relaxed than I had been in weeks. I had started working for two twenty-two year old basketball players for the Charlotte Bobcats as their Personal Assistant, so running around for them and their "boys" was a bit trying at times. I was also an Events Planner for a new soda company called Urban Lite, and we were working on getting the concerts and introduction of the company set-up in St. Thomas. With all that stress in my life, I needed a massage and a drink. I opened my eyes for a minute and looked at the floor, studying the small dots of color in the tile and thinking how beautiful the colors were. Yeah I was trippin! That is what happens when you've had too much wine and all of your stress rubbed away; you think about the smallest things in life and see their beauty.

After the rub down was over, we were dressed and decided to have lunch at the Cheesecake Factory. The food was good and the cheesecakes were off the chain. There were so many flavors to choose from, strawberry, vanilla bean, French vanilla, that it was hard to decide which one to get. I really enjoyed eating there. The line was usually long and I was starving, so I was hoping that it wasn't going to take all day.

We both got in our cars and drove across the street to the mall. We parked in the garage right next to the restaurant. When we turned into the mall to go to the parking garage, I could see people standing around outside of the doorway to the Cheesecake Factory, which only meant one thing—the waiting list was at least 45 minutes to an hour. We walked from the parking garage onto the sidewalk leading to the restaurant. People were standing around talking and laughing and just relaxing and waiting to hear the host call their name. I walked passed two fine-ass niggas standing there in jeans and t-shirts and we made eye contact. I just looked at them, and the cute pecan brown-skinned dude gave me the biggest smile. I nudged Lucky, "Girl did you see that fine-ass pecan brown, sexy motherfucker we just passed by?"

Lucky looked at me with her lips turned up, "Girl, too late! I peeped them brothers when we first walked up, and the one with the dark jeans and curly hair was checking a sister out. I think we need to go back and holla at them for a minute, while you playin!"

Lucky and I laughed and we walked into the restaurant and put our name on the list.

Unfortunately, as expected, the waiting list was at least an hour, so we decided to walk into the mall to pass some time. Being the shoe lover I was, we stopped in Nine West. Lucky told me that she didn't really shop, but we had to do something to make the time go by faster. Lucky walked in and looked at a couple of pair of shoes and then she sat down while I shopped.

I turned around to ask Lucky if she saw anything she liked. "Damn Lucky are you tired, why are you sitting down?"

"Paris, I told you that I don't like to shop and besides, I don't see anything in here that would look good on my feet."

I just shook my head and continued to look. I found some pink lace-up sandals, but just when I started to reach for them, I saw this hand grab them off the shelf. I was shocked at how quickly she got to them before I did.

The tall slim, brown-skinned woman looked at me and said, "Oh were you going to get these?"

"Yes, I was!"

She started laughing and said, "Girl I am so sorry, do you want them?"

I asked her what size shoe she wore. She told me a size 8 1/2 to a 9. I laughed and said "Good, 'cause I wear a size 6 ½, so you straight."

We called the salesperson over. She only had my size left, and I was too happy about that.

"Girl, I am so sorry they didn't have your size," I said.

She smiled and jokingly said, "I am sure you are! What is your name, just in case we meet again?"

"Paris."

"Paris, huh?" she repeated, raising an eyebrow.

"Yeah what's your name?"

She told me that her name was 'Lolita Marcus.' I said, "Okay, and you are having a problem with my name… hmmm."

Lolita was a very pretty woman with brown skin and neck-length brown hair with blonde highlights. She stood about 5'6 ½", and had the

v

same figure as Lucky, but with a little more ass. Unlike Lucky, though, Lolita had pretty feet. Her toes did not have one bump on them, and she had them polished with little designs on her big toe. She had the perfect face with chestnut brown eyes and small features. She was dressed casual in jean capris and a black halter-top, with black sandals. Lolita was very friendly. We spent some time talking about shoes and traveling, and I learned that she was the owner of seven spas, including two overseas in France and Germany. I never would have guessed she was so rich by just looking at her, and she was so down to earth. I told her about my business and trips that I had taken.

By that time, Lucky reminded me that it had been an hour and a half, so our table at Cheesecake Factory was probably ready. I introduced her to Lolita and Lucky invited her to join us for lunch.

When I was ready to leave, the salesperson had my shoes waiting at the desk so I purchased them. She looked at me and asked me if my eyes were green and if they were mine. I got that shit all the time so I just answered her with a firm "Yes!" I wanted to say *'Bitch, is that long ass ponytail yours, or Mr. Ed's?'* I just wished people would realize that black folks come in all shades colors and eye colors too. Hell, I had twin cousins with one eye green and the other blue. So what the fuck was the problem?

I just grabbed my bag and gave the salesperson a look as if I wanted to slap her face, without saying a word.

Lucky, Lolita, and I left Nine West, and headed towards the restaurant. By the time we got in the door, they were calling our names, so we followed the host to our seats. The host told us that adding Lolita to our party would not be a problem, because we were sitting in a booth that seated four people comfortably. We ordered drinks and sat in the booth talking for what seemed like hours. We all exchanged numbers and decided that we would get together again soon. That day was the first day of a long friendship between the three of us.

Skeletons,

Deceit to the Bone

Charlotte, NC, August 2003 was hot as hell outside, and I was in no mood to be waiting for my fiancé to pick me up from Charlotte-Douglas Airport. His ass was already on shaky ground, and I had pretended everything was fine. I was having the time of my life. I had just returned from France with my girlfriends, Lolita Marcus and Lucky Blue. Lolita had a grand opening party in Paris for her new 24 hour spa. That shit was off the chain, and we had a ball. It was a 16-hour flight back to the states, so we were all tired as hell. It was a long trip home, and I was ready to get into my king size bed and get some serious sleep after partying for a whole week straight, non-stop. The next four months were going to be busy as hell for us because our new club was opening in Miami; Club Dubai was going to be the first state-of-the-art club ever! We had a lot of work ahead of us. I could not wait to get to Miami and hang out on South Beach; people down there were wild and just doing whatever they felt like doing. Miami was the money town, and we were about to be paid.

I finally arrived home after a 30-minute drive from the airport and listening to Trevor explain to me why he was late. I was too exhausted to argue with him about it so I just listened to him go on and on. I told him that we could discuss it in the morning. I just wanted to go to bed.

We pulled into the garage and I saw something that was not there when I left—a motorcycle, and I was wondering to whom it belonged.

I asked Trevor, "Whose bike?"

He told me that was why he was late getting to the airport, because Lucky had her bike delivered to the house. I was in shock because Lucky did not ride a bike. *'So what is this chick up to, now?'* I thought.

I immediately called her on the phone, and I was like, "Nigga, who's bike did you have delivered to my house, and *why*?"

She started laughing and told me that she bought the bike as a surprise for a nigga she was dealing with that played for the Oakland Raiders.

I said, "I hope it's not Ron's punk ass!" I did not like him that much and I had never even met the nigga. I asked, "So why is the shit in *my* garage?"

She said that he was coming over to her house in the morning and she was going to bring him by to meet me and to get the bike. It was his birthday, and she knew he wanted to start riding again. I told her next time she might want to tell somebody before she had stuff sent to their house.

I hung up the phone from that trick and got my stuff out the trunk, and Trevor grabbed my suitcases and took them in the house. I immediately took a long hot shower and started to shampoo my hair, when the shower door opened.

Trevor was standing behind me and he said, "Let me do that for you."

The one thing I could say about that man is he sure knew how to make a woman feel like a woman. He started to press his body up against mine as he lathered the shampoo in my hair and gently massaged my scalp. That shit was so erotic, until my shit was wet as hell. He continued to lather my hair and I could feel his stiff, fat, long, 10-inch dick rubbing against my butt. I turned around to face him so I could rinse the shampoo out of my hair. He pressed his body close to mine, wrapped his arms around my neck, and kissed me slow and deep. With every move of his tongue, I could feel my body shake. Trevor moved my legs apart and as the water was running, he was sucking my lips and licking my clit with his tongue. I could hardly contain myself as the chills ran through my body like electricity. He looked up at me and said with a soft voice, "I missed you so much and I love you even more."

Lord have mercy, I could see myself melting like hot butter right in front of him. Just as I was about to cum, he started to lick my clit faster and faster and I came so hard until my toes curled, tightly gripping the tile on the shower floor. After that, he turned me around so that he could penetrate me, from the back, sliding that long hard dick inside of me and it was as if it was the best fit ever. He started thrusting back and forth; that shit was feeling so damn good, and finally we both came together in a passionate explosion.

I could not even put my nightgown on. I just got into bed and snuggled up against Trevor's warm body, falling fast to sleep.

The sun was shining so brightly into our bedroom the next

morning, that it woke me out of a deep sleep. I got up to take a piss, when I heard some old school R&B playing downstairs. It sounded like Voyage to Atlantis, by the Isley Brothers. You know you could tell that sound by the way Jasper played the hell out of that lead guitar. I heard the voice of Ron Isley, *'I will always come back to you, always, always, come back to you.'* That was the shit back in the day. Please don't smoke a joint with your man while that song was playing cause it was about to be on up in there—panties dropping, butt naked, pure love making!

I started singing along with the song as I walked toward the bathroom. I could also smell breakfast cooking, so I knew my baby was feeling very good that morning.

I sat on the toilet day dreaming about the events that took place over the weekend when the phone rang. I could hear Trevor yelling for me to pick up the phone so I hurried up and wiped myself, flushed the toilet, and washed my hands. I picked up the phone and heard Trevor talking to Lucky and I said, "I got it baby."

He said, "Okay, but hurry up and come eat your breakfast before it gets cold."

Lucky informed me that she was on her way over to pick up the motorcycle she bought for Ron and to introduce me to him.

I said, "Damn, Lucky, that nigga must be putting it down for you to be buying him a bike."

Lucky said, "Girl, he is *all that!* I've been talking to him on the low for about a year, now. I'm really just checking him out to see if he's worthy to meet my peeps."

We talked for a few more minutes, and then she said that she was 15 minutes away from my house, so we hung up. I started brushing my teeth. I at least wanted to have fresh breath when she got to my house. Trevor was yelling for me to come eat breakfast, so I slipped on some jogging pants and a tank top. I looked at myself in the mirror before heading downstairs and I looked damn good—shit, I was fine as hell! I was not conceited or nothing like that, but a woman should have confidence in herself, that way no man can pull her down and take away her self-esteem. I loved me some *me*! That was the bottom line.

By the time I was walking down the stairs, the doorbell was ringing, and I could see Lucky and this black, deep dark chocolate, midnight-looking brother standing on my porch. As I opened the door, I was surprised at how good her man looked. To my knowledge, this was the first time that Lucky had a fine nigga, and this dude was black as the night, with white pretty teeth and a low haircut. He was about 5 foot 11, and a swoll, cock-diesel nigga.

As I told them to come in, I whispered, "Damn Lucky this nigga is swoll!"

She started giggling like some schoolgirl, and said, "This is my baby, Ron Brown, but everybody calls him 'Diesel.'"

I said, "You got that shit right, because he is *that*."

Trevor walked in the room and said, "What's up Lucky?"

She introduced Diesel to Trevor and told him that he played professional football, so they started talking about the game and all the players, so we knew what time it was then.

Lucky and I walked over to the kitchen and I offered her some breakfast. As we sat at the kitchen table, eating, she told me all about Diesel, and how she met him. He was with one of her clients, some new rap artist that she had met for a business lunch to go over his contract before he signed.

Lucky started telling me all the shit that Diesel was doing in the meeting. "Girl I was in the meeting trying to concentrate on what I was doing and I promise you, Diesel was standing behind my clients sticking his tongue out and moving it like a damn snake.

I was giving him that look as if I was going to kill him if he didn't stop. That nigga just kept on doing it the entire meeting. I closed the deal and shook the guy's hand and left the meeting."

I asked, "Lucky, girl what was wrong with him, and what did he say to you after the meeting was over?"

"Paris, that nigga called me on the phone before I could get in the car, and then he had the nerve to ask me out to dinner. I told him that I don't date my client's friends and hung up in his face."

I looked at Lucky and started laughing at her and she was frowning up at me.

"Paris, what is so fucking funny?"

"Lucky, you and I both know that you were feeling that nigga when he first started sticking his tongue out at you. I know you were sitting there with your nasty ass wondering how that tongue would feel between your legs, bitch please, I know you!"

Lucky fell on the floor laughing, "Girl you are right about that, he was making my pussy wet as hell in that meeting, and he knew it."

"Well what happened, did you finally give him your phone number?" I asked.

"Yeah after that motherfucker sent flowers and cards to my office, and begged me everyday to go to dinner with him until I finally gave in. And now I can't get rid of his punk ass."

After listening to all the exciting details, I told Lucky that she seemed happy, so I was happy for her. We finished eating our breakfast and I heard Trevor in there laughing loud and talking plenty of shit, which I knew he loved to do when he got a listening ear. Lucky and I interrupted their conversation.

"Diesel I got you something for your birthday, but you will have to close your eyes when I tell you, because it's a surprise."

Diesel looked at Lucky and then he looked at Trevor and me. I threw my hands up as if to say *'Why you are looking at me, I don't know what it is.'* Trevor was talking shit the entire time, so I kept putting my hands over his mouth to shut him up. Diesel just looked like he was about to sit in Santa's lap and be granted the best gift in the world.

"Lucky, what did you get me?" Diesel asked.

"Baby you will have to wait until we get in the garage to see what it is, just calm down."

We all headed to the back door in the kitchen that led to the garage. Lucky was holding Diesel's hand and told him to close his eyes. When she opened the door, I saw the motorcycle parked in the corner of the garage.

Trevor, with his smart ass, was still talking shit, "Man all I am going to say is that you must have beat the brakes off that pussy!"

I was telling him to shut the hell up, but he was steady talking shit.

"Diesel, man I don't know you, we just met, but you are a bad man, you are a bad motherfucker. Teach me the secret nigga, please, 'cause I want to know what I am doing wrong."

"Trevor shut your damn mouth and let Lucky do this, she don't need your help, thank you," I said.

When Diesel opened his eyes and saw the bike, he started yelling, "Oh shit! Oh shit, baby, you got me the Busa, *damn* that shit is hot! Thank you baby, this is the best birthday present ever."

That bike *was* hot. It was black, silver, and chromed out, with the matching helmet, jacket and gloves. And to top it off, she had 'Diesel' on that nigga's license plate.

Diesel grabbed Lucky and picked her up as if she weighed 2 pounds. He was so happy, until I thought he was going to start crying. Lucky handed him the keys to the bike and he grabbed his helmet, jacket, and gloves, jumped on the bike, and told Lucky he was going for a little ride.

Lucky said, "Enjoy your new toy, baby! Call me later!"

After Diesel left, Trevor was still running that damn mouth of his, "You better be glad you told me that the shit was coming to my house and it was for your man, because I would have rode the shit out that Busa."

"Trevor, take your ass in the house!" I yelled.

"Paris, who in the hell you think you talking to? Don't let Lucky see you get your ass whipped out here."

I waved my hand at him as if to say 'Go away.' Trevor went in the house, I talked to Lucky for while, and we made some plans to get up with each other later on in the week. I gave her a hug, and she headed out the door.

Lolita

    Spa Margarita in Balentine was the first of seven spas Lolita had opened. That location was one of a kind with its ultra-modern look and feel. It was mint green and white throughout the entire spa, and when you first walked in the door, the waiting area had a big plush lime green sofa with matching white leather chairs. The receptionist desk was a huge half moon shaped with a white marble top, and the chair was a one-of-a-kind lime green leather chair. The receptionist area had one of those big rocks with the water running, but the unique thing about it was the water ran up and down with small white lights behind it. There was a plasma 32-inch T.V. on the wall, and the surround sound was off the chain. While you waited for your spa treatment, there was a margarita fountain, so you would be nice and *right*, about time you left the spa. There were three levels; the first level was for manicures and pedicures, the second level was mud baths, body wraps, deep tissue treatments and skin peels, and on the third level was the full body massage and Jacuzzi. There were over five massages to choose from, and clients had their pick of male or female. Also located on the third level was the VIP room, a room that cost $1500 for 3 hours. The VIP room hid behind doors that looked like giant mirrors on the wall, and in that room, there was more than massages going on. In order to get into the exclusive VIP room, you had to be on the list and have big dollars because once you went over 3 hours, the cost escalated to $400 for each additional hour.

The VIP room was designed for pleasure from porn on the big screen T.V. to all kinds of lotions, potions, and toys, you name it. There were all kinds of big fur rugs with huge pillows on the floor and fluffy ones on the sofas. Lolita had the spa looking like an old James Bond movie, which everyone seemed to love. It kinda reminded me of the 70's with black lights, colorful pictures on the walls, you smoked a little weed and got your drink on, and just let nature take its course. That was the model in the VIP room. Even though it was costly, people who had the money were paying to have that fantasy night to be anybody they felt like being.

Yes, sex and any fantasy that you had that was not too crazy went on in the VIP room. Lolita was a straight freak, and she did not mind letting you know that she was. She really enjoyed anal sex, and she owned several devices to help her reach her highest level of satisfaction.

This was the most frequented spa that Lolita owned in the United States. Overseas Lolita was a big hit. She had just had her grand opening in Europe and that spa sat on 400 acres of land and was fully equipped with anything you needed from body waxing to mud bathing. You named it and that spa had it. It even had a horse ranch.

Lolita had outdone herself this time. She had the money, fortune and fame to prove it, but she still could not get over her past and the type of family she came from. She only spoke to one family member—her baby brother Leland.

Paris

Trevor called me at 4:00 pm on Sunday to ask when I was coming home. I had gone to church with one of my old friends, and the service was different from any service I had been to. I had stayed there until 2 pm, talking to some of Jackie's friends who attended the church. They where asking when was my husband going to come to church with me. I said that it was my first time there and I was going to ask him to come with me the next Sunday. I did not want to tell them that we were not married, but we lived together, and had plenty of sex, just to hear them say, *'You know that is a sin right?'* I just did not want to come across as a bad person without them knowing who I was inside first.

I had come from a dysfunctional family and I had been involved, well participated in, or maybe I was molested. But I guess in a sense you could say that it was more like a game. My cousins were much older then I was; I was in the fourth grade and they were nineteen and twenty-one years old. All

I ever heard was that I was 'so pretty' and that I was going to be 'a heartbreaker' when I grew up. And how I had the 'prettiest smile' and the 'prettiest hair' and the 'prettiest green eyes,' which I got from my grandmother. I was 5'2" at the time, and I did not get much taller as I got older, but I had what they called a 'coke bottle shape.' I used to hear my cousin's friends say that I had a body like a brick shit house, whatever the hell that meant. I was born in the late sixties so it was a thing to be "light-skinned" as the black people would put it. I then had it from the other side of the coin as well. My mother used to always tell me *'Don't act pretty then you are not pretty, if you act ugly then you are ugly – pretty is as pretty does, so be pretty inside and out.'* I thought that meant try to please everyone and make him or her like you. Let's just say it started out that way, until I found out most of the people where lying to me including my relatives. *Especially* my relatives.

On a pretty summer day when I was about eight years old, my cousin Sandy asked me if I wanted to play a game with her, and I told her, "Yes, I would like to play a game, what is it called?" Sandy told me that she would tell me how to play first, then she would tell me the name of it. She told me to get under the covers with her, to open her legs, and then to put my tongue in her vagina. I asked her what kind of nasty game was that. She told me that it was not nasty; it feels good.

She said, "Let me show you first, so you can see for yourself."

Sandy pulled my panties to the side and she started licking my vagina. Her tongue felt warm, and at the time, I did not know why, but it felt good, just as she told me it would. I told her that I liked playing that game, and once again, asked the name of it. She said it was 'the pussy-lick' and then said, "Now it is your turn to do me."

Paris Love

I was eight years old and I did not know what she was doing to me was wrong or what she was teaching me to do to her was wrong. I thought since it did not hurt and she was not hurting me then it must be okay, so we played this game for sometime, until one day I told my mother what Sandy had taught me. My mother called my cousin's mother on the phone and told her what Sandy had been teaching me. Her mother was furious; she could not believe that her nineteen-year-old daughter would take advantage of a little girl like that. My aunt beat the crap out of my cousin, and she told her that she had better not even think about touching me again. I was upset because I looked up to my cousin, she was so pretty and I thought she was so nice. She used to buy me candy and take me shopping, but I later realized that it was all for her own sick pleasure. That's why that bitch never had any children.

Anyway, I stood on the church steps, thinking about all the shit that happened to me when I was a little girl, and I could feel my skin boiling, 'cause I was so damn mad. I forgot that I was still standing in front of the church. I had started talking to the Lord a long time ago and He was the only reason that I was still there that day. I did not have to go to no church to have a bunch of so-called 'Saints' judge me to know that God loved me no matter what. I just talked to Him as if I was talking to anybody else. Just regular conversation about how messed up this world was.

Anyway, I got in my car and I asked the Lord to help me to forget about what happened. Oh, and I had forgiven those who wrongfully used my innocence, but I just could not forget for shit. I called Trevor as soon as I got in the car. See, he knew all that shit about my past, but he still loved me, which I knew was a blessing from God. I was on the phone with Trevor and when he asked me how was church service, I was trying to explain to him that it was so different and the people seemed real. The pastor was talking about deliverance and being set free from past hurts, and all that and I was in tears. He told me that it must have been really been something, because I very seldom cried. He also said he was waiting for me to get home so we could go out to dinner. Trevor was the best boyfriend that I had ever had, because the ones before him were so full of shit, until no one would even believe the shit I went through if I told them.

I remember that after my cousin abused me, I thought you expressed love that way, so when I got to the age of thirteen, I had my first real sexual encounter. His name was Willy Jones, and he was soooo cute. He had good hair, you know, that curly shit, and he was black and his skin was as smooth as a baby's bottom. I can remember being so nervous when I would see him, and he would always have something for me. I remember one time he gave me his mother's diamond ring, and he told me that he loved me. We were behind the school on the playground, and they had one of those tunnels that kids played in. So we went in there and he had me up against the wall. I was standing there all-warm inside and my panties were soaking wet but I did not move. Willy started kissing me all on the neck and then put his tongue in my mouth, and I put my tongue in his mouth too. He was twilling his tongue against my tongue. I was doing the same thing, and we were in harmony with each other. I thought that I was in love, not knowing it was lust, but it felt good.

I dated Willy until we were in the 10th grade, and then it started. I can remember the first time we had got into an argument. Willy thought I liked some guy at school and everyday he would accuse me of cheating on him. I don't know when he had become so jealous, but it was starting to get on my nerves. I told him that I did not want to be his girl anymore and the nigga hauled off and slapped the shit out of me, started talking crazy, and said he was going to kill me and all this shit. I had to get myself together because this took me way off guard and at first, I didn't know how to respond to it. Then it happened. I saw a bottle on the ground next to where I was standing and before I realized it, I picked it up and busted that nigga upside his damn head. He was bleeding all over the place. I was ranting and raving and walked around him in circles saying, "I know you didn't put your hands on me, my daddy don't even put his hands on me." I left his ass on the ground holding his head, and I ran back into the school and told some of my homeboys that were in gangs and carried guns, what that nigga did to me. They went outside and had their guns cocked at that nigga's head. I told them not to kill him, but they beat the shit out of Willy that day, and after that, he would not even look my way.

Well this started a trend as far as dating went. It seemed like every nigga I met after Willy's ass was a damn fool and always wanted to put their hands on me. I did not play that shit. You did not fuckin touch me. I would kill your ass or have you done fa' sho! The last time I could remember my boyfriend hitting me was the last time I was going to deal with that shit and that was when I was twenty-one years old. I was dating this man named James Johnston and he was a Baller (drug dealer). I never knew what he did exactly. All I knew was he was taking care of a sister big time—bought me a four bedroom house, Mercedes Benz, two mink coats, jewelry, the whole nine. Gave me thousands of dollars on a weekly basis and took me all around the world. I did not ask any questions and did not care about them other bitches he was seeing, because I was wifey in that motherfucker. I was not a dummy though. I knew he had to be up to something illegal, so I stashed some of that money he was giving me, because I was working in the bank and in school pursuing my degree. I had that shit in a safety deposit box that no one knew about, and before it was all said and done, I had over a million dollars saved in that bitch. I can remember that shit like it was yesterday. JJ came home and he was looking like he had seen a ghost or some shit. I said, "What the fuck is wrong with you?"

He said, "Pack yo' shit, we got to get the fuck out of here, I mean leave the country and lay low."

I was going *no* damn where. I had school to finish and my career to get off the ground. I was not trying to hear that shit. I said, "I am not going no damn where."

And that nigga punched me in my stomach.

While I was bent over, I started to see red. Now I told you about the last motherfucker that put his hands on me and from then on, I was taking self-defense classes and a regular at the shooting range. I got myself together, ran in the bathroom, and locked the door. I had my purse in the bathroom because I was getting ready for school before JJ came home. My gun was in my purse. I wanted to shoot that nigga so bad, until I was about to explode in that damn bathroom. He was kicking the door, telling me to come out, telling me he was sorry for hitting me but something bad had happened, and he needed to get out of town right then.

I said, "You need to get out of town, not me and I don't want to know nothing about it".

He yelled, "Bitch, all I have done for you, and you going to leave me hanging like this," and before I could respond, I heard gunshots and a bunch of niggas yelling, "Get that nigga, get him for Rocket too!"

I jumped my ass in the linen closet and hid; they never came in the bathroom. I guess they thought he was there by himself. I was waiting in that closet for about an hour or two, shaking like a leaf. When I opened the door, JJ's body was lying in a pool of blood and he was dead as shit.

I called the police, and when they arrived, I told them that I was in the restroom and the whole story on how we argued before the people showed up. The police were asking me all kinds of questions about JJ's life, who was his friends and what he did for a living, and that was when I found out the whole story. It seemed that JJ was one of the top dealers in the U.S. and he had apparently gotten himself involved with some Cubans that tried to stick him for his drugs. He retaliated by killing them outside of a restaurant in Miami. He was on the run, and that is why he tried to get me to go with him. I told the police that I had no idea of what JJ did for a living, we never talked about it, and he was not home most of the time anyway. I was glad I never really knew what that nigga did, 'cause my ass would have been spending my 22nd birthday in prison. Not!

Lucky

    Lucky Blue, Attorney at Law LLP, she had come a long way from the country where she was a little farm girl and everyone in the town knew everyone. Lucky lived in a town where everyone went to the same church and shopped at the same grocery store and strip mall. When she first came to Charlotte, she was so nervous because of the so-called "BIG CITY," though Charlotte was not that big, but compared to where she came from, it was a huge change in her life. Lucky left her hometown after graduating from high school, and attended Chapel Hill and Duke for Law school. While studying law, she met a few entertainers and decided to become an entertainment lawyer. When we met, she owned an office uptown in the Bank of America bldg. on the 30th floor and had a clientele exceeding 800. She was working a deal with a new record company to be their lawyer for the entire company. Lucky had 3 paralegals and 10 lawyers who had two of their own paralegals, 2 receptionists, and several new clients coming in daily.

Lucky was not close to her family because they had no ambition, and that just drove Lucky crazy. She had always set high goals for herself, and she never wanted to grow up and become another country girl sitting on her ass and having babies for some nigga that dealt drugs for a living. Lucky wanted much more for herself and she worked hard to get where she was. Lucky never told anyone, but she used to work in a strip club while she was in college—the kind of club where you got completing butt naked. It was also a place where lesbians hung out. So Lucky was stripping for women, and she even did a few private parties when she was trying to make ends meet and pay for Law school. She also used to deliver 'packages' for one of her old boyfriends from her hometown. She was determined not to be broke and living at home with the rest of her schoolmates. Bottom line was she wanted to be successful, so she did whatever she had to do at the time.

Now that she was on top, though, she had been receiving calls from some strange number asking for money and threatening to put her pictures on the internet and call the news to put her out there about the life she lived before she became the top entertainment lawyer in the world. One day, Lucky got home and found a letter in her mailbox put together with cutout letters. The letter read that if she did not come up with 2 million dollars, the pictures and the video tapes were going to be sent to the tabloids. In addition to the threatening phone calls and letters, she received copies of the pictures she had taken when she was a stripper. Naturally, Lucky did not want what was on those pictures to get out to the public. She was trying to think of something to do to keep that information in the deep past. She had always viewed it as something she just had to do to make it through school.

Chapter One

Lolita and I called Lucky, "Attorney Lucky Blue's office, how may I help you?" Her paralegal was such a cheerful person.

Lucky had a huge office with marble finished floors, a huge cherry wood desk with plush leather chairs. I could picture her in my mind, sitting in her chair all suited up, looking like a million bucks.

Lucky picked up the line with her "white" voice and said, "Attorney Blue."

I said, "What's up, Blue?"

Then the ghetto voice came out of her, "Hey what's crackin? Are we going out tonight, because I could sure use a drink? It's been one of those days."

"Girl we are going to this club in Houston, so we were calling you so that you could leave work early. I have already made our reservation, and the flight leaves Charlotte at 7pm tonight, so what's up, you down?"

Lucky said, "Hell yeah, you know I'm down for whatever!"

We all loved to travel and with no kids, it was on and poppin. I told Lucky that we would send the car to pick her up, because she lived on the South side of town, and Lolita and I lived on the North. I had already told Trevor that we were going to Houston for the weekend and he just said 'Have a good time.' Trevor never was the type to try to tell me what to do, so it worked out well between us. I loved him, and I was not looking for anybody to take his place.

I got home around 12noon on Friday, ran upstairs, and jumped in the shower. The phone rang and it was Lolita and Lucky on a three-way call.

"What time are we headed out, and are we going to have time to get lunch?" Lolita asked.

"Well ladies, I am in the shower right now, and I will call you back once I am dressed, so start getting ready. Especially you Lucky, because you are slow as hell." I hung up the phone and finished my shower. The phone rang again, and I could see from the caller ID that it was Trevor.

"Hello", I answered.

"Hey baby, is you still getting dressed? I was on my way home to give you a little traveling lovin, so what's up!"

"Trevor, you had better be pulling in the garage as we speak because a sista is running on borrowed time."

"I am already in the garage and on my way in the house now so don't get dressed yet," he said

I hung up the phone. I was putting on my lotion when Trevor walked in the bedroom, butt-bald naked. I said "Damn baby, whatcha do, get undressed in the garage?"

He said 'Come here' and hmm, hmm that boy knew how to make a woman feel good. He went straight for the jewels, lickin, suckin,

Paris Love

and caressing every inch of my body. I felt his warm soft tongue going faster and the next thing I knew, my toes curled and I just let the juices flow.

Trevor looked at me and said, "That's all I wanted to see on your face before you left for the weekend was the look of satisfaction. Now you can get dressed."

I asked him if he wanted me to give him the same pleasure and he told me, "Naw baby I just wanted you to be satisfied and we can pick up where we left off when you return."

Damn, I almost wanted to stay home, and I could not wait to get back from Houston, so I hurried up and put my stuff in my bag so I can get on with this trip. I drove over to Lolita's house and used my key to let myself in. Lolita lived in Lake Norman in this big ass 500,000-dollar house with a house cleaner to boot. She had a four-car garage, swimming pool both inside and outside, six bedrooms, four bathrooms and a movie theater. My girl was *paid*, but she was so down to earth that you would not know she was sittin on millions.

The Limo driver arrived at Lucky's house around 2:30pm and Lucky called Lolita on the phone and asked, "Where is Paris?"

Lolita, with her valley girl voice said, "Girl, let me tell you, Paris came over here glowin and shit with this big cheese-eaten grin on her face, so you know what that heifer been up to. Girl, she is downstairs in the kitchen waiting on me, do you want to speak to her?"

"Lolita, tell Paris I said get her fas' ass on this phone, pronto!" Lucky said.

"Paris!" Lolita screamed down the steps, "Girl pick up the phone, it's Lucky."

"Hola, ma, que pasa", I said.

"Don't 'hola' me heifer, whatcha smiling 'bout?"

"Lucky, girl you know my baby had to put it down before I left him for a weekend, pleezeeeee believe! He don't even play, so do I need to go into details, 'cause you know how you like to hear all the details so you can be over there playin with yourself, nasty heifer."

Lolita screamed in the background, "Lucky, don't pay any attention to Paris' ass, 'cause she is the nasty one."

I told them both to 'shut the hell up'. By that time, Lucky was pulling up in the driveway. Lolita and I grabbed our bags and headed for the door, "Houston here we come!" we said in unison. The driver opened the car door and took our bags to put them in the trunk.

When we got in the car, Lucky was making apple martinis, and she looked at Lolita and me and said, "Have a glass ladies."

And you know we were ready to get our drink on.

I called to check on our hotel reservations to make sure that everything was set for our arrival. The clerk on the phone said that our room should be ready before 8pm, because the house cleaners had already cleaned it. Lolita was screaming in the background while I was on the phone asking about an ocean front room.

I said, "Girl we are not going to the beach. This is downtown Houston, so we will be staying in a suite with a small kitchen. The only view we will be overlooking is the city."

Lolita gave me that, *'well okay, excuse me'* look and I gave it right back to her, and then we started laughing at each other. When we got to the airport, it was mad crowded. It seemed like everybody in Charlotte was at the airport, or maybe it could have been because it was NBA All-Star weekend in LA, and I promise you everybody at the airport was going there. Fortunately, we already had our tickets and seat assignments, so we just dropped our bags off with the porter, gave him a tip, and headed toward the gate where our plane was departing from. I was so excited because one of my clients had arranged for us to have VIP treatment at all of the hot spots, and we were going to meet some of the basketball players. I had been a personal assistant for one of the football players for his first six years in the league, and we had a real good relationship.

I remember when I got my first client. I had gotten 100 cards made at the Office Depot for about forty bucks, and the cards read – *Paris Love – Personal Assistant with a special touch, specializing in "you" and all of your needs. For more information, call 704-555-0989.* I was so proud of myself when I got my first client. He was an executive out of New York and we had a good working relationship. I got paid 60, 000 dollars a year for a part-time position. Damn that money was good. When I opened my own office uptown, I gained two more clients, the newest being Ray, a basketball player for the Charlotte Bobcats. He traveled a lot and I took care of all his personal affairs as well as the other guys. Johnny Case was the one of my clients that set-up the weekend for my girls and I, and all we had to do was get there. Hell, why wouldn't I pay for my airfare to enjoy a free weekend in VIP and all the free food and drinks I could want?

The airplane landed in the Houston Hobby airport, and it was a very smooth landing. As soon as the fasten seat belts light went out, we anxiously gathered our things and began departing the plane. Johnny was waiting at the gate for us, and as soon as he spotted me, he grabbed me, picked me up, and spun me around.

Johnny said, "Hey baby, I am so glad you and your crew could make it!"

I was so excited. I forgot that I had not told the girls about Johnny. I had promised myself that I would not ever get involved with any of my clients, but somehow I ended up with Johnny's lips on mine. Lolita and Lucky were looking at me like *'what the hell'* and I was looking at them, with a glaring, *'I will tell you later.'*

We headed toward the baggage claim. While we were walking, Johnny pulled out this gift box and handed it to me. I said, "What's this?"

Moreover, his look toward me said *'Open it.'* So I opened the box, and inside were some diamond teardrop earrings. They were the most beautiful pieces of jewelry I had ever seen. I said, "Baby I love them."

By that time, Lolita and Lucky were really giving me a look of *'Damn, bitch, what is really going on?'* I just shot them a quick smile, knowing that I would a lot of explaining to do later.

We got downstairs to the baggage claim area and stood at the carousel where our bags were going to come out. The carousel started up, and the first bags started to come out. After standing there for 15 minutes, we finally got our bags and headed for the outside to the limo. Johnny was carrying my bags, and he got a few steps in front of us when Lolita grabbed one arm and Lucky grabbed the other. "Okay girl tell us what the hell is going on between you and Mr. Fine Ass Johnny," Lolita demanded.

I said, "Nothing, why y'all trippin?"

"Bitch, please," Lucky, said.

I tried to walk faster to catch up with Johnny so I didn't have to answer their stank asses, but of course Lolita had a tight grip on my arm.

She said, "Look heifer you had better start talking or else I will ask Mr. Fine what is going on between you two."

I whispered, "I will tell you after Johnny's gone, now shut the hell up, and get in the limo."

Johnny got in the front seat of the limo, we hopped in the back, and I asked him why he was not riding in the back with us. He told me that he was going to let us enjoy the ride over to the hotel, and that he had another surprise for me. I told him that he was doing too much, but you know we liked gifts, so I just smiled at him and gave him a kiss on the cheek. Lolita and Lucky were looking at me as if to say, *'You know we are going to kick your ass once we get in our hotel room.'*

I sat across from the two of them in the limo. The bar was stocked with all types of liquor, and there was plenty of shrimp cocktail, strawberries, cheese and crackers. We ate, drank, laughed, and joked all the way to the hotel. The car stopped in front of the hotel and I could see the bellhop coming towards the door. I looked at Lolita.

Lucky said, "This is not the hotel I booked for us, what is Johnny up to now?"

We stepped out of the limo and stood in front of the Houstonian Hotel, Club & Spa. This plush hotel had everything you could want.

I said, "Damn, Johnny, are you trying to impress me, because the shit's working?"

We all laughed and walked inside the hotel to the front desk. While Johnny checked us in, we looked in the little boutique that was across from the front desk. They had the most expensive, beautiful items in that little place. I saw the ruby and diamond necklace that would make my red Vera Wang dress look even sexier on me than it already did, but it cost 5,000 dollars. I wanted it bad, but I thought about the price that I would have to pay to play that game. Granted, Johnny was fine as hell, but I still loved Trevor, and I did not want to hurt him.

I put the necklace on and looked in the mirror, when Johnny walked up behind me. He handed me the key to our room and said, "You sure do make that necklace look good…do you want it? It's yours if you want it."

As I stood there in contemplation, he added, "Paris you know there is nothing that I wouldn't do for you or give you. All you have to do is ask me."

I looked at Johnny, smiled at him, and said, "I know." I thought to myself *'why couldn't I have two men, one in Charlotte and the other in Houston? What is so wrong about that? A woman would be considered a whore, while a man a player. This world is twisted.'* I told myself that I was going to change the game and be the female player, but my game was going to be tighter then these niggas out here that was fa sho. I smiled to myself as I thought of the way I could stack my stable of thoroughbreds, 'cause that's all I would have in my stable—no room for lames and old mules, just them young, strong-backed horses. Damn, the thought of it was making me shake and shiver with excitement.

"Paris!" I turned around and Lolita was standing there. "What in the hell are you doing, I called your name five times! What la la land was you in?"

I looked at Lolita and said, "Bitch, don't you ever walk up on me like that again, you could get yo' wig split!"

She said, "Pleeeeze, you were so far away from reality I could have busted you in the head several times and you wouldn't have seen it coming."

She was right. I was in the zone for a minute, and Lolita's ass scared the shit out of me. She was so stupid.

I walked out of the boutique leaving the beautiful ruby and diamond necklace behind. I watched the salesperson put it back in the case and lock it. As I waved good-bye, the woman smiled at me and said, "It will be here waiting for you, if you want it."

I said, "Naw, that's too expensive for my pocket." Not that I couldn't afford it, but I didn't like to spend my money on that type of stuff, besides I thought that was what God made men for.

Johnny was standing at the elevator waiting for us, "Will you women come on, we have a lot of events to attend, and I want to show you guys around Houston and introduce Lolita and Lucky to some of my friends."

"Are they fine?!" Lolita yelled.

Lucky asked, "Are they rich? Hell, I don't do fine no way."

And Lolita and I both said, "That's the gospel, 'cause them niggas you be messin with is fugly."

Lucky looked at me and snapped, "They're not that ugly. I think they're cute, so that's all that matters."

I said, "You got that shit right, 'cause I couldn't wake up to no ugly ass man laying in my bed."

Lolita and I fell out laughing and Johnny was shaking his head at us. He said, "Y'all some crazy ass women, come on let's go."

Lucky said, "Fuck you, Paris, and the horse you rode in on."

I just laughed at her some more, but after a moment, I felt that I had hurt her feelings, because she was dating one ugly nigga, at the time, and he had the worst skin I had ever seen. I called him 'Moon,' because that nigga had so many craters in his face until it looked like the moon. Lucky definitely dated some ugly guys, but they were usually arrogant too. I never understood it, because if I had to put up with your shit you needed to be fine, rich, or something. But that was just my attitude about it.

Now she used to date Diesel's ass, the fine one that she bought the motorcycle for, but that nigga ran off and got engaged to some white chick. That was how it was with some of those football players when they got the big dollars. Shit, he would have given me that Busa back before he carried his ass with some white bitch to the altar. He married that bitch six months after Lucky bought his bitch ass that bike. I would have cut his punk ass for that shit. My girl took it like a champ, but I knew when she was by herself she was hurting very bad behind that shit. I knew because we have all been there with those sorry ass niggas.

We got in the elevator and Johnny pushed the button for the 30th floor; all the suites in the hotel started at the 25th floor up to the 40th floor, and we were on the 30th floor. The ride in the elevator was surprisingly smooth and we were in one where you could see the outside as you rode up to the top. I did not want to look down, because the shit made me dizzy, and I felt like I was going to call Earl in a minute if it did not stop soon. No one was doing much talking on the elevator and I was not sure if it was 'cause our asses were all scared, or if it was because Lucky had that 'I'm pissed' look on her face ever since I made that comment about her boyfriend.

I asked, "Lucky are you mad at me? You know I was just playing with you, but I guess the truth hurts sometimes, huh?"

Lucky didn't respond, so I said, "Well I am sorry if I made you mad, but don't let that keep you from having a good time this weekend, girl we are FAM and you know how we do, so quit trippin."

The elevator stopped on the top floor. When the doors opened, we were all standing there with our mouths open except for Johnny.

I said, "Oh my God, this is beautiful!"

Johnny looked at me and said, "Wait until you see the room I have for us."

Lucky and Lolita were staying in the suite across from our room, and no sooner than he directed them where to go, they were already in the room popping the cork on the Moet that Johnny had waiting for them. I thought they were going to jump out of their skin, the way they were in that room bouncing around like two little girls. It was not like both them heifers didn't make good money and weren't used to nice places, so I did not understand what the excitement was about.

As if she could read my thoughts, Lucky said, "Girl it's nicer when you don't have to pay for anything, and you are being spoiled by somebody else."

I said, "I guess, because you can do all of this for yourself so it should not be a big deal, but okay."

I was ready to go to the restaurant to get something to eat, so I wanted everyone to hurry up and put their bags down so we could go to dinner. I told Johnny that I was starving, and he assured me that we could leave whenever I wanted. I sometimes wished that I did not have to make a choice between Johnny and Trevor because I loved them both, and they were both good to me.

I thought about Trevor, how sweet he was, and just as I was thinking of him, my cell phone rang. I answered the phone and it was Trevor on the line.

"Hey baby," he said. "Baby when are you coming home, I miss you so much."

I said, "Trevor, baby I miss you too, but I only been gone 6 hours." I walked toward the bathroom so that Johnny would not hear me on the phone with Trevor. I told Trevor that I loved him and that I would be home in a couple of days, gave him phone kisses, and quickly said 'goodbye.' Just as Trevor had done a few hours earlier, Johnny walked out of the bedroom butt-bald naked with his anaconda hanging down his thigh.

I looked at him and said, "Boy put your clothes on before we don't make it to dinner, and I am not trying to spend the whole evening in here. I will charm that snake when we get back to the room."

Johnny called downstairs to the front desk and asked the clerk to have the limo brought around to the front, because we were going to Willie G's Seafood & Steak House for dinner. I loved seafood and Johnny knew that. He told me this place had some of the best seafood in town.

We walked across the hall to Lolita and Lucky's room to see if they were ready to go to dinner. Those fools where in there tipsy and laughing at everything they said, I told Johnny that we might have to leave them heifers in their room 'cause we were not going to be embarrassed at the restaurant.

Johnny stood at the door waiting for us while I fussed. "Lolita, Lucky, *out!*" I said.

Lolita was looking at me with that big grin on her face, and she said, "Girl I am fine, let's go, because I am hungry as a hostage."

I looked at Johnny, and he just stood there smiling at me.

I said, "Let's go before I have to kill somebody in here."

We took the limo to Willie G's Seafood & Steak House. When we arrived at Willie G's, the place was packed and we thought that we would have to wait in a long line for hours. The limo pulled up to the front door and the driver got out and came around to the passenger side to open the door for us. Johnny got out the car first, and like the gentleman he was, he helped each of us out of the limo. I told Johnny that we did not want to wait an hour to eat, and he assured me that he had all of it under control. The driver pulled off, and Johnny walked into the restaurant and the way the people in the restaurant were responding to him, you could have sworn we were with royalty. We walked right in and they told Johnny that his private table was ready.

I leaned over and jokingly whispered in Johnny's ear, "Damn, baby, I didn't know you had it going on like that, I would have gave you some pussy a long time ago."

He said to me, "I told you that I was the man in this town, and you know I wouldn't have got that pussy if I was broke."

We started laughing and holding hands as if we were the fucking couple of the year. We sat in the back of the restaurant in this cozy little candle lit room. When we sat down at the table, two of Johnny friends walked in. Lolita and Lucky were looking at them with their mouths opened and to be honest, I had to stare at them myself. We were all thinking, *'Damn, they fine as hell.'* Men who were good looking usually rolled with niggas that was ugly as hell. We were shocked to see these two fine ass black men standing in front of us.

Johnny introduced them to Lucky and Lolita. Johnny told Lucky that he thought Jackson would be a great match for her, because he was a doctor and he was down to earth. Johnny told Lolita that Jackson's brother Jaylan would be perfect for her because he had his own franchise of sports medicine clinics and he was a physical therapist.

Jackson and Jaylan Belmont were twin brothers, thirty-three years old and childless, which made Lucky and Lolita even happier. Jackson had a small mole above his top lip and he had the smoothest pecan brown skin with not a scratch on it. He was 6 foot even, with his hair cut short with waves. You could see that he had a decent grade of hair, and he was so fine and clean cut, until it should have been against the law. Jackson wore a cream linen button-down shirt with linen pants and he had on some Kenneth Cole, brown leather, and slip-ons with the squared toe. Those shits were so hot, we women love a nigga that could dress and wear some nice ass shoes. Jackson had it going on and his teeth were so fucking white, that when that nigga smiled, I could have sworn we were in a Colgate commercial.

I thought to myself *'damn, Johnny is fine, but Jackson's ass is a beast up in this motherfucker.'*

Lucky was *on* that nigga. She pulled out the chair next to her, and said "Come here baby, sit right here next to me, 'cause I need to be close to you tonight."

I just shook my head because I knew we were going to have a wild weekend in Texas.

Jaylan was the duplicate of his brother, because they were identical twins, so it was double trouble, because we could not tell them apart except for the part that was unseen. Jaylan told us that he had a birthmark shaped like the state of Florida on his ass and Lolita asked him if she could see it. Jaylan told her that he would show it to her later that night if she still wanted to see it by then.

A birthmark separating the two, damn that shit was crazy.

We ordered drinks and our food, and coincidentally, everybody got steak and shrimp with potatoes and veggies. We ate and laughed for hours. Jackson, Johnny, and Jaylan told us crazy stories about the groupies that they had in Houston, and how they would do anything to get with them. Johnny said that one girl had two of her friends show them their breasts and began to get each other off right in front of them. That shit happened in a limo that they had rented for a night on the town. I asked him if he knew them, and he said that they just came up to them and asked if they wanted to be entertained, and you know those niggas were down for whatever.

After very interesting conversation, we finished our food, Johnny paid the check, and we headed to the club to shake a little something. When we got into the limo, Johnny told the driver to take us to Main Street between Congress and Capitol so we could hit several clubs in one night. Inside the limo, we had Apple Martinis, Hypnotic, Grey Goose and all the juices that went with it. I was feeling good, and Johnny was kissing all on my neck and rubbing the shit out of my thighs. I was thinking, *'damn I could fuck his ass right now,'* 'cause my pussy was hot like fire, but in the back of my mind, I kept thinking about Trevor's ass, and how much I loved him. That thought only lasted for a minute 'cause Johnny had me twisted, and I could not escape that feeling that he was putting on my ass at the time.

I glanced over at Lucky. She was already in the mix, kissing the shit out of Jackson's ass, and I thought, *'damn if the walls had eyes we would be in some deep shit right about now.'* Lolita had her arms around Jaylan while he was whispering something in her ear. As she laughed, he was rubbing her legs and squeezing her arms, which were the weak spots for Lolita. And that nigga had some biceps out of this world. I could see the look of lust on her face, because she was in the zone, laughing and grinning all up in Jaylan's face like that motherfucker gave her a million dollars. Jaylan started kissing her on her neck, and it was a wrap 'cause she was wrapping them long ass legs around that nigga like it was legal as hell.

We hit about three clubs on the main strip and party. Lolita and Lucky were in the corner dancing and grinding on Jackson and Jaylan, and I thought I saw Lolita kiss Jaylan in the club, tonguing that nigga down as if she had known him for years. I just shook my head, knowing that she was going to fuck that nigga that night, and there was no stopping her. Lolita had money, a fat-ass crib, and the whole nine but she had never taken to a nigga like that. She was usually the laid-back one, but she was ready to handle that shit in an instance, and it was going to be handled correctly. I had to stand back and just take the night all in, because although I knew we would have fun, that shit was crazy. And I knew that it wasn't over yet.

I was dancing to 50 Cent's "Just a Lil Bit" when I felt someone pressing all up against my ass. I thought it was Johnny, so I started rolling my ass and backing up into that nigga's crotch like he was mine. I felt his dick getting hard. I turned around, but to my surprise, it was not Johnny. I backed away from the strange man and said, "Damn, I'm sorry, I thought you were my friend."

The nigga was fine as hell. He told me there was no need to apologize because he loved every minute of it. I had to catch my breath because he had the sexiest voice I had ever heard, and my panties got wet just listening to him talk. Out of the corner of my eye, I noticed Johnny walking towards me with two drinks in his hand, so I had to get myself together with the quick. I told ol' boy that I enjoyed the dance, too, but my man was coming over so I would holla at him later.

Johnny handed me an apple martini and asked me who the dude was that he saw talking to me.

Brushing him off, I said, "We just danced together, he thanked me for the dance, and that was it."

He said, "Cool, I did not know if you knew him or not, because I see that cat out on the town a lot."

Now you know that is the fourth rule in the playett's handbook: do not mess with a dude that your man sees out all the time, because as soon as you do, those niggas will be friends. The next time you see him, he will be hanging out with your man, playing basketball, and the whole nine. It was best to keep the side dick on the sideline and out of town far away from home plate.

The music in the club was off the chain, the DJ was doing the damn thing. He took us from old school to new school and back, and we danced until our feet were bleeding and I mean toes cramped up—we could not walk out of that joint.

Paris Love

It was 4 o'clock in the morning, when we headed back to the hotel. We had a damn good time, and we were all tired as hell. Once we got inside of the limo, Lucky and Lolita were all cozy with Jackson and Jaylan. Lucky was lying in Jackson's lap and he was rubbing her head, because she told him that she had a headache. Lolita had Jaylan rubbing her feet, and I could not believe he was not complaining about those spoiled milk-smelling things. I could smell them, so I knew he *had* too. That brother was rubbing her feet and grinning as if he had a bouquet of roses in his hand. I gave Lolita that *'your feet stank'* look, and she gave me the *'fuck you, he likes it'* look and we just burst out laughing. Jaylan did not know what we were laughing at but he was over there just busting a gut right along with us. The things that a brother will do when he thinks he has a chance to get some, is amazing. I mean he was pouring on the charm, but Lolita already had a plan for his ass and he did not have a clue. He thought it was all about the bullshit that he was feeding her, but the decision to give him those draws was made on first sight.

I was sitting next to Johnny in the limo and he was whispering in my ear all kinds of nasty shit that he is going to do to me when we got back to our suite. I was giggling like a schoolgirl, and he had one hand on my thigh, giving it this long slow squeeze. I got wet and hot as a summer thunderstorm, I mean smoking! I was purring by then, and he loved every minute of it.

The limo finally stopped in front of our hotel, and we all got out of the car. One by one, we walked into the lobby of the hotel and headed for the elevator. Lucky and Jackson said their good nights before we could get on the elevator, and I thought *'damn when the doors open again they must plan on b – lining straight to Jackson's room.'* I thought that he was going to rub and kiss her to death before we could get on the elevator.

I said, "Damn can you two wait until you get to the room?"

Lucky was laughing and hugging up on Jackson like I just told the funniest joke ever. It was obvious that those two were like some horny little teenagers, and somebody was going to get hurt that night. When the elevator finally stopped at the top floor, we all headed towards our rooms and all you could hear was giggling and doors closing.

Johnny looked at me and said, "Did I do good or what? And your girls really got attached to Jaylan and Jackson quick."

I told him don't flatter himself because those two weren't nothing but some little tricks looking for a good fuck. We started laughing and Johnny told me that I was shell. I was just kidding, but sometimes that was how shit went down out of town. You did shit you wouldn't normally do in a city where you were well known, so you had to be undercover and buck wild when you got a chance.

Lucky and Jackson yelled down the hallway, "Good Night," as they closed the door behind them.

Once inside, Jackson pushed Lucky up against the door, and started to pull her dress up around her waist as he kissed her deeply on the neck and down to the nipple of her breast. She sighed with pleasure, and pulled him close to her. Jackson reached up to her panty line and pulled her panties to the side as he slid his fingers two at a time inside of her wet pussy. Lucky arched her back and pushed her body out against his hands and Jackson continued to stroke her wet cat back and forth. He pulled his fingers out of her pussy, and began to suck her juices from each one.

He pulled her close to him and whispered in her ear, "It tastes just as good as I imagined it would".

Jackson lifted Lucky up to his shoulders with his hands cupped underneath her ass, pulled her pussy to his mouth and started twilling his tongue around her clit. Lucky wanted to scream but when she opened her mouth, nothing would come out. He moved a few inches back away from the door and laid Lucky on the floor of the hotel room. She had her eyes closed as she enjoyed everything he was giving her. Jackson pulled Lucky even closer to him as he buried his face in between her legs. His tongue moved faster as he licked every inch of her vagina until she exploded with pleasure.

Jackson pulled Lucky up off the floor and carried her to the bed. Lucky fell back on the bed with her long hair flowing on the pillow, and Jackson laid his head on her stomach with his arms underneath her hips.

"I love the smell of you", Jackson said as he looked up at Lucky. "Tell me where this leaves us because I would love to get to know you better."

Lucky told Jackson that she would like to come back to Texas to visit him and spend some time getting to know him as well.

The two of them fell fast asleep in each others' arms and all the while Lucky was thinking about what she was going to do when she got home, and how was she going to see both men in her life, because she definitely wanted to see Jackson and make him her man.

The phone in my hotel room rang so loud until I jumped straight up in the bed. I was looking for Trevor. I realized that I was still in the hotel room in Texas with Johnny. I quickly grabbed the phone and said "Hello?"

It was Lolita's retarded ass on the other end. "Girl, you ain't up yet? I am ready to get back home because Jaylan is getting on my nerves, but he has the biggest dick I have ever seen and when that nigga dropped those draws, I was like *damn*, that is what Paris was talking about when she said ANDACONDA. His shit was hanging like a log, and girl you know I was a little nervous, but I handled my business and that shit was good."

I looked at the clock and said, "Will you please stop screaming, it is 7:30am, and I am not feeling this early morning shit."

Lolita said, "Girl you know how excited I get, but he put it down. He picked my big ass up and handled me like a newborn up in this piece. I was like Flo Evans, *'damn, damn, damn!'*"

"Lolita girl you stupid, but I am going back to sleep because our flight doesn't leave until 3pm, so I am sleeping until check out. So good bye."

"Bye, Nigga!"

We hung up the phone and I pulled the covers up, moved closer to Johnny's warm body, and fell asleep thinking about Trevor.

12 noon came sooner than I was hoping. It was time to check out of the room, and I was just hopping in the shower. Johnny was up, packing and ordering me room services, steak and eggs with hash browns, biscuit, orange juice and coffee. As I stood in the shower, a little guilt flashed over me, so I had to give myself the talk. I was still holding on to the fact that Trevor did not tell me that he was married when we first met, and how I never got a chance to see him while he was going through his separation. I tried to justify what I was doing with the fact that he lied to me, but I knew better, and I knew that he loved me. I guess in my own way I was trying to protect my heart from getting broke, but I could not stop loving him even when we were trying to see other people. After he got out of his marriage to old girl, we moved in together, and it had been that way ever since. I was afraid to marry him, because I did not know if the same thing would happen to me, but I could not ever leave him no matter what.

I heard a knock on the bathroom door, and it was Johnny telling me that the food was there and to hurry up so we did not have to pay for another day in the room. I grabbed the bathrobe, slipped it on with the slippers that the hotel had provided, and turned off the water. I quickly brushed my teeth, washed my face, and went into the dinning area to eat. When I sat down, Johnny had poured me a cup of coffee and some juice. He was so attentive and sweet but he was no Trevor, especially in the bed. I really enjoyed Johnny's company and I just wished I could keep the both of them because he liked to do things that Trevor did not. It just balanced my life out so wonderfully. I knew that all good things must end, so I was going to try to enjoy it while it lasted.

We finally checked out of the hotel and arrived at the airport an hour before our flight was beginning to board. I checked my bags, gave Johnny a hug and a kiss goodbye, and told him that I would call him once we arrived in Charlotte.

Lolita and Lucky were standing there waiting for me to board the plane, and I said, "You heifers could have gotten your asses on the plane, I am not helpless, thank you."

Lolita started laughing and told Lucky that I was walking funny, and I gave both of them the finger as we boarded the plane.

Chapter Two

Trevor had the day off and was out shopping when he ran into one of his co-workers from his previous job. They had not seen each other for about a couple of years, and the two had met when he was married. Maria Santiago was her name, and she was a very short woman with long black hair and deep black eyes. Trevor noticed her right off because they used to be very attracted to one another, but never crossed that path.

Trevor walked toward her and tapped her on the shoulder. She turned around and her eyes lit up like fireworks. She grabbed him and gave a deep sexual hug as if she wanted to fuck him right then on the spot. Trevor pulled back and said, "Damn, girl I didn't know you would be that glad to see me. How long has it been? Two, three years? A lot has happened since then. I am divorced from Erica, and I have a new girlfriend that I live with now."

Maria told Trevor her story about her last boyfriend. She always wanted to get with Trevor but never had the chance. Trevor remembered how freaky she was, because she used to tell him stories about her boyfriends and girlfriends and how she was once at an orgy and some guy had his dick in her ass while the other one had his dick in her mouth. While he stood there talking to Maria, Trevor smiled to himself as he noticed his dick getting hard. She noticed it too, and asked him if he wanted to have lunch with her. Trevor said that he did not see a reason they could not have lunch, because he knew that he had about six hours to spare before I got home.

Well, Trevor invited Maria to come to the house after they had lunch because they had sat and drank wine for the entire lunch, and both were feeling horny. Trevor knew better than to bring some trick into the house, but the wine had him by the balls, and he wanted to bust a nut.

Maria and Trevor got to the house in 20 minutes tops, and on the way there, Maria gave Trevor a blowjob. He could hardly keep the car from running off the road, but he made her stop before he nutted all in the bitch's mouth. He pulled into the driveway, and slammed on the brakes, didn't even put the car in the garage, ran straight to the door, and that bitch was on his heels all the way to the front door. He took her in the spare bedroom downstairs next to the kitchen, and before he could get to the bed good, that bitch was pulling his clothes off and reaching for his dick to finish the job she started in the car. Trevor asked her if he could put his dick in her ass since that was a fantasy of his, and I would not let him do it. She told him that she loved anal sex—what didn't the bitch like? She was such a nasty ho, but of course, Trevor felt he could do anything he wanted to her. Trevor slipped on his Magnum extra large condom and told her that it might hurt a bit because he was working with a monster, and to his surprise, the bitch didn't even make a sound. She pushed her ass back further for him to jab it in there deeper, and I guess since he was not making her scream, he was not getting a thrill out of it. Her ass muscles were a bit loose, and that just turned him off.

Trevor said, "Turn over bitch, damn your ass is wide enough to stick a horse's dick in it. What the fuck have you been doing? Never mind, forget I asked."

Trevor put the girl in a leg lock, and started fucking her so hard he almost broke her damn back. She was yelling at this point because he was practically standing up in her pussy with a hump in his back so deep you could have sworn he was a cat about to defend himself in a serious battle. The boy was gangster fucking the shit out of Maria, and she loved every bit of it. He finally busted a nut and when he was done, she tried to pull the condom off him so she could drink his juices.

Trevor was like, "Naw bitch, you had better get your shit and get out of here because my woman will be home soon, and I cannot be caught in here with your tired ass. I will call your trick ass a cab and you can hit the bricks, bitch."

Trevor thought about the shit and started laughing because he did not think that Maria was such a trick-ass bitch. He was glad that he did not fuck with her on a real tip; that was just sex. He was not going to lose me over that bullshit but at least he finally felt what it was like to fuck a ho in the ass. He had just wished it were a tighter ass.

Trevor put Maria's ass out on the front to wait for the cab, and she was cussing his ass out from A to Z, telling him that she was going to tell his woman and all this shit. Why did she say that, 'cause Trevor lost it.

Trevor grabbed Maria by her throat and choked the shit out of her. Trevor said, "Bitch don't you ever play like that, because I will have your ass killed if you ever say anything to my woman about this. I don't even play and you really don't want to see my bad side, because I can be the nicest guy in the world, but I can be a motherfucker if you piss me off."

Maria's eyes grew as big as grapefruits, she started to cry, and Trevor look at her with that *'I am not moved by your tears'* look and told her to sit her ass on the curb until the taxi got there.

Feeling guilty, Trevor went back in the house and called the florist to order me some flowers. He made dinner reservations at Mickey and Mooch in Lake Norman. He cleaned the downstairs guest room, washed the sheets, and put on clean ones. Trevor looked out the front window and saw Maria getting in the cab. He had given her the money for the cab, and he thought to himself, *'that bitch better not ever show her face around here again, but damn, I shouldn't have brought her to the house.'*

Trevor started smiling when he heard the phone ringing. He looked at the Caller ID and saw it was my cell phone number.

"Hey baby, are you in Charlotte yet?"

"Hi Trevor, I am getting in the limo now baby, I will see you in about 30 minutes."

Trevor said, "I have a surprise for you when you get home and we have dinner reservations at Mick and Mooch."

"Okay baby, let me get off this phone so I can pay the baggage handler, and I will see you soon."

Trevor hung up the phone and finished cleaning up the downstairs. He jumped in the shower, and threw the clothes that he was wearing in the wash just in case that bitch left any signs of her scent on him. Trevor was no fool because when he was married to Erica, he cheated on her the entire first five years he was married. He would send her shopping and call one of his tricks over to fuck in their bed, and then he would cuss her ass slap out if she questioned him about his whereabouts or anything else he felt she should not be asking him. Trevor was a motherfucker back in his twenties, and he did not take any shit from a man or a woman, definitely not any nigga. He would beat the brakes off any nigga that stepped to him wrong. He was no punk and that was the gospel.

I finally arrived home and it was so good to see my house and my garage. It seemed like I was gone forever. I opened the garage and saw Trevor standing there with a bouquet of flowers and this big cheesy grin on his face.

I slowly pulled the car up and put it in park. I let down the window and he said, "You better get yo' ass out da car and bring me my pussy."

I just started laughing at him because he was such a fool. I jumped out the car, wrapped my arms around him, and started rolling on him while saying, "Slow motion for me, and do it slow motion."

He said, "Alright now you don't want to wake up the monster, because I can't do anything with him once he raises his head."

I said, "Too late!"

We both started laughing and I took my flowers in the house while Trevor got my bags from the car. When I came in the house, I had a strange feeling come over me like another women had been there, but I thought to myself, *'naw he ain't that crazy to bring no bitch up in here.'* I went upstairs to our bedroom and there was a box lying on the bed. By that time, Trevor was standing behind me. He wrapped his arms around my waist and pulled me close to his body and whispered in my ear, "That's just a little something I picked up for you while I was out shopping today. Open it. I am sure you will like it."

It was the diamond and ruby set that I had seen in the hotel in Houston. I stood frozen as my heart damn near stopped. How in the hell did he know I was looking at it, and how did he know that I even tried it on? Damn, was he there spying on me or did he have one of them shady niggas from his past following me?

I just looked at him and said, "Baby this was the necklace that I tried on in Texas, how did you know?"

Trevor told me that he had called Lolita and Lucky to ask them what to get me for a "just because," gift and they had told him that I was looking at that necklace. He called the hotel and asked them to ship the necklace to him. The woman told him Tiffany's in South Park had the same necklace in their store so he went and picked it up. I knew that he could be a bit much at times, but when he was good, *damn* he was good. I figured either he must have missed my ass something terrible or he had did some shit he had no business doing. But what the hell, I had my fun in Texas so it was all good.

I kissed Trevor's lips slowly and passionately until I could feel that Anaconda busing out of his pants. I undressed him and we moved toward the bed.

As I was pulling my top over my head and taking off my bra, Trevor whispered in my ear, "Let me do that."

I started whimpering like a small animal as Trevor lowered my body down on top of the pillows on the floor. He pulled my thong to the side and I could feel him entering me deep and slow but then he began to thrust his body into mine and I could feel him fill my vagina with his big ass penis. I was thinking, *'damn this is some good dick,'* and while he was asking me if I missed that big dick inside of me, I was about to lose my mind, 'cause that shit was so good.

We both came long and hard. I could feel my legs shaking and Trevor let out the loudest scream of ecstasy that I had ever heard. We laid butt naked in each other's arms.

Trevor looked at me and I just started smiling at him and said, "Damn, baby you put it down!"

He told me, "That's what I do, that's my job!" We talked for a while and then we took a little nap because we both were feeling good and relaxed.

Chapter Three

Lucky entered her office on Monday morning to find a stack of shit on her desk to do. She called in her assistant and began to sort out her day. Her office phone rang, and it was some female on the other end of the phone asking Lucky all about that nigga Ron 'Diesel' Brown. Now that nigga had been calling her like crazy, especially since his ass was cut from playing football. His ego had been broken down, and he wanted to bring Lucky down with him. I had called her one day and that nigga was in the background calling her all kinds of 'bitches' and telling her that she was 'not the only pussy in town' and shit like that. I could have busted him in the head to the white meat, but when your friends are in love, they have to see the light for themselves. Lucky was trying to get away from him because he had put his hands on her on more than one occasion, and she was really starting to get sick of his shit.

Now this bitch was on the phone asking her if she was still fucking that nigga, so Lucky cussed her ass slap out.

Lucky was screaming in the phone, "First of all you stank ass bitch, I don't want Ron's ass! You can have that broke ass bastard, and I wish you'd stop calling me about this shit!"

Lucky slammed the phone down and went into the bathroom. She had been having anxiety attacks lately, and she was feeling that sweating-could-not breathe attack coming over her. The room started to move, faster and faster, and Lucky was trying to run some water to put on her face when she collapsed and fell to the floor. When Lucky finally came to, she was sitting in her chair in her office and staring at her secretary, and asking her what happened.

Tanya told Lucky that she had found her on the bathroom floor and she had been in there for an hour, so she called the security guard to help bring her to her office. Tanya asked Lucky if she had been taking her pills. Lucky had a hard time accepting the fact that she was not feeling well because she was so afraid of losing her mind, until she was starting to do just that.

Lucky asked Tanya to bring her some water. As she sat at her desk, thoughts of her sister ran through her mind. She never understood why she killed herself and left her mother and father to take care of her five small children. The people in her hometown said that her sister was crazy and all the pressures of her life caused her to snap. Lucky had dreams of her that still haunting her to date. She could see her sister hanging by her neck from the ceiling fan and her limp body going around in circles as the fan spun. She would always let out a loud scream and that was when she would wake up from her nightmare. Lucky was so afraid of becoming the next female in her family to have a nervous breakdown, but she did not let any of us know that she was having anxiety attacks.

After Lucky had gathered her composure, the phone in her office rang. It was Ron on the other end.

Ron said, "Lucky you stupid bitch, why are you telling lies on me to my family? When I see you, I am going to beat yo' ass bitch!"

Lucky slammed the phone down and told Tanya to screen all of her calls. She then made a phone call to one of her police friends to get some advice on putting a restraining order on Ron and his stupid ass wife. That white bitch thought she was black, and she was going to get her ass kicked like Rodney King if she kept fucking around, bottom line.

Lucky hung up the phone and told Tanya to hold her calls for the rest of the evening, and if any client emergency came up, to call her on her cell phone.

Lucky headed for the elevator in her building. When she reached to touch the button, she felt like someone was watching her, but turned to see nobody there. Lucky got to the garage where she parked her Mercedes. She jumped in the car and locked the doors when she saw Ron's wife standing by the elevator, just staring at her with this demonic look on her face. Lucky was so scared until her hands were shaking as she put the car in reverse and backed out of the spot where she parked. Lucky sped pass the girl almost hitting her with her car, but the girl just stood there, as if she didn't almost get hit.

Soon after, Lucky called me on the phone and was just crying hysterically, "Paris, this bitch is crazy; she has brought her ass to my office and following me to the garage to my fucking car. Girl I am going to kill her ass if she doesn't leave me the fuck alone."

I did not know what to tell her because when people are crazy, calling the police on them will not stop them. I told Lucky she needed to get her a gun, go to the range and practice 'cause the next time she saw that bitch, she should shoot the shit out of her, and then call the po-po.

"Lucky, meet me over Lolita's crib in an hour because this shit is getting out of hand, and we might need to get some of our peeps to handle this shit for real," I said.

I hung up the phone with Lucky, called my cousin Pookie, and told him the shit that was going down and that we were going to meet Lucky's ass in an hour. He came with some of his boys, because we had to handle that shit ourselves. Fuck the po-po. We had to put the professional, educated shit down and take it to the 'hood. I got on the phone with Lolita, and she was telling me that she knew that bitch was following Lucky because she had seen her when they were at the mall, but she didn't think anything of it at the time. We talked a little more and then I told her that I would see her later that night.

Ron had become Lucky's worst nightmare, because he had turned into a total crack head, and he was really losing his mind. His so-called wife was some corporate bitch that he met when he was big time, and he turned her into a straight base head. She would do anything for that nigga and when I say anything, I mean *anything*. The trick stole millions of dollars from her company before she was caught, and the bitch only spent two years in jail for the shit. Now if that had been a black girl, she would have been sentenced to life without bail. I just could not understand how a man on top of his game could fall that hard into some bullshit.

Lucky took a long time to get over that nigga, too. I remember when she caught that nigga fucking some white chick in his apartment, all up in the pussy when Lucky walked in the room. That shit was bananas. Lucky threw the glass ashtray off the nightstand to bust both their asses in the head, but she forgave that nigga, and once again, he was back over her crib within a week. I thought, *'damn, she has not had enough of this nigga's shit yet.'* After that, they were all lovey-dovey and two months later, that nigga was telling his friends about all the women he was fucking while he was with Lucky's ass. She found out that he was talking shit about her, so July 4th Lucky and Lolita went to a party Ron's cousin was having. Although they had asked me to come with them, I was not feeling that nigga nor was I feeling Lucky at the time, so I chilled. I got a phone call at 1am in the morning with Lucky's ass screaming in the phone talking about Lolita not to have her peeps jump on Ron's ass, and I was sitting up in the bed wondering what the hell went down. Lolita grabbed the phone from Lucky and told me that Ron's ass had pushed Lucky and had her by the throat in the bathroom. Apparently Lucky came to the party and Ron had some fat white bitch at the joint grinding all up on the chick on the dance floor. Lucky was trying to play the shit off, but Ron showed his ass even more and started kissing the girl in front of Lucky. Lolita was trying to get Lucky to leave the party because she saw that some shit was about to pop off, but Lucky claimed that she was fine, and that she was not going to let Ron ruin her night. Lolita told me that Lucky confronted Ron in the bathroom and he grabbed her by her neck and started choking her and calling her all kinds of 'bitches.' Lolita said that she jumped up, ran over to the bathroom door and was trying to push it open, while Ron was trying to close it on her. However, before he could, she had that ass by the neck and she was trying to choke the shit out of him. Ron pushed Lolita out of the bathroom and shut the door on her foot, and when she was trying to get in the door, again she could hear Lucky and Ron in the bathroom straight scrappin. The door to the bathroom finally opened, and when Lucky came out her lip was bleeding and Ron's nose was bleeding. Lolita said that those motherfuckers looked like Ike and Tina Turner coming out of that bathroom, and Lucky was limping and yelled at Ron that the shit was not over. Lolita said that Lucky was full of shit, because when they got to her peoples crib, she was begging them not to hurt that nigga, and she didn't want to go back over to the party to give that nigga a proper beat down. Lolita was hot about that shit and she wanted to kill that nigga, but she said Lucky was acting all scared and shit because she did not want Lolita's people to hurt Ron's sorry ass.

After hearing that long dramatic story, I told Lolita that I was glad that I didn't go to the party with them 'cause I knew some old crazy shit was going to go down. I listened to Lucky's ass whine some more in the background while Lolita was telling me how she tried to choke the shit out of Ron's ass, and then I was just done listening to the shit, because she was going to be with that nigga regardless of what Lolita said. I told Lolita that I would get with her later because that shit was starting to get on my nerves.

I hung up the phone, shook my head, and just thought about the first time I met Ron. Lucky had bought his ass a motorcycle and she told Trevor to put the shit in my garage. They used to call that nigga Diesel because he was swoll as hell but those drugs had that nigga looking like a hot mess. He was small as hell, shit he look like his waist was a size 28. His face was all ashy and sucked in, making his eyes look like some fucking marbles. His ass went from sugar to shit quickly and he was blaming Lucky for all of that.

Chapter Four

    It had been six weeks, and Lucky had not heard from nor had she seen Ron or his wife. She figured the restraining order she filed on them had kept them from contacting her and trying to show up at her job. Lucky pulled out her plush leather chair from her desk and sat down in the seat. She slowly leaned back in the chair to catch a moment before she started going through the messages on her phone. Lucky got a voice mail from Chuck Brown out of Miami, he was the owner of a hot club down there called "Shine" and he was meeting with us in two months to get our club running.

    Lucky, Lolita and I were finally going to Miami to get our business together to open a nightclub in South Beach called 'Club Dubai.' We were going to fly down in a couple of weeks to go over the floor plans to make sure everything we requested had arrived on time, and that our opening date was confirmed.

    Lucky finished listening to the message from Chuck and started dancing around her desk and yelling, "We're going to Miami, we're going to Miami!" When her assistant came in her office to see what was going on, Lucky grabbed her and had her skipping around the desk practically dragging her. Lucky told her that the construction workers started building our club and it would be ready for the grand opening in May.

Tanya looked at Lucky and shook her head. She said, "I am going to lunch. I will see you in an hour."

Lucky said, "Bye!"

I was going in the house when I heard the phone ringing. I yelled out to Trevor to answer but he was not at home. I put the grocery bag on the counter and grabbed the cordless phone off the wall in the kitchen.

"Hello? Hello?" I could hear noise in the background and then I heard Lucky's ass screaming in my ear.

"Girl we are going to Miami in two weeks to check out our new club! I just got a message from Chuck and things are going as planned. Guess what else? All of the shit we want and ordered is there on time, can you believe this shit? I am so freaking hyped!"

I said, "Bitch calm down and tell me nice and slow 'cause we are about to put this shit on the map."

Lucky gave me all of the details. Everything was falling into place. I was cheesing my ass off as I sat down in the kitchen chair. I told Lucky to get Lolita's ass on the three-way 'cause this shit was about to be on and poppin.

We got on the phone with Lolita and told her about the club. That bitch started yelling in the phone and she was laughing and talkin about how we were about to do the damn thang in Miami, and how they weren't ready for what we were about to put down. The club was going to be *hot*, everybody and their mother was going to want to come to Club Dubai. That shit was going to be stupid!

The design was a duplicate of the hotel Burj Al Arab in the Middle East but on a smaller scale. The club was the replica of the billowing sail, the profile of an Arabian sailing ship - design with the same choreographed color sculptures of water and fire. The club's external lighting schemes, from white light to a multicolored one, changed from one to other every 30 minutes, expressing the evening's progress. There were 10 floors in the club, 4 dance floors, 2 VIP's, 2 theatres, 1 main floor and 2 private suite levels. When you first walked in the club, there was the front entrance where two bouncers stood and opened the door to the club. Inside there was security who patted everyone down to make sure there were no guns or knives on the person. The main floor had two coat checks—you could check your personal items in a room that had a security lock box and the coat hangers had numbers on them that matched the security lock box key number. The coat check was in a huge walk-in closet that had rows and rows of space like in cleaners, but with more class. The cashier's window and meet and greet lounge were on the left of the front entrance. Once you made it through the security checkpoint, a red rope led to the cashier's window.

In addition, the main floor had its own private dining and lounge with a full service bar. There were several plush leather sofas and love seats in red, black, gray, pink and white and a bar on each side. The carpet was multi-colored swirls of reds, blacks, pink and gray. There were several glass cocktail tables with candles on each of them. The lights were dimmed and cozy to give that soft elegant look and feel. The lounge area was a big open space and the first level where the dance floor and bars were was sunk in with three steps leading towards all the tables with white tablecloths and candles on each of them. The dance floor was in the middle, with the DJ booth above the floor in all glass. There were lights coming from the ceiling in all different colors and going in every direction you could imagine. There were four cages on each corner of the dance floor for whoever was feeling "free" to get in and show the crowd what they were working with. When you stood in the middle of the dance floor and looked up at the ceiling, you could see all the way to the top of the sail with all of the other nine floors circling up from the bottom floor. The space was like a big open vaulted ceiling with the private VIP on the 10th floor. On the second and third floors were king-sized suites with a wet bar and Jacuzzi in each room. The fourth floor had two dance floors, two bars, jazz and old school music for the more mature crown. The fifth floor had two theaters for movies, plays, and concerts. The sixth and seventh floors were for the 21-35 year old crowd with nothing but hip-hop and go-go music. The eighth had a VIP for the small ballers with security and plush furniture, DJ, soft lights, food, big screen TV and restrooms. On the ninth floor was a ballroom area with a big dance floor—we used this room for charity balls, banquets, weddings, and special events. Finally, as I said, the 10th floor was where the money-makers hung out. This VIP level in the club was private, had its own entrance away from the normal crowd. The elevator stopped on the ninth floor, and a private elevator took the VIPs to the 10th floor. Guards were on the 10th floor, therefore VIP status was checked out before guests could enter.

The 10th floor had a glass bottom floor where you could see the other floor levels beneath it. There were two DJs and four bars with lounge areas, and the guest could order from a huge selection of foods. The floor has its own kitchen and private chef. There were two huge restrooms, and the roof opened or closed depending on the weather. The 10th floor overlooked the city of Miami, and you could see the beautiful ocean from every angle.

There were plush soft butter leather sofas with lounge chairs and ottomans to rest your feet on. There were private suites on this floor as well, but only the people with access knew about them, just in case guests were with someone that they were not supposed to be with. Needless to say, the 10th floor was the place to be if you could afford to indulge in its luxury and pampering.

We were hyped about the club all the way up until we were ready to go to Miami that night. We had two weeks to go before the grand opening. This club thing had been in progress for 2 years, and now it was finally coming together.

We hung up our three-way call, and I just sat in the kitchen daydreaming about the grand opening of the club. What I was going to wear. And all of the famous people who were going to attend, appearing on Oprah, and then Trevor walked in the house calling my name and took me from my daydream back to reality with the quickness.

Trevor came in the kitchen, I told him all about the club and the opening date, and he was more excited than I was. He started talking about what he was going to wear and his boys were going to come, and all this and that.

I was looking at him shaking my head, and he looked at me and said, "What, I can't fantasize!"

"Naw, baby you can, I am just trippin on how you got your boys coming and all that. It's all good, we are going to set Miami on fire opening night, now come here and let me kiss those soft lips of yours."

Trevor loved it when I talked about his lips or any part of his body for that matter, he was just a big old freak, and I loved every bit of it.

Lolita

Jaylan was in Texas at his brother's house. He was daydreaming about Lolita and wanted to see her, yet he had not called her in two weeks. All Jaylan could think about was that night in Houston and how the sweet taste of Lolita's pussy was still on his lips. Jaylan looked at the contact list on his phone, saw the initials HP (Hot Pussy) with the cell phone number, and pushed the send button on the phone. Jaylan heard the phone ringing a couple of times and then a sweet voice on the other end. It was she, Lolita, and an instant smile came across his face as he said, "Hello Lolita, this is Jaylan, and how have you been?"

Lolita was shocked that he was calling her, because she had just asked me about him the other day. Lolita said, "I am fine Jaylan. I must have talked you up because I just asked about you the other day when I was hanging out with Paris. I am glad you called because I want to see you. When can you come to Charlotte?"

"Damn Lolita, you don't waste any time do you? I was just about to ask you what your weekend was like. That's funny, because I was thinking about flying in on Thursday and staying until Monday."

Lolita held her Blackberry, as she checked her schedule. "Well Jaylan, looks like you're a lucky man, because I had to cancel two appointments which allow time for me to play with you for the weekend."

Jaylan was smiling so hard on the other end of the phone until his jaws hurt. "Lolita, that's wonderful news and I am looking forward to playing with you too…shall I bring anything special for you?"

"Naw baby just bring yourself and we will handle the rest when you get here. Call me after you make your reservations and I will pick you up from the airport," Lolita said.

"Okay baby I will call you tomorrow with my flight information. I can't wait to see you again with your sexy ass," Jaylan responded.

"Jaylan you might not want to go back to Houston, hell I might not let you!"

"I will talk to you later Lolita but in the meantime, keep it hot!"

Lolita chuckled, "Jaylan, you are so nasty but I like it in you! Bye boy!"

"See you soon, baby."

Lolita hung up the phone and started reminiscing about the time her and Jaylan spent in the hotel room in Houston. She thought about how he was so good in bed, and his dick was as big as a horses' dick. It was unreal to Lolita! But they also argued a lot because Lolita was so used to having everything her way, but Jaylan wasn't haven't that. He was just as head strong as Lolita, but she was sprung on that dick and she knew it. No doubt, Jaylan was putting it down and the passion was just crazy between the two of them.

After hanging up with Jaylan, Lolita just sat there still with the phone in her hand thinking about how Jaylan was hittin that ass from the back and making that pussy talk. She got chills just thinking about it.

The phone rang and it startled Lolita. She nearly jumped out of her chair. Lolita answered the phone, "Hello?"

"What's up girl!" a voice shouted through the phone.

Lolita held the phone, puzzled, because she did not recognize the voice on the other end.

After a moment, the strange voice said, "Oh, you don't know who I am since you all high and mighty. Bitch this is your cousin, Renay. Oh I am sorry *Laquesha*, or I forgot its Lolita now!"

Lolita turned three shades of red and she snapped, "Bitch, how the fuck did you get my phone number, because the last time I remember seeing you was on top of my boyfriend, you stank ass ho!"

Renay was in the background laughing, which just infuriated Lolita.

Lolita asked, "Bitch what the fuck is so funny?"

"What's funny is you still holding on to that shit. We were in high school, and that nigga was not your man. I know you don't want to talk to me Lolita, but I need you to help me out because I don't have anyone to turn to."

Lolita just sat there looking at the phone and wondering how in the world that nasty bitch cousin of hers got her number, because the only family member she dealt with was her baby brother, and she knew damn well he had not given her the phone number.

Lolita never liked her cousin because she was taking shit from her since day one. That bitch would steal the draws off your ass if you did not keep a close eye on her. Lolita was hot about her calling to ask her to do anything because she hated Renay with all she had.

Renay said, "Lolita did you hear me? I need you to help me because I don't have any money or a place to stay. Your brother put me out, and you know how my mother is."

Lolita sat there for a moment and then began to speak slowly with every word coming out her mouth clearly. "Renay, hear me when I say, bitch I am not giving you a damn dime, because you are a trifling ho, and I will not have nothing to do with you. If you need some money then do what you use to do, steal it! Sell pussy, I don't give a damn, just don't ever call my house again!"

"Lolita, I see you are the same bitch you were when we were kids—you don't give a damn about nobody but yourself."

"Whatever! You can't say shit about me, because I used to do everything for your ungrateful ass, you and your damn family, and all you did for me is fucked every man I brought around you, stupid bitch! And I don't give a damn if your black ass starves to damn death, DON'T FUCKING CALL ME AGAIN!" Lolita slammed the phone on the hook and told herself that she was not going to let that bitch get to her because she had pulled herself up out of that shit hole of a life with her family and managed to take care of herself and her baby brother.

The upsetting call from Renay triggered unpleasant memories of Lolita's tumultuous upbringing. Lolita remembered the dirty clothes she used to have to wear and how half the time, her stomach hurt from being so empty. She couldn't even go to school, because her clothes were not clean and the kids would make fun of her. She could see the small slave-like shack in her mind where she stayed with her mother, father, and little brother. Her father was always drunk or high and used to beat the crap out of her mother. Lolita was raised down south in a small town outside of Columbus, South Carolina. She hated her life and promised herself that she would never live like that when she was grown and old enough to get away from them. Her life back then was a living hell and her relatives where crazy as hell. She would have to fight them to keep her uncles from trying to rape her and her brother. Lolita had to stay with her cousin Renay's parents when Lolita killed her father, because he beat her mother to death. That 9mm blew a hole in his head and splattered his brain all over the kitchen wall. She had to go to therapy for years to get that image out of her head. Recurring nightmares kept her up for years following that incident. Luckily, though, the court dropped the charges against Lolita, because they had determined that she acted in defense of her mother and was not the blame for killing her father.

Renay's parents were terrible people. They mistreated Lolita and her brother and had them cleaning up and doing everything around the house that they did not want to do. On Sundays, Lolita would go to church with her cousin's family. Church was the only place where she found peace. She would pray to God that he help her with her schoolwork, and make her smart enough to never have to need money, clothes, or food again. The church youth choirs would sing "I Won't Complain," and she would just cry her eyes out, because she always knew that someday God was going to bless her.

Renay was Lolita's favorite cousin when they were little. She did everything for her, but as they got older, Renay became very jealous of Lolita and started stealing everything she had from clothes and money to jewelry and boyfriends, just because she did not want Lolita to be happy. Renay was jealous of Lolita's looks, because she was very pretty and tall with pretty skin and long legs, so Renay was always trying to hurt Lolita. One day Lolita caught Renay fucking her high school boyfriend. She could not take it anymore, so she beat the shit out of both of them and sent their asses to the hospital with bruises to prove that she was not playing.

After that, Lolita's aunt put her out, so she went to stay with a friend until she could figure out her next step. While staying at her friend's house she met Raymond. Now Raymond was a very good looking tall dude and Lolita thought he was cute. That was the first time that she paid any attention to a man's looks or anything else for that matter. She was always studying and trying to make good grades in school.

It was summer and Lolita had to think of something to do before school started back. This would be her sophomore year and she was determined to finish school and go to college. Her baby brother was still staying with her aunt, he was five years younger than she was, and she knew it was best for him.

Lolita planned to go to get him when she got a place for them to stay because she wasn't going to leave her brother then for them to mistreat. Lolita sat on the sofa in her friend's living room and watched Raymond talk to the women that he had brought to the house with him. One of the girls looked as if she was only seventeen or eighteen and when he told them what to do, they moved quickly without question.

Raymond walked over to Lolita and sat on the sofa beside her, "What's your name little pretty thang?" Lolita looked around the room as if he was speaking to someone else and he said, "Yeah, I am talking to you sweetheart, what is your name?"

Lolita looked him in the eye and said, "My name is Lolita." In his smooth silky voice Raymond said, "That's a pretty name, almost as pretty as you."

"Thanks I guess," she said.

Raymond took her hand and said, "I hear you having family problems. Why don't you let me be of some assistance to you, I could help you get on your feet so you can finish school and take care of your little brother."

Lolita sat there with her mouth hanging open, she had just turned fifteen and this man was talking to her, wanting to help her. Not knowing that he had a motive for his actions, she was infatuated with the fact that he was paying attention to her when he had two beautiful women with him. Lolita had big dreams and she always wanted to own her own business someday. That seemed like the perfect opportunity for her, so she listened to Raymond.

In a matter of months, all was well, she was back in school and everything seemed to be going great. Raymond was 25 years old, had lots of money and he took care of Lolita. He had Leland in an after school program. It was beautiful, until Lolita discovered she was pregnant the spring of her sophomore year.

Raymond talked her into selling the baby, so when she gave birth to a healthy baby girl, Raymond sold the baby to a couple in another state and he never told Lolita any information about the people or where they stayed. Lolita didn't even give the baby a name. Raymond told her that she shouldn't do that, because then she would become attached to the baby and that was not a good thing to do. They never told a soul and when school started back, Lolita was there on the first day. All of that shit had happened to her because of her bitch-ass cousin Renay.

Lolita thought about all the shit her family put her through and how they would not help her when she was struggling to take care of herself and her brother. She was not about to let none of their asses near her again.

Lolita called her brother to find out how her cousin got her number, and when she dialed the number, it rang several times until the voicemail picked up. She left a message for her brother to call her ASAP!

Lolita hung the phone up and fixed her a Goose and juice before she headed out to pick up a few things for Jaylan. She wanted to make sure he was comfortable when he got to Charlotte. Besides, she did not want to think about her stupid ass cousin and Raymond's dumb ass; thinking of Jaylan would take any thoughts of her family off her mind.

She thought now that she had some peace in her life, her stupid ass cousin found out where she was and had her phone number, but Lolita was not going to let that phone conversation ruin her week. She was not going to give Renay shit, and she meant that.

Lolita quickly drank her glass of Grey Goose, and poured another one for the road, grabbed her keys, and headed to the garage. She decided to drive her Mercedes. She was feeling hot and sexy, so she jumped in the Mercedes and let the top down. She wanted to let the wind blow through her hair and listen to a little old school, so she popped in her Keith Sweat CD and turned the volume up. *"There's a right and a wrong way to love somebody, you love me right..."* Lolita sang along as she pushed the garage opener to open the garage and back out of her driveway. Letting her top down all the way and heading for the mall made her feel extra good.

Lolita's phone rang and it was Jaylan on the other end. "Lolita my plane lands in Charlotte at 2pm, will you be able to pick a brother up, or do I need to rent a car?"

Lolita told Jaylan to stop trippin, because she was on her way to the store to pick up a few items to make his stay a little bit more comfortable. She did not want him to feel like a stranger when he got to Charlotte.

Jaylan said, "Hmmm, I wonder what goodies you have in mind, you know I got a sweet tooth!"

"Boy, stop! I am going to pick up some wine, strawberries, and cool whip, is there a special request?"

"Yeah Lolita, pick up some chocolate syrup to go with all that, and I will do the rest when I see that hot tail."

"Okay now why I got to be hot? Anyway, I will be there to pick you up at 2pm, now get off my phone."

Jaylan said in a very low sexy voice, "Bye HP!"

Lolita hung up the phone, turned the music up, and continued singing the lyrics to Keith Sweat. She sang as loud as she could, snapping her fingers and rolling her hips to the beat. Lolita pulled into the parking space at the Super Wal-Mart. When she got out of the car two young tenders walked passed her and said, "Damn, Ma that you?"

They were pointing at the Mercedes and holding their hands over their mouths when Lolita said, "Yeah, that is me!"

The two men told Lolita "We like your car, can we go with you?"

Lolita just smiled and told them, "Y'all ain't ready!"

Lolita walked towards the entrance to Wal-Mart, grabbed a shopping cart and headed towards the fruit section in the store. By the time Lolita finished shopping, her basket was full of all kinds of stuff—candles, strawberries, whipped cream, chocolate syrup, body oil and wine.

The woman at the cash register looked at Lolita and smiled, "Somebody is going to have a good time."

Lolita smiled back at the woman and handed her the cash for the items. She watched as the cashier placed her items into the bags, and Lolita told the woman 'thanks', grabbed her bags and headed to the car.

In the parking lot, Lolita reached into her purse for the keys, pressed the button to pop open the trunk, and then the car started up. She had some on-lookers watching as she approached the trunk to put her bags in the car. Lolita was a very proud, confident woman and it showed in every step she took.

After placing all the items in the car Lolita looked at her watch as she closed the trunk. She called her brother again to see if he had given her number to Renay's stupid ass but she got his voicemail again. "Leland your black ass had better call me back!"

Lolita hung up the phone and headed back to her house to make sure that the house cleaners had cleaned and to check the stock of food and wine. Lolita didn't want to leave the house for no reason once Jaylan got there; she wanted everything they needed to be in place. Lolita turned the music up louder as she flew down 85N, headed towards Lake Norman.

Lolita pulled in her driveway and she saw the housekeeper leaving, "Hi Ms. Marcus, everything is clean to your liking, is there anything else you need me to do before I leave?"

Lolita got out of the car and popped the trunk. "Sophie, can you help me bring these bags in the house?"

"Si, Ms. Marcus."

Lolita and Sophie carried the bags in the house and sat them on the kitchen table. Sophie started to put the things away, and she smiled at Lolita. In her thick Spanish accent, she said, "You planning to have a good time, yes?" Lolita smiled at Sophie, "Si, si, mucho good time!"

Sophie and Lolita laughed. Lolita said, "I guess sex is sex in any language."

Sophie responded, "Si."

Lolita made sure there was enough food and wine before she told Sophie she could leave.

"Thanks Sophie, see you next week!"

"Okay, bye Ms. Marcus!"

Today was the day that Lolita was going to see Jaylan and she was more than excited about it. She walked towards her car and looked at her watch, it was 1:45pm and she needed to get to the airport. Lolita jumped in the driver's seat and pulled out of the driveway, blasting her music. She started to sing and dance as she headed to the airport to pick up Jaylan.

The airport was not as busy as Lolita thought it would be when she arrived. There was hardly any traffic in the arrival section of Charlotte Douglas. As she approached the US Airways terminal, she saw Jaylan standing there with his one bag in hand. It was amazing to Lolita how men traveled with one suitcase for the weekend and women traveled with two, three bags full of stuff.

Lolita watched Jaylan; he was looking around and watching every car that rolled passed him. Lolita smiled to herself and she studied the tall handsome pecan brown man standing at the curb waiting for his Lolita to pick him up. Lolita rolled slowly up to the curb. Her tinted windows kept the outside from looking in. As she pulled up to the curb where Jaylan was standing she slowly let the window down. Peeking over her Chanel shades, she said, "Well handsome are you going to stand there all day or are you going to get that fine ass in this car?"

Jaylan saw Lolita and said, "Damn Ma, can I ride with you!"

Lolita gave Jaylan that sexy smile of hers, "Yeah baby, let Mommy take you for a ride. Hop yo' fine ass in this car!"

Jaylan put his bag in the back seat and jumped in the front. Leaning over the armrest, he put one hand between Lolita's legs and turned her face towards him with the other, "Give daddy a kiss. Did that cat miss daddy? Hmmm yeah it did, it's all wet."

Lolita started to blush and told him in her soft kitten-like voice, "Stop, you know I have to drive."

Jaylan looked at her and said "Drive, I am!"

Lolita smiled at him, put the car in drive, and headed towards the exit of the airport. In 25 minutes flat, Lolita was in Lake Norman. The Mercedes rode so smoothly she did not even notice how fast she was going. She and Jaylan talked all the way from the airport reminiscing on the time that they spent together in Texas. Lolita told Jaylan that she wanted his lips all over her lips and she didn't mean the ones she spoke from.

She said, "Boy, just wait until we get in the house, I am turning the phone off and double locking the doors, and we are not coming out until it's time to go to dinner."

Jaylan leaned in for a kiss, "That's fine with me Ma; you know we can do whatever you want."

Jaylan and Lolita had a great weekend. They stayed in and watched movies, ordered food, and just enjoyed each other's company.

On Sunday, Lolita drove Jaylan to the airport. His plane was leaving at 11:30am so they had breakfast and headed to the airport. Lolita arrived at Charlotte Douglas and pulled up to the departure area of US Airways. She put the car in park, got out, and walked around to the passenger's side.

Jaylan opened the door and grabbed Lolita around the waist, "Girl I had a good time and I am so glad I came to see you. When are you coming to Texas again?"

Lolita gave Jaylan a kiss on the lips ever so softly and said, "I will come after the club's grand opening, will you make it to the opening?"

"I have to work but I will definitely try to be there." Jaylan opened the back door to the car and grabbed his bag. He gave Lolita another kiss and rushed off to his gate to catch his flight. Lolita stood there for a moment and then she jumped in the car and called me on the phone.

Paris

It was a pretty day in Charlotte. The sun was shining brightly through my office window as I stood there day dreaming about my life. I had just hired a male assistant two weeks ago because my clients had increased 50% from the previous year, so I needed the help to keep everything in order. My daydreaming came back to reality when I heard Palmer Benton calling me on the intercom. Palmer was a college graduate from the University of Chapel Hill; he majored in Marketing and Advertisement. Palmer was very smart and he knew a lot about the sports industry. I enjoyed his work, not to mention he was fine as hell.

"Ms. Love, are you in there? Stefan is here to see you," Palmer said.

"Palmer let him in, please."

Stefan walked into my office just as fine as he had ever been in life. I remember when I first met him three years before. I was sitting at a red light and he was in the left turning lane headed towards the University YMCA. I looked at him and smiled. He waved at me, but the light turned green. I looked in my rearview mirror and could see that he was following me in his red mustang. Stefan followed me to the Food Lion on Sugar Creek and then we both pulled into the parking lot. I could remember that fine thang getting out the car and walking towards me. When I let the window down, he told me how beautiful I was and immediately asked me out to dinner. We exchanged numbers and he called me that night.

We talked for about a week before we ever actually went out. At the time, I did not know that Stefan was in the Anaconda family until one day he stopped by to see me. Stefan had called me on the phone and asked me what I was doing. I told him that I was getting ready to shampoo my hair. He told me to wait until he got there because he wanted to do it for me. I had never had a man shampoo my hair before so I was excited, to say the least, about him coming over.

Stefan arrived 30 minutes after we had talked on the phone, and when he came in the house, he looked like a million dollars; his skin brown like a pecan, his eyes chestnut hazel colored, his lips full and soft as cotton and the wavy hair on his head—beautiful. Stefan had nice sized muscles and a nice back. He had three tattoos; one was the Kappa symbol and his chest was beautiful. Not a scar on the man. I thought about how he stood behind me at the sink, as he began to wet my hair, his breath was warm against my neck as he pushed his body up against my ass.

"Is the water too hot?" he whispered in my ear, as I felt chills run up my spine.

I replied in a soft low voice, "No, it's just right."

Stefan applied the shampoo to my wet hair and began to massage my scalp as the shampoo lathered up on my head. Stefan had the strongest hands and they were big too, but he was so gentle with his touch and with his body up against mine was damn near erotic. I knew that it would not be long before the two of us would be butt naked and all over each other.

As I snapped out of the pleasant memory, Stefan was standing at my desk, probably wondering what I was deep in thought about. As I stood there, I could hear him breathing, and I could smell his cologne. I remembered he wore Black by Kenneth Cole, and the shit smelled so good it made you want to eat him up or lick him like a lollipop, damn!

I turned around and said, "How long have you been standing there?"

Stefan looked at me with this deep sexual look and said, "Long enough to see you were not on Earth. Where did you dream off to?"

"I was reminiscing about a place that had me in heaven and feeling like a woman alive and sexy."

"Well now," Stefan said, "let me see if I can guess where that was and who could have had you feeling so good." Stefan looked at me and gave me that half grin which made me want to kiss him right there where he stood.

I said, "You know exactly who that was. It's been a long time Stefan, what brings you to town?" I hoped that he would say that he was married or something to that effect, because he was the only man in Charlotte that could make me turn my head from Trevor, because Stefan was the best lover, I had ever had. Even better then Trevor.

Stefan pulled me close to him and whispered in my ear, "Let me hold you tonight, because I miss feeling your soft skin next to mine. And no matter how long it's been, I can't get you out of my head."

I was floored, because I knew I could not go there with him. It could jeopardize all that I had built with Trevor. The way that Stefan traveled it would not be worth the trouble, anyway, but I thought that if I just told myself that it was only for one night, maybe I could do it and not look back. I knew that I could not tell a soul about this, not even my girls. This could not get out, and I hoped that Stefan was leaving for good, because the two of us could not live in the same city.

Stefan gave me a kiss and told me that he would call me to find out if I had made up my mind about spending a night with him. Then he turned and headed towards my office door. I told Stefan that I would definitely have an answer for him when he called, but I was hoping that he didn't, because some things were better left alone.

He had even cooked for me and fed the food to me. I could remember how his dick was so big that I was in shock when I first saw it. I thought to myself that it could not be real, because it was thick from tip to the bottom, and he knew how to work the shit out of that thing. Damn, the memories of all of that was getting me wet as hell, so I decided to take the rest of the day off.

Palmer was out in the receptionist lobby when I heard him flirting with Stefan and I thought to myself, *'Is Palmer gay? He seems to like women, but there are a lot of these down low brothers out here these days.'* I heard Palmer tell Stefan that he liked his jeans and the pink button-down he had on, and I could hear Stefan telling Palmer that he did not swing that way, and if he ever approached him again, he would put his foot in his ass. Palmer was telling him not to knock it if he had not tried it, and Stefan told him, "Don't get your ass beat in this motherfucker."

I stepped out of my office and I was livid. I looked at Palmer and said, "I know I didn't just hear you trying to come on to my client, did I?"

Palmer told me that he was 'sorry' but he could not help himself, because Stefan was so fine. I could not believe Palmer was tripping like that, so I just told him that he needed to keep his thoughts to himself, because he could lose his job if he ever stepped out of line like that again.

I went into my office and I heard my cell phone ringing in my purse. When I finally found it, the caller had hung up the phone. I called home to speak to Trevor, but I just got the voicemail, so I tried him on his cell phone, and it too went directly to voicemail. I did not know why Trevor was not answering his phone, but I just figured he was busy and would get back to me as he always did.

I grabbed my things and was headed towards the door when I heard my cell phone ringing, "Hello, hello?"

I didn't hear anything on the other end, so I hung the phone up and looked at the Caller ID. It was a 219 area code, but it wasn't any of my people's number. I thought that maybe it was a wrong number. I walked over to Palmer's desk to let him know that I was leaving the office. "Palmer, hold all of my calls for the rest of the evening because I am going to do a little shopping. Call me on my cell phone *only* if it's something important."

I walked out of the office and headed to the garage where I parked my BMW. My cell phone rang again, and this time it was Charles Brown.

"Hello Charles, how are things in Miami?"

Charles told me that everything was going just as planned and he wanted to let me know that the club was ready for inspection before the big opening in a couple of weeks. "Paris do you think you and your girls could come down next weekend to check things out?"

Charles was always a businessperson and had his shit on point whenever you did business with him.

Paris Love

"Charles we will be there. I will get with Lolita and Lucky and we will call you back with the details," I said.

I hung up the phone with Charles and opened the door to my BMW. As I sat in the seat and cranked up the car, I started to think about my day and the surprise visit from Stefan. Once again, my cell phone rang. I glanced down at the Caller ID and saw it was a restricted call. I did not answer the call, but the caller kept calling, so I finally answered, "Hello?"

"Paris!" It was Trevor on the other end.

"Baby, where are you calling me from?" I asked him in my nervous voice.

Trevor said, "Calm down baby, I'm all right I just left my phone on the dresser at home."

I did not know it at the time, but he was lying to me, because he was doing some shit that he knew I would not approve of. He was in too deep to stop, until the deal went down. Trevor knew that he could not tell me until it was all over, because he had been working undercover for the FBI and did not know how the shit was going to turn out. He was praying that once he finished that shit, he was done with their asses for good. Trevor hated the po-po and wanted no part in this shit with their asses, but he had no choice because they were holding some shit over his head that happened a long time ago. He wanted to get the shit off his record for once and for all.

Trevor told me that he would be home late that night because he was going to play poker with the boys, and he usually did not come home until 3 to 4am in the morning.

"Trevor you know as long as I know you're okay, it's cool. I will be in the bed when you get home so wake me up if you want me to break you off a little something – something."

Trevor laughed and said, "That's what's up! I love you Paris!"

"I love you too Trevor, be safe baby. I will, see you later."

"Okay baby, bye!"

77

I hung up the phone and put the car in drive. I thought for a minute about Stefan, but I decided that I was not going to go there with him and turned on the radio to drown the thoughts of Stefan out of my mind. I hit the button on the CD player for track number 6. I was feeling a little gangster so I wanted to hear the baddest bitch, Trina. The base was blastin, and I was feeling very good. I put my cell phone on speaker and said, "Dial Lolita."

The phone rang, Lolita picked up, and shouted, "What's the deal Paris!"

"Girl you know it's all about you. What the hell are you doing because I have left the office early because I need a damn drink, so you down?"

Lolita was in her office in South Park. She had been looking at a new location for another spa because business was off the chain, and she had so many people wanting her to open a spot in their city.

"Paris you know I am down. Let me get Lucky's ass on the phone to see if she wants to roll with us, because you know she has been tripping lately, so we might need to get her ass out for a drink."

Lolita called Lucky, but she got her voicemail so she tried her office and was told that Lucky had taken the day off because she was not feeling well. I was thinking that the shit sounded crazy because Lucky never took off work without letting us know, especially if she was planning to be out of town or if she was sick.

"Lo, that shit sounds crazy, do you think we need to drive over to Lucky's to see if she is okay?" I asked.

"Paris, I don't know because she has not called us before when she was at home having one of her pity parties. So let's just wait until tomorrow to see if she calls."

Lolita always was the one to give a person time to deal with their issues. So we figured Lucky was just tripping, and I told Lolita to meet me at Maggiano's for drinks in an hour. We said goodbye, and I headed towards 85S.

Chapter Five

Three hours had passed since Trevor got off the phone with me. He was ready to leave but had no choice but to sit his ass in the black SUV with three FBI agents. Trevor had stumbled on some shit that he was not supposed to see. He knew the names of all the guys connected to a gun smuggling ring, but he only knew them because he had a friend that was dating this girl who worked for the telephone company. Her name was Sheila, and she had put taps on all the phones in the house, because her boyfriend was a major thief; this motherfucker stole shit like expensive jewelry and paintings, shit that the average brother would not think about taking.

Trevor had only met Sheila once, but he knew Brandon from grade school. Trevor did not fuck with Brandon like that because he knew that nigga was in some deep shit deeper than where Trevor wanted to go. Brandon had some connections overseas. He knew that these Germans were arms dealers and they were into money laundering. Brandon had been watching them for a month and recording all of their conversations from the phones that he had Shelia tapped. Most of the shit was in German so they figured no one would know what was going on if they heard them. Brandon was a different type of nigga. He could speak three different languages, and he was smart as hell with computer shit, but the motherfucker was a straight thief. Everything he had, he got with shit he had stolen from other people. Trevor used to buy little shit from him back in the day, like DVD players, computers, shit like that, but that nigga flipped the script on him and changed the game for real. Now Trevor's ass was sitting up in the Feds shit watching that nigga because they found out that Trevor knew Brandon's ass, who just happened to get his ass caught up in some bullshit and didn't even know the extent of the shit that was about to go down.

Trevor sat there listening to the audio feedback from inside of the house. The name that one of the men kept saying was 'Hans,' and apparently Hans was the leader, because he was the only name that was used the most in the conversation between the men in the house and a few Iranian men. Now Brandon had told Trevor that he was going to wait until the Iranian dude came with the money, and he and a couple of his boys where going to rob them. Trevor was like 'Word,' and he was thinking at that time that Brandon was shell, (meaning he was crazy) but he was just having some drinks with him. Brandon told Trevor that he had a few friends coming from Greece who were in on the deal, and he asked Trevor if he wanted to get in. Trevor never turned down easy money, and all Brandon wanted him to do was to put a small video camera on the button on Shelia's blouse. When she went to check the phones, she could get pictures of the inside of the joint to know what kind of shit Brandon was going to be up against when he hit the place. Brandon told Trevor that he would pay him $50,000 just to do it, and he promised that he did not have to be involved in nothing after that.

Trevor said, "That's all? Shit, hell yeah I will do that shit!"

Trevor never thought that he would end up sitting in an undercover SUV with the damn Alphabet Boys. He just wanted the money and to be done with the shit. Trevor was not the type to snitch on anybody, but Trevor hated prison more. A nigga had to do what he had to do, besides that, Brandon had already given Trevor the money, so it was a done deal, and he wasn't trying to give that money back. So Trevor was trying to think of a way to tell this nigga what was going to go down without getting caught by the Feds.

They had sat in the SUV for hours, which seemed like days to Trevor, but he was a thinker, so he was trying to come up with a game plan. He only had three days to get that shit together, because that was when the shit was going to hit the fan. Trevor had to get home to pack. He had a plane to catch out to Miami for the grand opening of my club, and he knew if he was not there, I was going to have a damn baby. The Feds told Trevor that he had better be back in town on Monday morning because they were going to need him to identify Brandon once they busted him. Trevor was not feeling that shit at all, so he had to come up with a plan to get the word to Brandon, even though they were not boys. Trevor didn't want to help the po-po with shit.

The Feds dropped Trevor off at the parking garage on E. Trade Street, across from the Civil Court building. Trevor jumped in his truck and stared at the black SUV. As it pulled off, he sat there for a while before he started the truck and thought about how he was going to take care of this shit without telling me. Trevor glanced at his watch and noticed it was 1pm, and his flight departed for Miami at 6pm. He had to hurry home to shower and change clothes. He needed to pack a small bag for the weekend and pick up a gift for me and the girls for our grand opening.

Trevor pulled out of the parking garage and turned onto E. Trade Street. He headed towards the transit station, came to a red light and turned left onto Brevard. As he headed towards 277N to 77N, his phone rang. Babyface's 'Never Keep Secrets' was playing when Trevor smiled, because that was the song he had set on his phone for whenever I would call him.

"Hey baby, how are things going in Miami?" he asked.

 I was so excited, that I could hardly get everything out. "Baby, wait until you get here, the shit is off the hook! What time does your plane land? I am going to send the car over to pick you up when you get to the airport."

Trevor said, "The car, oh you ballin like that? Let me find out!"

We both started laughing and I told him that I missed him, and he needed to hurry up and get there.

Trevor said, "I can only get there as fast as the plane gets me there Lamont!"

I started laughing and said, "You know what I mean punk, just hurry. I love you, bye!"

Trevor told me that he loved me too, and he would see me when he got to Miami.

Opening Night Club Dubai

July 2, 2004, was opening night at Club Dubai and Lolita, Lucky and I had spent the first week in Miami with Chuck making sure everything was the way it was supposed to be. I thought that we were going to have to postpone the club's opening, because Lucky had a bit of a breakdown. She had stayed in the house with all the lights out, shades closed, phones off, and did not even get out of bed to go to work. Lolita and I had gone over to her house that night after we had drinks to check on her, and when we walked in, the crazy ass girl was in the bed crying her freakin eyes out. It took a long time, but we finally convinced her that she had a lot to live for, and that her life was not over, so to get her ass up and get it together. That night was just crazy all together, because Lucky had really freaked me out. But the bitch was all better now, and she had been binge dating ever since. I was glad she was doing something other than sitting her ass in a dark ass house crying over Ron's worthless ass.

Now we were all in Miami happy as hell, and we are about to have the biggest crowd ever in one place. The shit was about to be crazy.

Lucky came in the room and asked, "Paris have you seen Lolita? We are supposed to go to the store to get some last minute items for the VIP rooms and time is running out."

I said, "She is on the first floor with one of the waiters going over some details about the food, so why don't you go down there and grab her, or I could go with you as soon as I finish checking the suites out with Chuck."

"Naw, that's okay, she will probably be ready once I get to the first level. We are going to run out for about an hour and then that should be the final touches on everything. Girl are you ready for tonight?"

"Hell yeah, I *been* ready. And I got this hot ass outfit too!"

"Will Trevor be here tonight?" Lucky asked.

"Yeah, he just called me from the road. He is on his way to the airport, so he should be here around 7pm."

"Good, I was wondering if he was going to make it, since he has been working so late these days."

"I know but he promised he wasn't going to miss the grand opening of our club, so he is on the way."

Lucky said, "Well let me grab Lolita so we can go and get back, because I want to make sure I look extra good tonight. Got something hot coming in town!"

"Alright now, don't hurt anybody! Girl I will see you later!" I said.

Lucky jumped on the elevator and pushed the button for the first level. As soon as she got off the elevator, Lolita was standing there.

"Where the hell you been? You know how I hate waiting on people, damn!" Lucky said.

"Calm your ass down bitch, and let's go. I was looking for your dumb ass first!" Lolita said.

Lolita and Lucky pushed the button for the main level at the same time and started laughing at each other.

Lucky said, "You nervous ain't you, bitch?"

Lolita said, "Hell yeah, yo' ass is too!"

They laughed even harder at each other, and when they reached the main level of the club, there were workers everywhere, from waiters, waitresses, bellhops, and people bringing in flowers and stocking alcohol in the bars, to the front desk clerks. The club was in motion, and it all was looking lovely.

Lolita and Lucky stopped and just stood in the middle of the lobby for a few minutes watching everyone run around preparing for the grand opening. It was so exciting until it was breath taking.

Lucky said, "Lolita are you ready, because I am ready to go back to the club so I can get dressed. I am so excited about tonight!"

"Girl, I was just thinking the same thing. I am so excited too!"

Lucky and Lolita headed towards the revolving doors and once they were outside standing on the red carpet, the bellman whistled to the valet park to bring Lolita's car to the front. In 5 minutes flat, Lolita's Boxster S convertible Porsche was in front of the club with the top down and all. She decided to drive the Porsche while she was in Miami because she wanted to floss as she drove through the city. It was a beautiful day in Miami and everything was going perfect. Lolita gave the valet person a one hundred-dollar tip, and told him that he picked a good day to work valet parking, because she was in a giving mood.

Lucky opened the passenger door, gave the valet a *'Please-do-not-even-try-it'* look, and said, "That tip was from both of us, so don't even think I got something for you."

Lolita said, "Girl you're crazy as hell!" Lolita started laughing at her.

Lucky said, "Girl, you know he wasn't getting a dollar out of me!"

"Lucky, stop being so cheap, 'cause us about to be some even richer bitches up in here!"

"I know girl, but we ain't given nothing away either," Lucky said.

"I know that's right!"

Lolita shifted into second gear and turned onto Washington Avenue. She hit track 2 on the CD player and blasted Trina's 'Diamond Princess.' The music was so loud, that Lucky could not hear her phone ringing, but she felt it vibrating in her purse.

"Hello, hello!" Lucky said, and she heard breathing on the end of the phone. "Who the hell is this?!"

Lucky had that panic look on her face. When she asked who the caller was again, she heard a voice that sounded muffled say, "I'm going to kill your bitch ass!"

Then there was silence.

Lucky looked at Lolita and her face was ghost white.

Lolita asked, "What's wrong? Who was that on the phone, Lucky?"

Lucky just stared out the window with tears rolling down her eyes. She looked at Lolita and said, "I don't know, but I've been getting threatening phone calls for the past two months."

"Girl, why didn't you tell us about the calls? Did you call the police?"

"Yes, Lolita, I did. But they said that I should put a tap on my phone, because they needed more information to find out who has been calling me, and where they are calling from."

"Lucky, don't worry, because me and Paris will look out for you. And don't let that phone call ruin our grand opening night."

"Lolita, I am scared, because I don't know who has been calling me. I am just trying not to think about it. Maybe when we get back to the club, all the excitement will take my mind off the threats."

"That's right, we will forget about that call for now and deal with it after the club's open," Lolita said.

Lucky wiped the tears from her eyes and she said, "Turn up the music," and she started dancing in her seat.

Lolita knew that it was going to take a lot for her to get Lucky through that night, but with my help, they would get to the bottom of the phone calls and who was threatening Lucky.

Lolita turned into the parking lot of the Creative Parties and VIP store. She quickly parked in the empty space in front of the store, leaving the top down. Both Lolita and Lucky went inside of the store.

Ray Shawn greeted Lucky and Lolita at the counter, "Can I help you ladies find something?"

Lolita told him that she had spoken to someone the previous week about getting an ice sculpture for the VIP rooms in the new

Club Dubai. He asked her for her name, and then went switching off to the back of the store.

The clerk was gone for about 10 minutes, when he came bouncing back to the front of the room. "Girls, oh I think you going to love this, come see, come see!"

Lucky said to Lolita, "Damn he is flaming! Girl he is *too* sweet!"

Lolita started to laugh. The two of them giggled all the way to the back of the room, but when they walked into the entrance they were standing with their mouths opened. The ice sculpture for the VIP rooms where these beautiful statues designed like the boat sail, with blue ice for the water at the bottom surrounding the sail. It was breathtaking and they all had a different view. Ray Shawn turned the lights off in the room and all of the sculpture lit up with mulit-colors to match the design of the club. Lucky was just saying repeatedly how beautiful the sculptures were, and she and Lolita stood there for about five minutes just looking at them.

Lolita gave the balance for the sculptures to Ray Shawn. He asked her if she needed them delivered, and she told him that he should have them there by 7pm, because they needed to be set up in the club before 9pm. Ray Shawn finished the transaction and asked if they knew the owners of Club Dubai, and Lucky looked at Lolita and said, "Well we are two of the owners, and the other one is back at the club preparing for tonight's grand opening."

With a doubtful face, Ray Shawn looked at the two of them and said, "Okay, you can tell me the truth."

Lucky said, "We are not playing, but since you don't believe us, you can come by the club and see for yourself."

Lucky gave him a VIP pass and told him that she was going to let him in free, and also let him check out the VIP rooms. After that, he could tell her what he thought of the club when the evening was over.

"Thanks!" Ray Shawn gave Lolita her credit card back, and smiled at her, as she put the card in her purse.

Lucky and Lolita were walking out the door when Lolita's phone rang, "Hello?"

"Lolita, this is Paris. Where in the hell are you two bitches?"

"Girl shut up! We are on our way back to the club, and girl wait until you see the ice sculptures for the VIP rooms," Lolita said.

"Well hurry up because everything is ready and we need to make sure we are looking lovely tonight."

"Okay, quit trippin!" Lolita hung up the phone and opened the door to the Porsche, when she put the key in the ignition the seats adjusted to where she had it when she first got in the car.

Lolita pulled into traffic and headed towards Washington Street when she spotted a car in the rear view. It seemed like the car was following them but Lolita didn't say anything to Lucky because she didn't want her to be alarmed for no reason. Lolita continued to watch the car as she drove to the club and when she turned into the club's parking lot, the car continued going straight. But Lolita could have sworn she saw Lucky's ex-boyfriend looking at them when she drove up to the valet parking.

Lucky and Lolita got out of the car and walked to the front entrance of the club. The bouncers where standing there laughing and joking when they noticed Lolita and Lucky.

"Let me get the door for you lovely ladies," one of the muscular bouncers said.

The shorter bouncer with all the muscle, looked at Lolita and said, "Girl you know you are fine as hell. Can I buy you a drink tonight? You know I can get you in for free."

Lolita looked at the little swoll man and told him, "Nigga pleazeeeee don't go there, and I don't need you to get me in nowhere, okay!"

The bouncer standing next to the short one elbowed him and whispered, "Man, she is one of the owners!"

The short bouncer gave the man a look like *'why you did not tell me,'* and said, "Oh excuse me! I didn't know I was talking to the boss. I wasn't expecting someone as fine as yourself to be one of the owners, my bad!"

Lolita could not do nothing but laugh at the little swoll pitbull looking person, so she looked at him and said, "That's okay, you cool! Just make sure that there is no trouble in my club tonight and keep out the riff – raff."

The bouncer looked at Lolita and Lucky as they walked inside of the club and shook his head, "Damn, 'em some fine ass bitches, and rich too!"

Lolita and Lucky took the elevator to the VIP room on the eighth floor. When the elevator doors opened, security was standing there to greet Lolita and Lucky. "Hi ladies, looks like we are going to have a hot night tonight!" the security man said.

Lolita said, "Hey Joe, I am glad we got you and your boy to work this floor, because you know how those young ballers can be. I know you will have everything under control."

Joe pulled his jacket back revealing the 9mm glock in his holster. "Yeah, I got everything under control right here."

Lolita and Lucky smiled at him, "Yeah, that's what we talking bout, boy!" They both started laughing as if they had made the joke of the year, and walked into the VIP room where I was talking to the bartender.

"Top Shelf only in this room, and keep all the Cris, Patron and Moet stocked. And make sure we don't run out of anything," I said. I was giving orders because I was the boss.

"That's right girl, you tell him!" Lucky said while Lolita gave her the thumbs up.

I turned around to face Lucky and Lolita, "Y'all bees are a trip. Now let's go to our suites so we can get our drink on and put our shit on, 'cause it's about to be on and poppin in this bitch tonight!"

Lucky, Lolita and I jumped on the elevator to the 10th floor where the private VIP room and several suites were. We each had a suite of our own, and it had all the luxuries of a five star hotel. I went into my suite to get dressed for the party when my cell phone rang.

"Hello?" I answered.

"Hey baby, I am just getting off the plane and headed to the baggage claim. What time are you coming to pick me up?" Trevor asked.

"Trevor, sweetie I am sending the car over for you right now. Baby I am so excited that you are here with me. Can't wait to see that fine ass 'cause mama needs some of that daddy dick right about now!"

Trevor smiled and said, "Yeah, and daddy is going to make sure you get it all too!"

I told Trevor that I would have the car pick him up outside at the arrival gate in front of US Airways. We hung up the phone and I started laying my clothes out on the bed to look them over one last time before I jumped in the shower. I dialed zero on the hotel phone and the front desk clerk picked up, "Front desk!"

"Hi, this is Paris. Can you please have Rick go to the airport to pick my fiancé up, and he will be waiting in front of US Airways arrival gate."

"Yes, Miss Paris, I will have him go right away."

"Thank you."

The girl on at the front desk was very pleasant and helpful. I hoped she would be like that when the crowd appeared, because it could get very frustrating when you were working. Especially when you worked around a bunch of drunken people. I was so excited about that night. Everything had run smoothly so far, and all of the employees, including the DJ, were there, so it was all good.

I jumped in the shower, and while the water ran off my body, I thought about Stefan. Why now, why was the image of Stefan in my mind? I really did not understand, because I had not thought about him since he had left my office. Stefan was a forbidden fruit in my life, and I was not about to ruin my relationship with Trevor just to see if something was still there with Stefan.

As the soap from my body ran down the drain, so did the thoughts of Stefan. I was determined not to even think about being with him because I didn't want to take the risk the outcome would be too devastating for either of us to endure.

Chapter Six

Lucky's assistant Tanya Jackson was the ex-girlfriend of Ty. Now Ty and Lucky went back before Lucky ever attended Law school and became a major lawyer. Lucky was working at a strip club, and Ty used to give Lucky big money to strip and do private dances. Lucky never knew that Ty wanted her like that, she just needed the money at the time to get through school, so she just did what she had to do. Now Ty had sent Lucky flowers and even paid a couple of semesters of school for her. Lucky was involved with Ty after work hours, and she did enjoy the attention, but it was only because of the stress of trying to go to a Law school that cost an arm and a leg to attend. Ty began to be wherever Lucky was, showing up in her class and waiting for her after school. Lucky was feeling as if Ty was stalking her, so she refused to see Ty again, and that was when it all happened.

Ty sent Lucky letters telling her that she loved her more than life, and that she was going to kill herself if Lucky did not want to be with her. Those threats added stress to Lucky's life because she did not want to have anyone's death on her hands or in her heart.

Ty hung herself from Lucky's living room ceiling fan, and Lucky found her when she came home from school. When Lucky opened the door to her apartment, she dropped her books on the floor and fell to her knees. She couldn't believe what was in front of her—Ty's lifeless body going around and around with the sound of the rope tightening on Ty's neck. The way Ty killed herself was the same way that Lucky's sister had died. That made things even harder for Lucky to deal with. She needed to get away for awhile to sort things out.

After the death of Ty, Lucky had to take a semester off from school and return to her hometown in the mountains to get her mind together to finish school. For a long time after Ty's death, Lucky would get a phone call and there would be no one on the other end. Lucky finished Law school and moved to Charlotte, but she still had flashbacks about Ty.

Tanya sat in her bedroom with a picture album filled with pictures of Lucky and Ty, with Lucky giving a lap dance and wearing very provocative clothing. Tanya truly, deeply loved Ty, and when she passed away, Tanya wanted revenge. But she never thought she would get that close to Lucky. She never thought she would be her personal assistant. She went to Lucky's office as a temp and overheard the conversation between two paralegals that Lucky was looking for a Legal Assistant. Tanya jumped at the chance, and now, it had been two years, and Tanya had gained Lucky's trust to the point where she had access to her house and all of her personal accounts at work. Tanya blamed Lucky both for Ty's depression and for her death. She hated Lucky and everything about her to the point that she would use her clothes and perfume, and fix her hair like Lucky.

Tanya stood in the mirror dressed in the dress that Lucky wore on the picture the day of Ty's birthday, which was the first night that they met. Tanya took Ty to the strip club to celebrate their one-year anniversary, and Lucky was dancing on the stage in the red dress that wrapped around her waist like a big red silk ribbon. Her hair flowed as she moved her hips in slow circular movements. Tanya stood in the mirror and wrapped her arms around herself as if she was dancing with someone, and she closed her eyes and hummed the sound out loud, "Slow motion for me, hmm I like it like that, slow motion for me, do it slow motion."

Tanya stopped dancing and started talking to herself in the mirror, "Lucky, I love you so much, why you don't want me? Lucky, Lucky, that bitch ruined my life. Why Ty? Why did you think she was prettier than me? Look Ty, I can look like her if you want. Well then Ty, let's see how much you love her when her face is dismembered, and I cut all of that beautiful long hair off, and then the two of you can go to Hell together!"

Tanya turned into this angry enraged person. She started throwing things around the room, and then she took her fist and broke the mirror. With blood running down her arm, she fell to the floor and started crying hysterically. "You are going to pay for what happened to Ty! Lucky you are going to pay with your life!"

Tanya picked herself up off the floor and headed to the bathroom to wash the blood from her arm. She wrapped her arm in gauze and sat on her bed. She reached in her top drawer of the nightstand and got the scissors. She began cutting out letters from the magazines and pasting them on a blank sheet of paper. "It's not over. You will pay with your life bitch!"

One by one, she pasted the letters on the blank paper and once she finished, she cut out the numbers and letters for Lucky's address at work and pasted them on the outside of the envelope with no return address. Tanya had planned to ask Lucky to come help her pick out a place to hang a picture that Lucky had given her for a house-warming gift. She was planning to cook dinner and share some of her photos with Lucky. Tanya thought that it would be a good plan, and she was going to make sure that she had everything in place. Once she got Lucky to her apartment, she would have rope and the same outfit that Ty wore the day Lucky found Ty's lifeless body hanging from the ceiling fan in her apartment. Tanya knew that Lucky didn't remember her because they only met once, and Lucky didn't show up at Ty's funeral. Besides, Tanya had lost weight and changed her hair color, so she didn't look the same as she did when Lucky met her.

Tanya could remember Lucky just looking passed her not really acknowledging her as being with Ty. She hated Lucky the first day they met, and she just knew that she was going to end up ruining everything that she had built with Ty.

Tanya picked up the phone and dialed the number to the office. When the voicemail came on, she left a message for Lucky. "You are going to die soon, and you will finally pay for what you did!" Tanya removed the voice distorter from the phone and she put the device in the back of her top dresser drawer. With an evil grin on her face, Tanya headed out her apartment door.

Club Dubai

I put the final changes on my outfit for the grand opening and stood in the full-length mirror in the VIP suite, "Damn I'm looking good and feeling even better!" I said to my reflection.

I poured myself another glass of Goose and juice and took a long sip. I stood in front of the mirror a little longer, admiring my hourglass shape in the white linen halter pants suit that had the low dip in the front and back. I slipped on my silver stilettos sandals, which showed off my fresh French manicured toes. I was a very stylish woman, and I loved to dress up and look as rich as I was. I took one more look at my entire outfit and gave myself a big love-you-kiss in the mirror.

I heard a knock at my door, so I grabbed my purse and walked into the living room of the suite. When I opened the door, their stood a man with two dozen blood red long stem roses in his arms hiding his face. I was smiling from ear to ear and I asked, "Are those for me?"

When the flowers where handed to me, the face behind them through me off. It was Stefan standing there looking extra good and fine as ever.

"What the hell? Stefan what are you doing here?"

Stefan looked at me and said, "Are you going to invite me in, or are you going to let me stand here holding these roses?"

I looked at him and I thought, *'Why am I being tempted like this and how did Stefan find out about the grand opening?'*

Stefan looked at me with that *'I know what you are thinking'* look and said, "I called your office on Friday and spoke with Palmer. He told me that you were here at your grand opening, which I was wondering why you never mentioned it to me."

I knew that I was going to cuss Palmer ass out on sight because I was trying to avoid seeing Stefan, and now he was standing in my hotel suite. "Stefan, I am going to put the flowers in a vase and then we have to go, because the club will open in an hour, and I have to get with Lolita and Lucky to do a final check on everything. But you are welcomed to stay at the party and enjoy the festivities."

Stefan handed the flowers to me as I walked over to the kitchen area, opened the cabinet, and got a big round glass vase. As I was filling it up with water, I could feel Stefan's breath on the back of my neck.

"Paris you know that I want to be with you not just tonight but forever. I love you."

Stefan grabbed me by my waist, turned me towards him, and gently kissed me. He kissed me first just with his lips pressed firmly against mines. Then he gently moved his tongue in my mouth and slowly moved it against mines and in a circular motion, our tongues twilled as the passion blazed inside of me. I wanted to pull away from Stefan but I just could not get my body to move.

Stefan began to suck on my lips and pull me closer to his muscular chest. The ringing of my phone made me jump and pull away from Stefan. I walked over to the desk and got my cell phone out of my purse I saw that it was Trevor calling.

"Hey baby where are you?" I said as my voice trembled.

Trevor answered, "I am pulling into the hotel, are you going to meet me downstairs and show me to our room, or shall I just come up?"

"You can come up baby I will wait here for you and then we can meet up with Lolita and Lucky."

I hung up the phone and turned and looked at Stefan, "Please leave now and enjoy the party if you want, but I can't see you. Trevor is on his way up and if he catches you he will flip."

Stefan looked at me and said, "I will be waiting for you, because he is not the man for you Paris, I am."

Stefan walked out of the suite and I ran quickly to the door to lock it and tried to get myself together before Trevor got to the room. I reapplied my lipstick and put the flowers on my desk. I hid the card that was attached and straightened the room while looking for any evidence of Stefan left behind.

I heard a knock at the door, and when I opened it, Lolita and Lucky were standing there.

Lucky said, "Girl what is wrong with you and why do you have that 'I got caught with my hand in the cookie jar' look on your face."

Lolita charmed in and said, "Yeah girl you look like you were up to no good!"

"Both of you bitches shut up because Trevor is on his way to the room and I got to make sure he doesn't notice anything different and I need to get my mind right. Where's my glass, because I got to get another drink before Trevor gets up here," I said.

"Paris what happened in here? And someone smells good. Smell like Black by Kenneth Cole, I know that scent anywhere," Lolita said, as she walked over to the bedroom. "Who you been fuckin!"

I turned towards Lolita, "Bitch that is not funny. I had a surprise visit from Stefan and girl he tongued me down. My pussy is still wet and I am about to see Trevor's ass in less then a minute. I got to get my composure back! I told Stefan that I could not see him. He went on and on about loving me and all this shit about us getting back together. I can't go there with him, and we both know that, but girl he had me straight twisted up in this piece!"

Lolita and Lucky started laughing at me and my cell phone rang, "Damn, this phone is ringing like I'm da president, HELLO!"

"Baby what's wrong with you, I'm on the 10th floor which suite are you in?" It was Trevor again.

"Hey Baby, I'm sorry just a little frustrated. I'm in Suite 11."

Trevor hung up the phone and seconds later, he was knocking on the door. Lucky and Lolita were standing their stank asses at the door when I opened it, just waiting for me to have that same look I had on my face earlier, but I was determined not to let it show that I had another man on my mind. I opened the door and before I could get anything out of my mouth, them two heifers where screaming "Hey Trevor!"

I gave both of them a dirty look and gave Trevor a hug and a kiss, "Hi baby I am so glad you are here now, maybe I can relax and just enjoy the evening."

It was 8:15pm and the club was opening at 9pm so I had to get downstairs to check everything one more time before opening. I told Trevor to get dressed and meet me in the main lobby. Lolita, Lucky and I headed downstairs to get everything jumpin. When we got in the hallway, I told Lucky and Lolita that Stefan was coming to the party. He had checked into one of the suites on the eighth floor, and I was not comfortable about him being there, because I could not trust myself to be alone with him. I loved Trevor, and I knew I did not want to be with Stefan like that, but damn that man brought out a passion in me that I did not even know was there. I was glad that we were not in the same city because there would be trouble, trouble.

Lolita and Lucky were looking at me and they both knew what was going on in my head, and the only way I was going to get rid of the images was to kill that stupid cat, 'cause curiosity was fucking me up right about then.

We got to the elevator and the guy that was working the VIP elevator had changed shifts so he asked to see our VIP passes to be on the 10th floor. I said "Honey we are the owners of this here establishment, I am Paris Love, this is Lolita Marcus and Lucky Blue."

The man looked at me and said, "I am so sorry. I didn't know, I was just doing my job."

I knew he did not know who we were, but I just wanted him to see that three beautiful, intelligent and rich black women could own a club and not just be the hired help or the eye candy on some nigga's arm. We all just looked at the man and smiled with that *'I know you did not know'* look and *'its okay, but make a note of it for next time.'* I just laughed to myself, because he was so nervous, and I guessed he needed to be, because we could have been three bitches and fired his ass on the spot for trying to check us. But that was not the case, so we let the brother off the hook.

The elevator came to a stop on the main floor and when the doors opened old boy said, "You ladies have a good night, and this is a very nice club you all have."

We all said 'thank you' at the same time and headed towards the main desk to do our last check for the night before the doors opened to the public. Everything was looking lovely and the waiters and waitresses' uniforms were pressed and as clean as the board of health. Every one of the staff looked so well, and we were so proud of how things were going. It was 8:50pm and we were getting ready to open the doors to the club. There was a line wrapped around the building. The limos were pulling up one by one with all the ballers and their women on their arms dressed to the tee. We were so excited and ready to get the party jumpin. The staff was ready and with a wave of our hands, the doors opened to the club.

We had complimentary strawberries dipped in chocolate and champagne all night for our guest. Lucky and Lolita both wore pants suits. Lucky wore a red halter one-piece gaucho pants outfit and Lolita wore a black halter-top with black capris. Lolita loved to have her twins showing and bouncing freely so she made sure the top was cut low. Lucky on the other hand, was somewhat on the conservative side, so she was just elegant in her red with a twist of sexy. I had that white linen looking like a million dollars wrapped in white silk. Damn, I was looking so good, even Trevor gave me that *'girl if you were not going to this opening, damn what I would do to you' look.*

We were about to make history at our grand opening and the paparazzi was in full effect. The cameras were snapping and people where coming from everywhere. The club was packed with people. Both the VIP rooms where filled with celebrities and those who had the money to party like celebrities. We shook hands and met people all night long. I felt like I was a movie star and everyone loved me. That was the best night I had in years, and Trevor was really enjoying himself, too. I saw him talking to the other major defense lawyers in the room exchanging lies for lies. Trevor was having a good time but he seemed a little on edge. I could not put my finger on it, but I knew when something was going on different with him. We were just that close. I looked at him from across the room and smiled at him. He gazed at me and gave me a wink. He mouthed the words 'you are so beautiful'; that was my baby. I loved that man, but in the back of my mind, I was still thinking about that kiss that Stefan and I had shared before Trevor arrived at the club.

Lolita and Lucky were mingling with the crowd on the main level. The DJ had the whole floor hyped and everybody was dancing and just having a ball. The party was jumping on every level in the club. The people in VIP were eating, drinking and laughing. The waiters and waitresses were bringing drinks after drinks, the cash registers were changing and our pockets were getting fatter. Damn that shit was the bomb! We had outdone ourselves this time, and everything was lovely.

Trevor came up to me and said, "Baby this club is hot. I mean this shit is off the chain! I am having the time of my life, and babe, there are so many famous people at this joint. I swear I saw P Diddy in the 10th floor VIP room, but it was so packed in there I couldn't get over there to say 'hi.'"

Trevor was so excited and drunk, he was having the time of his life and he loved looking at pretty women, pretty half-dressed ones. And if he thought he could get away with it, he would have got him some stranger that night. Men, they all cheated in some form or fashion, but I felt that if he was taking care of home and paying all of the bills and he brought his ass home, what the fuck did I care. Whew, let them bitches help me out so that nigga wouldn't be trying to fuck me to death every night.

I just looked at him and said, "I am glad that you are having a good time baby, now come on this dance floor and slow dance with me."

I pulled Trevor on the floor, he put his arms around my waist, we danced to Jagged Edge's "I Gotta Be", and we just held each other close. I had my eyes closed but when I opened them, I saw Stefan standing at the dance floor just looking at me with those sexy eyes. Just then, "He Can't Love You" by Jagged Edge started to play, and Stefan was standing there mouthing the words to me. I thought I was going to melt and I just closed my eyes again and held Trevor tighter. I was thinking about Stefan and I was trying to focus on Trevor and our relationship. We had a good thing going right then, and I did not want to think about Stefan. But the thoughts of being with him naked in the shower, and him kissing me all over my body was just a thought that I could not shake, ever since that day he had showed up to my office, and now the grand opening. *'What does he really want from me?'* I thought.

The song ended and I was still holding on to Trevor. He pulled back from me and was looking at me.

He said, "What's wrong baby? You act like you never want to let me go, are you okay?"

I quickly gathered my thoughts, told Trevor that I was fine. I said, "I guess the excitement of the club's opening has me a little on edge."

Trevor walked over to the bar and ordered a drink for me and when he returned with the glass, he handed it to me with a smile. "Here baby, this should help calm you down. Relax and have a good time. This is a great party and everything has turned out fine, so there are no worries. Okay, baby?"

I took the drink out of Trevor's hand and drank half of it down and I looked at him and said, "Thanks baby, I am feeling better already. I am going to go find Lolita and Lucky to see what those tricks are doing. I will see you later." I gave Trevor a kiss and headed for the elevators.

When I got to the elevators, the doors opened and when I stepped into the elevator, Stefan was standing there.

He walked up to me and said, "I saw how you were dancing with Trevor, but I could see in your eyes when you looked at me that you wish it was me holding you instead of him."

I laughed and said, "Boy please, I wasn't thinking about yo' ass so don't even go there!"

Stefan looked at me and he pressed his body up against me in the elevator. He had me pinned up against the wall and I was trying to move to the other side, but he was blocking me in. Stefan took my arm and slightly twisted it turning me around so that my back was facing him. He pressed his crotch up against my ass, and I could feel that big ass dick of his growing.

Stefan whispered in my ear, "You miss all of these twelve inches don't you?"

I could not do nothing but moan and wiggle up against that Anaconda, whew! I was trying to fight the fire that was burning inside of me because I knew that it would lead to trouble if I gave in. I turned around to face Stefan and he told me that he wanted to take me up to his suite and he wanted to suck my clit until I came with ecstasy. Then he pushed the button for the eighth floor and started to kiss me. I wanted to run but I was feeling good from that last drink that Trevor had given me from the bar and the way Stefan was kissing me I was weak as a lamb. The elevator stopped on the eighth floor and Stefan took out his room key to enter his suite. 812 was the number of his room, and I could not stop myself from walking in there when he opened the door.

I did not even get into the room before Stefan grabbed me, kissing me harder with more passion. It seemed like the room was getting hotter. Steam was coming off the windows, and the lights seemed to flicker. I was spinning and I could not control myself, so

I just gave in to every touch, squeeze, and caress that Stefan was giving me. He untied the string to my halter-top, cuffed my breast in his hands, and started licking down the middle of them. Then he sucked each of them so, so gently until I thought I was going to explode. Before I could blink, my clothes were on the floor, and I was left standing butt naked in my heels. I couldn't catch my breath fast enough when Stefan swooped me off my feet and carried me over to the bed. He turned me over on my stomach and proceeded to lick my clit from behind; my legs were trembling as I came so hard until I collapsed on the bed. He then turned me over and penetrated me deep and hard, back and forth, in and out. Stefan was stroking my pussy until we both came at the same time, screaming in ecstasy.

Afterwards, I laid there on the bed, as Stefan was kissing me on my neck and asking me to be with him and leave Trevor.

"Stefan, you know I can't do that and that is the reason why I didn't want to go there with you, but the alcohol and the extra heat had me twisted."

Stefan stood up and looked out the window at the city of Miami. "I know it's a lot to think about right now, but you and I both know it's more to this than sex and we might need to see where it takes us," he said.

I couldn't help but stare at his chiseled body standing at the window and every inch of him was just beautiful. And he was packin like a horse. I thought to myself, *'damn this shit is crazy wrong.'*

I looked at Stefan and said, "I got to get back to the party before Trevor starts to look for me. I will think about what you said Stefan, but my heart is with Trevor right now."

"Fair enough, I can only hope you make the right decision and choose me."

I grabbed my things off the floor, took a quick shower, and sprayed some of my Vera Wang perfume on. I lotioned down my body, reapplied my make-up, and gave Stefan a kiss on the cheek. "Thanks, I will see you at the party."

He did not say anything. He just gave me that sexy ass smile and locked the door when I left.

Stefan lay on the bed and smelled the pillowcase that I had laid my head on and he could still smell my perfume in the pillowcase. "She is going to be my woman, it's just a matter of time once she finds out what a liar and crook Trevor is she will come running to me."

Stefan closed his eyes for a minute and he envisioned the last time he saw Trevor. Trevor was meeting with one of the Columbian drug lords Pedro Ceros which he represented in a case that was thrown out of court because the main witness was murdered in cold blood several days before the trial. Stefan was an undercover DEA on the case, but he had never met Trevor in person. He just kept tabs on him after the trial and found out in his research what a dirty lawyer he was.

Stefan's baby sister was the witness in the case against Pedro. Pedro had dated her when she was a freshman in college and turned her out on cocaine and heroin. She had been in rehab and was trying to get her life together when she was going to testify against Pedro, but he had the safe house blown up, killing everyone that was there including her. Stefan swore he would get revenge.

After leaving Stefan I jumped on the elevator and pushed the button for the sixth floor. I was ready to get a couple of drinks and dance this mess out of my head, so that when I faced Trevor again, I would be straight. I got off the elevator and I heard Lil Wayne's "The Block Is Hot" playing in the background. I walked straight to the bar, and got me a Hypnotic on the rocks and started pumping my hand in the air and swaying back and forth to the music. This young fine nigga walked up to me and said, "Excuse me, you dancin or what?"

I looked at him and drank the rest of my drink down in one gulp, "Let's go pimpin!"

I grabbed his hand and headed to the dance floor. They started playing Missy's "Lose Control," and I was dropping it to the floor and the whole nine. I danced about five records straight and when I stopped, I was sweating and wiping my face with a napkin. I didn't use a regular napkin either; I had the special thick cotton napkins because I needed to make sure I was straight after I finished dropping it like it was hot.

I looked up and Lolita and Lucky were standing next to me at the bar.

Lolita said to me with her hands on her imaginary hips,

"Where the hell yo' white ass been?"

I said, "I was on the VIP floor with Trevor and then I came on the 6th floor. Why you tricks trying to find out where I been? Where in the hell have the two of you been? I hope mingling with our guest and having a good time like I am trying to do."

Lolita said, "Nigga, don't be new, you have been running around here and Trevor ass has been looking all over for you, and you know how that nigga likes to trip."

Lucky was standing there looking like she was not having a good time, so I asked, "Bitch, what is wrong with you?"

Lucky looked at me with those big brown eyes of hers and said, "Paris I am not feelin yo' shit right now, because I just saw Diesel's black ass up in here. And how in the hell did he find out about the opening is my question?"

I said, "Girl I didn't invite the nigga so we can have his ass put out!"

Lucky said, "Too late! I had security put that nigga out on sight, and he had the nerve to try to threaten me. I am going to call Pookie and 'em first thang in the morning, because he must think he can just do what the fuck he wants to do, and I am starting to get sick of being scared of that nigga. I was thinking to myself how did this nigga find out about the party, and I could not come up with nobody I knew that would have told him."

Lolita said that she thought she saw that nigga following them earlier when they went to check on the ice sculptures, but she wasn't sure, and damn if it wasn't his ass.

I was thinking that we had to get rid of that stupid nigga for real, because I thought he was done fucking with Lucky after that last ass whipping Pookie put on that ass. Something had to happen before things got out of hand and Lucky really lost her mind.

I gave Lucky a hug and said, "Girl don't worry about a thang, because I'm not going to let that nigga hurt you. Lolita and I got your back."

We had our group hug and then it was back to the party. It was 4am and people were starting to either leave or head to their rooms. We were getting all kinds of compliments from our guests and the media was there, so we figured it was going to be in the news and on Entertainment Tonight or some shit.

As we had hoped, the opening of Club Dubai was a huge success and we could not wait until the news came out the next day to see how big we were on our first night. Lucky, Lolita and I headed to the elevators to go to the main level to see our guest out. Everyone on the VIP floors had suites and they were still partying. When we got on the elevator, Trevor was standing there getting ready to get off on the sixth floor.

I said, "Hey baby you been having a good time?"

Trevor looked at me. He was drunk and talking a mile a minute, and he started rambling about how he was talking to some basketball players out of Chicago and how he'd danced a couple of times because some girls pulled him on the dance floor. Trevor was smiling and I could tell that he'd had a good time. He was like a kid in a candy store.

I said, "Baby I am glad you had a good time. Do you want to come say bye to our guest that are leaving, or are you going to the 10th floor to the VIP lounge?"

Trevor looked at me and said that he was going to play poker with a couple of the men on the VIP floor and that he would see me later. I gave him a kiss and pushed the button to go down to the main level.

Lolita and Lucky were standing there with that look on their faces as if to say, *'okay we know your ass was missing for an hour, where in the hell were you and where is Stefan?'*

I smiled at them and said, "Ah, I don't know what you heifers are talking about, I was on the 6th floor where you found me getting my drink and dance on, thank you! I haven't seen Stefan since earlier today, so stop sweatin me about him!"

"Nigga please," Lucky said as she gave me that *'I know what you did'* look. "We know you got the hots for that nigga so don't even try to play us like that. We know you!"

I thought about the night of passion with Stefan and decided to keep what happened between us and not even tell my girls. Sometimes you had to do that, just let it be between you and God.

I looked at both of them and said, "Well I'm telling you nothing happened, so let's drop the conversation about him, because I don't want to think about that right now."

With that, the elevator doors opened and we were on the main level of the club. There were so many people standing in the lobby and some were leaving and others where just politicking with each other. It was a beautiful sight and it was all peaceful.

Lolita looked at me and said, "Now this is how a grown folks party is supposed to be, fun and non-violent."

The party was still poppin on the VIP floors, but my ass was tired as hell. It was 7am, so I went to my suite and left Lucky and Lolita on the main lobby talking to some guys they met from Philly.

I got to the room and when I open the door, Trevor was not in there. I just figured he was still playing his little poker game, so I jumped in the shower and stood under the warm water for a while. Thoughts of Stefan filled my head again. I didn't know what it was about him but whatever it was I didn't want to think about it, because I had already crossed the line with him, and I didn't want to repeat the scene anytime soon. I finished my shower and wrapped myself in the terry cloth bathrobe, washed my face and put my Oil of Olay night cream and jumped in the bed. I was feeling a dream sleep come over me as I closed my eyes and drifted away.

I didn't hear Trevor come in and when I woke up to go pee, he was laying next to me but I didn't have the terry cloth robe on anymore and I guessed Trevor had took it off of me and put me under the covers. I stumbled out of bed and headed towards the bathroom. As I sat on the toilet, I rubbed my eyes, and the hot pee came out like a flowing river. It seemed like it was not going to ever end. I finally finished and wipe myself, flushed the toilet and washed my hands. I stumbled back towards the bed when I notice what looked like a lot of money on the table. As I walked over to the table, I tripped over one of Trevor's shoes and I saw the stacks of money. It had to be over four thousand dollars on that table and I was thinking to myself, *'damn he was playing with some sho nuff ballers tonight.'* Then I saw a business card with Stefan's name on it and I thought, *'Oh shit, they played cards together!'* I was praying that my name never came up because I didn't want them two talking about me in no kind of way. I looked at the card, and it had something about 'Real Estate Broker' and I knew Stefan worked for the DEA, so I wondered, *'What is this, his side job?'* I put the card back on the table and decided to leave all that shit alone and hoped when Trevor woke up he did not ask me anything about Stefan.

The alarm clock went off at 10am, and it damn near scared the shit out of me. I jumped and then reached over to the nightstand to hit the snooze button when I heard my cell phone vibrating in my purse. Trevor was still asleep so I grabbed my cell phone and went into the bathroom to answer it.

I glanced at the Caller ID and saw Stefan's name, "Hello Stefan, did you enjoy yourself last night?"

There was a dead silence on the phone for about 2 seconds before Stefan answered me, "Good Morning Paris, yes I had a great time last night. And I met Trevor. Did he mention meeting me to you?"

I paused for a moment carefully choosing my words, "No, as a matter of fact he didn't mention meeting anyone because I was asleep when he got in, and he is still sleeping now."

Stefan said to me with a voice of concern, "Are you sure this is the man for you Paris? I think that you can do so much better. He just doesn't seem to be your type."

I didn't know where Stefan was going with that, but I could not continue talking to him because I did not want to wake Trevor up. And I was not in the mood to discuss my situation with Stefan. I said, "Stefan what happened between us last night was nothing and we shouldn't have went there in the first place. I let the alcohol and the feeling of your warm soft lips on mine get me all twisted up. I love Trevor and I have to go now, please don't call me anymore."

Stefan sounded like he was furious when he said to me, "Look Paris I know how you feel about me, I could see it in your eyes but you will soon learn the truth about your precious Trevor and I will be here as a shoulder to cry on."

Without saying goodbye, Stefan hung up the phone and it was just as well because I could here Trevor waking up and calling me to come to bed.

After two hours of messing around with Trevor's horny ass, I finally got up and took a shower so that we could catch our flight back to Charlotte. I spoke to Lucky and Lolita for a brief moment. They were taking the red-eye home because they wanted to go shopping before going back to Charlotte. I told them that I would see them when they got home and to call me later that night. After checking out of the hotel Trevor and I rode the limo to the airport. Our flight to Charlotte was leaving at 2pm and we were so ready to get home and sleep in our own bed. We arrived at the airport with 30 minutes to spare before our flight boarded. There were several passengers going to Charlotte and we did not sit too long before the announcement for parents with small children and people in wheelchairs to start boarding the flight.

Our flight to Charlotte was smooth and comfortable. Thankfully, we did not have any problems with landing or our baggage. I felt blessed just for being able to get off a flight without them losing my luggage. After picking up our luggage, we caught the shuttle to the daily parking section of the airport. Trevor had parked his SUV there in section D and the shuttle stop was right next to the truck. We drove for about 30 minutes down I-85N and got off on Ext 25. We lived in the Birkdale area of Charlotte, which was not too far from the airport, so the ride was not long. Pulling in our driveway, I noticed a black SUV parked down the street and two men were sitting in the truck looking at our house. I asked Trevor if he knew who they were and he told me that he did not have a clue. Trevor pulled into the garage and turned the truck off. I got out of the truck and he was still sitting there staring into space.

I said to him, "Trevor what are you thinking about, get your butt out of this truck so we can go to bed."

Trevor thought to himself, *'Damn I can't even get home good and the FBI is sitting outside my house. I will deal with this tomorrow before the shit really hits the fan.'*

Chapter Seven

    Lucky and Lolita took the red eye back to Charlotte from Miami and had more bags with them going home than what they brought with them. Lucky was exhausted and she went to sleep on the flight while Lolita checked her Blackberry for messages from her managers, updates on up coming events, and emails. Lolita saw an email from Jaylan apologizing for not being able to come to the grand opening of Club Dubai. Lolita quickly responded to Jaylan and the two of them texted back and forth until the plane landed in Charlotte Douglass Airport. Lolita's last message to Jaylan was that she would go out to Texas to see him in three months. She just needed some time to catch up with her businesses.

    The plane landed and hit the runway a little hard. The noise woke Lucky and she jumped. When she opened her eyes, she realized that the plane had landed, and she quickly sat upright in her seat. Checking to make sure her seat belt was securely fastened, she asked Lolita how long she had been asleep.

Lolita said, "Bitch you been sleep the entire time, from when we first took off until now."

   Lolita laughed and said, "Girl I am so sorry. I meant to keep you company because I know how scared you are on airplanes, my bad."

   Lolita looked at Lucky and told her that she had spent the entire flight text messaging Jaylan and that he kept her company.

   The plane pulled into the US Airways Gate 15 and the passengers began to gather their things from the overhead compartments. Lucky and Lolita stood up and reached for their bags. They had taken up two overhead compartments and lucky for them, the flight was not full or they would have had a problem getting all those bags on the airplane. While the passengers were deplaning, Lolita called for her limo to pick her up outside of baggage claim. Lolita looked at Lucky and asked her if she needed a ride home, but Lucky had called her assistant Tanya to pick her up from the airport.

   Tanya sat behind the wheel of Lucky's BMW. The luxury car had leather interior, wood grain, navigation system, and was fully loaded.

   Tanya said aloud, "I should leave that bitch at the airport. Just who does she think I am, her fucking maid and chauffer?" Tanya looked at herself in the mirror on the visor. She could see that her face had aged and that she had dark circles around her eyes from not getting enough sleep. The very thing that others took for granted, like sleep, was a difficult task for Tanya, because all she could think about was getting Lucky back for what she did to Ty.

   Tanya's cell phone rang and she answered. "Yeah, I am on my way to the airport now. Just have everything ready, we are going with the original plan. YES, I said everything is ready!"

Tanya hung the phone up and made another call. "Yes, do you have the cabin ready for Mr. Ron Brown? You will leave the keys under the mat on the porch next to the old rocking chair. Thanks!" Tanya hung up the phone, opened the garage, and backed out of Lucky's driveway.

When Tanya arrived at the airport, she saw Lucky standing at the baggage claim entrance with all of her bags and smiling like the world belonged to her. Tanya pulled up to the curb, popped the trunk and got out of the car. "How was the grand opening Lucky?"

Lucky started telling Tanya all about the party and how it was the bomb and how everybody and their brother was there and so on and so on, until Tanya tuned her out while she put the bags in the trunk of the car. Lucky finally shut her mouth and Tanya was so relieved, because she just could not stand her whining ass mouth anymore.

They drove down 85N and then Tanya got off on the Beatties Ford Road exit and headed towards the 'hood. She pulled up in the back of the Rudd Deans. Before Lucky could ask Tanya why they were stopping, three men jumped out a black Cadillac and opened the door to the passenger side of Lucky's car. One of the men put a gun to her head and demanded that she get out of the car. A second man ran around to Tanya's side, pulled a gun on her, and told her to get out of the car. The two of them stood there shaking and wondering what was going on. The man that made Tanya get out the car got behind the wheel of Lucky's Beamer and closed the door. The other two men grabbed Lucky and Tanya and threw them in the back seat of the Cadillac.

When they got in the car, Ron Brown was sitting in there looking at Lucky with a crazy grin on his face. "I bet you thought you got rid of me because you and your bitch ass friends had me thrown out of Club Dubai, but I have been watching your stupid ass ever since you called the po-po's on me."

He did not say anything to Tanya; they just looked at each other and the two other men got in the front seat of the car. The driver of the Cadillac signaled to the man driving Lucky's car to pull off. Ron put duct tape over Lucky's mouth and her hands. He covered her face with a black cloth sack and the driver pulled off.

Lucky could hear Ron talking to the driver in the front seat telling him to go towards the interstate 40 to Black Mountain. Lucky was trembling, she did not know what to do because Ron looked like he was on something and she was never so afraid in her life.

Tanya leaned over and whisper in Ron's ear, "I have everything ready. My cousin used to have a cabin in a secluded area near Black Mountain that has not been occupied for years. The key is under the old mat in front of the door."

Tanya had planned to kidnap Lucky for years and she met Ron when he would come to visit Lucky in her office. After Lucky and Ron split up, Tanya contacted him. She paid him to help her with the kidnapping by convincing Ron that Lucky ruined his life just as she ruined hers and revenge was the only way to make her pay for what she did.

It took three hours to get to the cabin after driving through several winding roads and turning onto an unpaved road surrounded by large trees. The path led to an old wood cabin, and Tanya told the driver to stop in front of the cabin. There were leaves everywhere and when Ron and Tanya got out of the car, they walked towards the porch. Tanya walked up the three steps and in front of the door was a dirty 'Welcome' mat. Tanya lifted up the mat and found a silver key. She put the key in the lock for the front door, and it opened on the first turn. The door had a loud squeaking noise as it opened.

Inside, there was dust and dirt everywhere. The furniture was covered with old white sheets and the wood left in the fireplace seemed to have been there for several years. There was a little round wooded table with four wooded chairs and there was a lantern on the table. Tanya took the lantern and wiped off the dust with one of the old sheets, and then pulled the wick to straighten it out before lighting it. Tanya reached in her purse and pulled out a book of matches. She lit the wick and the flame brought light to the room. Tanya looked around the room and in the corner was a small bedroom room with a full-sized bed and night table. She went in the room and pulled the sheet off the bed. The spread was nasty and dirty, but Tanya didn't care.

She called Ron to the room and said, "Bring Lucky in here. We will tie her up until morning and then we will poison her and put her in the raft down the French Broad River."

Ron didn't want to hurt Lucky, but he felt that she did deserve to die after all she had put him through. He had lost everything and Lucky had done nothing to help him. All she did was give him her ass to kiss, as she flaunted her money in his face. Lucky would talk down to him and tell him that he was dumb and didn't have a pot to piss in, how he wasn't shit, and even when he was in the league he played like a girl. Lucky broke Ron down after she did not have feelings for him, and when she turned cold, it was like a blizzard. He would not stand a chance against her sharp tongue. Her words would cut him down so bad that he would just walk away with his head down, Lucky would talk about his whole family and tell him how they wasn't shit. It was terrible. And on the day that Lucky broke it off with Ron, he was down to nothing. The last thing Ron could remember was Lucky's voice telling him that he wasn't shit and that he never was going to be shit but a broke ass nigga.

The thoughts of her made Ron angry and he stormed out of the cabin and told his homie to open the door to the car. Ron snatched Lucky out of the car by her hair. "Come on bitch, let's see how smart your damn mouth is now!"

Ron pulled her hair tighter around his hand and jerked hard, almost snapping Lucky's neck. She tried to scream but no one could hear her through the duct tape. It only sounded like a muffled hyena. Ron dragged Lucky in the cabin and tied her to a chair in the bedroom. Tanya was in the living room clearing off a dusty old table. She reached in the bag that she had brought with her and pulled out food and drinks. Tanya told Ron that she had food for them to eat while they went over the details of Lucky's sudden death.

As Lucky was in the bedroom blind folded and tied to the chair with duct tape, her mouth was getting sore and she felt her lips swelling. She had the worst headache, and all she could think about was why Tanya was helping Ron. She did not even think that they knew each other. Just when she started to try to break loose, the door to the bedroom opened.

Tanya pulled a chair up in front of Lucky. Then she took the blindfold off her face.

"Lucky, I know you are probably wondering why I have done this to you and you might even think that Ron put me up to it. Shhhh, don't try to talk because you have said enough over the years. I know that you don't remember, but I used to be happy until you destroyed that happiness for me. I use to date Ty, remember Ty, Lucky? We were happy until she went to that strip club and saw you dance. Every night that you worked, she was there. Ty became obsessed with you, and you used her."

Lucky looked at Tanya with those big brown eyes with the look of fear on her face. At that very moment, Lucky remembered Tanya, as she stared into her dark blue eyes. But Tanya was 40 pounds heavier and her hair was dark brown, stringy and long.

When Tanya saw that Lucky recognized her, she said, "Oh now it's all coming back to you. Yes it's me, you sorry bitch, and I promised Ty that I was going to make you pay for what you did to us."

Lucky's thoughts ran back and forth to the time she met Ty and their relationship. Lucky was trying to pay for school and she had never experienced a lesbian relationship. Ty was a beautiful woman. Lucky somehow got caught up in her fantasy, which ended up a tragedy.

Tanya slapped Lucky across the face. She took the knife that she had hidden in her pocket, cut Lucky across her face, with one slice, and blood ran like a river down Lucky's cheeks. Before Lucky could regain her composure, Tanya sliced the other side of her face. With blood running down both sides of Lucky's cheeks, she was squirming in her chair trying to break free. Tanya took the bottle of rubbing alcohol from her pocket and splashed it on each cut, causing Lucky to scream in agony.

Ron came running in the bedroom and he found Tanya standing over Lucky with the knife in her hand dripping of blood. Ron pushed Tanya out of the way, grabbed a towel from the bed, and wiped the blood from Lucky's cheeks.

He yelled, "Get me some water in a bucket you stupid bitch! I told you that we were going to do this my way. Now how will it look like suicide if she has been cut in the face?"

Ron was trying to apply pressure to the wounds on Lucky's face but the bleeding would not stop. He was trying to wipe away the blood so he could see if she needed stitches. The cuts were not deep enough for Lucky to have stitches but she would have two bad scars on her cheeks. The tears rolled down Lucky's face and she was so afraid. She did not want to die. Not like that.

Chapter Eight

It was six o'clock Tuesday morning when my phone rang. It was Palmer. "Paris will you be coming in to the office today?"

"Palmer, why are you calling me at six o'clock in the morning to ask me if I am coming to work? Don't I usually get in at nine o'clock?"

"Yes, Paris, but I wasn't sure if you were feeling up to work. Especially after the long week you spent in Miami preparing for the club's opening. By the way, how was it?"

I said, "Palmer I can't begin to tell you how it was, there is not a word in the dictionary that even comes close."

Palmer was looking at the phone and turning up his nose. "Was it like that!"

"Yes, it was *like that*! Even better then you could imagine! Did you hold down the fort while I was away? What do I have on my calendar for this week?"

Palmer opened up the calendar on 'Lotus Notes, Paris Love,' "Okay missy you have an appointment with the President of Urban Lite, the new soft drink promotion party is in two weeks, and Mr. Minami wants you to call him as soon as you get to the office. He also left a message; he said to tell you that he had a ball at the grand opening and thanks for the VIP set up."

Palmer was upset because he wasn't invited to the grand opening of Club Dubai, even though he was only working for me for two months. He thought that I would have at least mentioned going to the club to him. Palmer knew that I was upset with him for coming on to Stefan, but he did not know that we were close friends and had a past together. Nevertheless, he still was upset about not attending the opening.

"Palmer!"

"Yes, Paris?"

"Palmer you have not heard a word I said to you, what are you doing?"

"Paris I was checking to see if you had any other messages and you had a call from Johnny Case. He said to tell you that he was sorry he couldn't make the opening of your club but please call him and catch him up on the details."

"Okay, Palmer I will see you at nine o'clock. Call Mr. Minami and ask him if we can meet at 1pm for lunch," I said.

"Yes Paris, anything else?"

"No Palmer, that is all!"

Palmer said goodbye and hung up the phone. He called Mr. Minami and spoke to his assistant. "Hi, my name is Palmer Benton and Ms. Love would like to set up a lunch appointment with Mr. Minami. Will he be free at 1pm?"

The assistant answered, "Mr. Minami is open. I will put Paris down for 1pm. Where would she like to meet for lunch?"

Palmer told the assistant to make reservations at McCormick & Schmick's Seafood Restaurant uptown on Tryon Street. He knew that was my favorite restaurant. Palmer put the date and time on my calendar. I was glad when he reminded me, because once I started my day it was busy until I left the office.

I arrived at the office at 9:30am and parked my car in the Three Wachovia building uptown. My office was on the 16th floor in the building. Palmer was waiting for me when I walked in the door. He handed me a cup of green tea, and I took my morning drink and grabbed an orange cranberry muffin from the basket on the table. I sat in my chair and called Lolita on the phone.

The phone rang several times before Lolita picked up, "What's good Paris?" Lolita was in her SUV going to her spa on the South-side. She had the music blasting as she always did.

I said, "Lolita, turn that music down so you can hear me."

Lolita pushed the 'down' volume button on the steering wheel of her SUV. "Okay, it's down, and this had better be good, because that's my song playing and you are making me miss it."

"Anyway, Miss Lolita, have you heard from Lucky? She was supposed to meet me for lunch. I called her four times today and I keep getting her voicemail."

"Well Paris I don't know what to tell you. She had Tanya pick her up from the airport yesterday and that was the last I heard from her."

I was getting worried because Lucky never missed an appointment, and she especially did not miss going to lunch. I had called Tanya but I did not get her, and when I tried the office, the phone just rang.

"Lolita I am a little worried because Lucky told me that she had got a phone call before she came to Miami and no one knows where that Ron Brown character is these days. He could pop up again like his ass did in Miami. Do you think she is alright?"

"Girl don't start that, you know how Lucky can be sometimes. We will go by her house tonight to see if she's at home."

"Okay Lolita but I just have a funny feeling about all of this and you know how I am when my spirit is feeling weird," I said.

"Okay Miss Dionne! I will see you tonight."

"Whatever!" I hung up the phone in my office and spun around in my chair to face the window. Looking out the window, my thoughts were with Lucky. "Girl where are you?"

I got on my knees in front of my desk and prayed that I would find Lucky at home when I went by there, but my spirit was telling me different. "Lord, do not let anything bad happen to my friend." I got up from the floor and stood at the window in a daze. I was startled when I heard Palmer's voice come over the intercom.

"Paris, Mr. Minami is here. Are you ready to go to lunch and will Ms. Blue be joining you?"

"No Palmer, Ms. Blue will not join us for lunch. Tell Mr. Minami I will be right out." I grabbed the mirror from my purse, reapplied my lipstick and headed out the door.

It was five o'clock in the evening, and I was exhausted from my first day back in the office. I had to make some arrangements for two of my clients who were having a huge party at Big Chill on Saturday and I needed to get a crew together to make sure the food, DJ, decorations, security and VIP were in order. That shit had almost taken up most of my day. In the end, everything was in place so that when Saturday came the only thing left to do was set up. I put Palmer in charge of making sure things ran smoothly for the party, because I had to fly to St. Thomas to make the final arrangements for the promotional tour of Urban Lite. Mr. Minami had a first class ticket waiting for me at the airport and he was meeting me in St. Thomas on Friday morning. I looked over my calendar and I made an appointment to call Johnny on his cell phone in the morning but now it was 6pm and I needed to go by Lucky's house to see if she was home. I called Lolita and we planned to meet at Lucky's by 7pm. I tried to call Lucky one more time before I left work but I reached her voicemail at home and on her cell phone. I knew that something was definitely wrong because this was so out of character for Lucky.

Lolita arrived at Lucky's house first, she got there at exactly 6:58pm, and she sat in her SUV and waited for me to pull up in the driveway. Thinking aloud, Lolita said, "Now I know Paris said to be here at 7pm, so where is she?"

Just as Lolita started to pick up her cell phone, I pulled in the driveway and parked behind her. I got out of my car first and walked up to the driver side of Lolita's truck, "Girl I am nervous. What if we find her body in there?"

"Paris don't say that, there is nothing wrong with Lucky and we are going to see that as soon as we get in the house."

"Lolita I am hoping and praying to God you are right."

Lolita and I walked to the front door of Lucky's house and I used my key to get in the house. The alarm was beeping so I hurried and punched in the code to turn it off. I turned to Lolita and told her to start looking around downstairs and I would look in her bedroom. I headed up the stairs and when I got to the master bedroom I noticed that the bed was still made and the clothes that Lucky had laid out before we had gone to Miami was still on the bed. The bathroom was clean and the shower was dry with the same towels that Lucky had used before the trip to Miami laying on the vanity chair. I knew for sure something was wrong because Lucky was a very neat person and her room was always tidy.

I called downstairs to Lolita, "Lo, come here!"

Lolita ran up the stairs to see what I had found. When she walked into Lucky's room, she noticed the same thing.

"Paris, Lucky's things are the same way they were when we left for Miami and this is not like her at all."

Lolita and I seemed to have the same feelings because we looked at each other and tears were wailing up in our eyes.

"Lolita, I just felt a big drop in my heart and it is not good, do you think we should call the police?"

Lolita told me that we should call the police because it was not like Lucky to not call us all day and not answer at least one of her phones.

I said, "I think we should try her office one more time to see if Tanya knows where Lucky is. Maybe she had to go out of town for something. Let's just do that first, and then we will call the police."

I went over to Lucky's nightstand and picked up the phone to call her office and the phone rang four times before Tanya picked up.

"Hello, Attorney Lucky Blue's office, how may I help you?" Tanya saw that the call was coming from Lucky's house and she knew it had to be either me or Lolita, so she had to play it cool so that her plan would work.

"Whew, thank God, Tanya where in the hell is Lucky?" I said.

"Oh hi Paris, Lucky told me to contact you and let you know that she had an emergency come up and she had to fly out to LA. One of her clients had got himself into some big trouble and she need to meet with him ASAP."

As Tanya talked, I was telling Lolita what she had said and Lolita was asking questions about why it took Tanya so long to call, and so forth.

"Tanya, I am glad that she is okay but when she calls the offices tell that stupid girl to call us, and ask her why in the hell hasn't she been answering her cell phone."

"Paris I don't know, maybe she is in a meeting and can't answer her phone, but I will tell her to call you as soon as possible."

I told Tanya that I would check back with her late that day but I still didn't like the feeling that I was having. It was as if Tanya was lying to me about Lucky's whereabouts.

Lolita and I checked the messages on Lucky's phone and we heard Lucky leaving a message for Tanya to pick her up at the airport, but Tanya picked up the phone before she could finish leaving the message. We could hear Tanya tell Lucky that she was on her way and then we heard Tanya say 'that bitch is going to get hers one day.' We figured Tanya thought the voice mail was turned off and not still recording.

Lolita told me that she did not trust Tanya, and we agreed that if we didn't hear from Lucky that night, we were going to have some questions for Ms. Tanya in the morning. Lolita and I left Lucky's house at 7:30pm, locked the doors and set the alarm.

It was 11pm when I got a call from Lucky's brother Kelley. "Hey Paris have you seen my sister? She was supposed to come to visit this weekend but she hasn't call to confirm."

I said, "I haven't heard from her, but Tanya said that she was in LA with a client."

Kelley said, "LA, she never told me anything about going to LA."

"Well don't feel bad because she didn't tell us either and she has not answered her cell phone in two days now."

"Paris I know my sister, and she would never go anywhere without calling and letting somebody know especially her girls, come on, something is not right with that picture."

"I know, I think I am going to go by the office in the morning and talk to Tanya myself."

"Yeah, you do that and make sure you let me know what that crazy bitch tells you because I don't trust her sneaky ass," Kelley said.

"Me and Lolita said the same thing and I am starting to think she is lying about the whole thing, but I will definitely call you tomorrow morning."

"You have a good night Paris, and I will be waiting to hear from you in the morning."

Chapter Nine

 Wednesday morning, Trevor called Brandon on his business cell phone and asked him to meet him uptown at the Fox and Hound bar on N. Tryon Street at 10pm. Trevor had found out that the bust was going down on Friday morning and he wanted to get to Brandon before the Feds did. Trevor had thought long and hard about how he was going to let Brandon know what the deal was without being caught by the Feds, because he did not want his picture in the newspaper nor on Fox's eleven o'clock news showing him being involved in a gun trade with the terrorist. Trevor was a high paid Defense Attorney and his reputation for getting the criminals off with a warning or 6 months to a year sentence was not going to be ruined with this shit. The Feds had had him by the balls because someone on their team had evidence that he was involved in a death of a young woman that was in witness protection and was the main character witness against a drug lord that he was representing. Trevor always had known that someday that shit was going to come back and haunt him because he didn't want any part of it, but he knew the location where the girl was being held, and he revealed that information to his clients' boys. Ultimately, that led to the girls' death, so basically it was as if Trevor pulled the trigger himself.

Trevor was getting out of the shower when he heard me calling him from the master bedroom, "Baby, are you done in there? I have to go by Lucky's office before going to work, so could you hurry up."

"Paris, you can come in. I am done in the shower and I am running late myself so calm down."

I walked in the bathroom, and Trevor was standing there with nothing on. Then he looked down at his dick, and as always, it was hard as a rock. I looked at him with that '*do not even think it*' look and he looked at me and said, "Come on, just let me stick the head in!"

I said, "No, nasty, now get dressed because I got somewhere to be, and so do you. I promise I will hook you up at lunchtime. I will stop by your office okay?"

Trevor looked at me and smiled, "I like that! So can I have you for lunch?"

"Of course you can, now get dressed!"

I took my t-shirt off and got in the shower. Trevor stood there and talked to me about the poker game, how he was going to give Stefan a chance to win back his money. I was trying not to listen to him talk about Stefan like that was his new-found buddy. That shit wasn't cute and that was the reason why I had to put a stop to the whole Stefan thing as soon as I came up with a plan.

Trevor finally was dressed, and by the time I got out of the shower, he was giving me a kiss and telling me that he would see me at lunchtime and not to make him look for me. I was just glad he was gone, because that boy was crazy.

I finished getting dressed and made a phone call to Lolita. "Lo, I am going to stop by Lucky's office today and I am going to get to the bottom of this, because I still say Tanya's ass is lying. I am going to make a guest appearance on that bitch this morning, so she had better have her shit together when I get there."

Lolita said, "Girl, call me because if we got to kick that bitch ass up and down Tryon Street, we will."

"I know Lo, but Tanya is a sneaky somebody and when I find out what she is up to, I will call you."

I hung up the phone and put my shoes on, grabbed my purse and headed for the door. I got downstairs and I found a card on the counter next to my keys from Trevor. I was wondering when he got the card because he did not mention it when he was in the shower. I started to open it but decided to read it after I left Lucky's office instead. I figured hell, I would probably need it by that time. I grabbed my keys and put the card in my purse. I gave the house a look over to make sure nothing was left on that would burn it down. I set the alarm and walked out of the door to the garage.

When I got in the car, there was another card on the seat and I was thinking *'Damn, did I miss a special occasion because I am getting all of this love from this man for some reason.'* I started the car and pulled out of the garage while hitting the redial button on my cell phone. The voicemail came on "Lucky Blue, please leave a message." I could not believe it had been three days and Lucky had not contacted Lolita or me. I then dialed Lolita, but I only got her voicemail, so I left her a message telling her that I was on my way to Lucky's office.

I turned on Tryon Street, made a left on 5th street across from Discovery Place, and parked in the IJL building parking deck. After I parked, I walked out of the IJL building and crossed the street to the Blumenthal Theater. As I was walking pass the theater, I saw Tanya leaving the bank building. I called her name. She looked in my direction and seemed to hurry to get into the parked car in front of the building. I ran up the street to get a closer look at the driver of the car and from a glimpse it looked like Ron's ass, but I knew Tanya didn't know him, so I thought that maybe my eyes were playing tricks on me. It had to be somebody else. I said to myself *'Maybe Lucky was in her office and I am just trippin about Tanya rushing off like that.'*

I got to Lucky's office. It was dark, and the doors were locked. There was not a soul in sight on her floor. I was in panic mode now, and I ran to the elevator and pushed the button for the floor below hers where all of her employees worked. Surely, someone had to know something. I talked to some of the paralegals and the other attorneys. Everyone seemed to think she was in LA with a client, so Tanya had told them. One of the women in the office said that she was on Lucky's floor yesterday morning talking to Tanya who she felt was acting a little strange, but she did not bother asking too many questions, because she thought she was just stressed out.

I called the police from Lucky's office and then I got Lolita on the phone. I told her everything that I had found, and that the police where on the way to the office to let me in, since they did not want me to go in the office without waiting for them to get there first. Lolita hung up the phone with me and said she would be there in 30 minutes.

The police arrived the same time that Lolita did, and when she saw all the police in Lucky's office, she began to cry. I put my arms around her and we just prayed that everything was going to be all right. The office was clean. There were no reservations made by Lucky to go to LA, and when the police pulled up her client contacts in LA none of them had an appointment with Lucky. By then, we were trying to figure out why Tanya would lie about Lucky being in LA and why was she acting so strange.

We tried to call Tanya's cell phone but we got a busy signal every time we dialed the number. I was not sure if she had anything to do with Lucky's disappearance, but she was surely acting as if she knew something, and she damn sure knew where Lucky was.

Lolita and I filed a missing person complaint down at the police station and they continued to investigate the information that we gave them. I was so scared, because we told the police how her ex-boyfriend Ron used to call and threaten her life until she had a restraining order filed against him. We had not heard from him, but we thought we saw him a couple of times stalking her. The police promised us that when they found out something they would let us know.

Lucky Blue was now on the milk carton as a missing person and soon it will be all over the news.

I dialed Trevor's cell and when he answered, he sounded like he was busy.

"Baby are we still having lunch today?" I asked.

"Naw Paris, maybe we can do it next week. I got something to handle right now and I won't have time to sit down with you for lunch."

"Okay baby, I will see you later," I said.

At 9:59pm, Trevor's SUV pulled up to the Fox and Hound on N. Tryon Street. When Brandon hopped into the front seat, Trevor quickly pulled off. Brandon was wearing a dark jogging suit with the hoody pulled over his head covering his face. He sat there with the hoody on—still not revealing his face—and he wondered what Trevor wanted with him that was so urgent.

Trevor spoke to Brandon in a low smooth tone, "Brandon, man what I'm about to tell you is going to either save your life or cost me mine, so listen carefully while I explain to you the reason why I asked you to meet me tonight. First, did you make sure you were not followed? Did you make sure nobody knew where you were going? And finally, did you take the bus to the transit and walk to the Fox and Hound?"

Brandon looked at Trevor from the side of his hoody so that Trevor could see his face. "Man, yeah, now what the fuck is going on?!"

Trevor drove the car towards 77S headed for Arrowood Road to park in the lot on the side of the DMV building. Trevor started telling Brandon the Feds were watching this terrorist group move arms from the US to Iraq for the last six months. They were going to bust the guys behind it when they discovered his ass trying to set up plans to rob their guy for the money that was supposed to pay for the guns. Some of the money was marked and the man that was making the deal did not know that his partner was part of the FBI. After they exchanged the money for the guns, the bust was going to take place, but now that his stupid ass had bugged the place and was planning to rob them. The Feds were after Brandon too, and planned to kill two birds with one stone.

Brandon was wanted for several thefts but they never had enough evidence to prove that he stole anything, so he always got off with the charges dropped each time. Now, though, it was a different story. The Feds had watched Brandon and his little girlfriend from beginning to end and they knew he had planned to steal the money from the gun trade. They had his black ass on tape and everything.

By the time Trevor pulled into the park lot at the DMV, Brandon was tripping on what he had just heard from Trevor for the last 30 minutes and his mind was going a hundred trying to figure a way out of that shit, because the money wasn't worth him being caught. Especially in some terrorist bullshit.

Brandon said, "Man they are not going to pin that shit on me, I found out about the money from a source and I never knew about no terrorist involvement. That's some bullshit!"

Trevor looked at Brandon and he told him about how they had some shit about him leaking information on the whereabouts of one of the main character witnesses that was going to testify against one of his clients a couple of years ago, and the witness was murdered. The Feds never found out who killed the girl so his client got off with six months probation for some minor traffic charges.

Trevor said, "Brandon they found out that we grew up together and were asking me all kinds of questions about you and wanted me to identify you when you showed up at the spot. They asked me if you paid me and all kinds of shit. Man I told them that I didn't know what the hell they were talking about, that we had met for drinks and that was it."

Brandon sat there shaking his head trying to figure out a way to escape without being caught by the Feds and without exposing Trevor.

"Trevor man I'm glad you told me but how in the hell are we going to pull this shit off without either of us going down?"

"We have to come up with a plan before Friday and that shit is not going to be easy to do," Trevor said.

Trevor drove back towards 77N with the radio playing low in the background. There was silence between him and Brandon the whole way, both of their minds racing trying to come up with a way to get out of the shit they were facing.

Brandon's cell phone rang which caused both of them to jump. He answered, "Hello?"

It was Shelia. Brandon told her about what was going down with Trevor, and the Fed's being up on the deal with the arms trade. Brandon told Shelia the whole story and she was listening to his words carefully as he spoke.

Shelia could tell that Brandon was upset and she wanted nothing more than to help him any way she could.

"Brandon, calm down baby and listen. The guy Hans is messing around with my friend Gina and that fool has been getting all kinds of gifts from him for a long time. She told me that he was involved in imports-exports but I saw him in front of her spot with the dude that let me in to fix the telephones."

Brandon had a smile on his face because he knew right then how he was going to get out of the shit he would be facing on Friday.

"Damn baby you sure about all this?" Brandon asked.

"Boo I'm sure as I am talking to you right now. My girl said that dude was going to come by her house tonight because the deal is going down on Friday."

"What, Shelia are they meeting at the spot I had you check out for me?"

"Naw baby they are meeting at Gina's crib at midnight! Gina told me that Hans got a man on the inside and he knows about the Feds watching the spot so that fool has switched the time and location on their asses."

By then, Brandon was really smiling and Trevor was looking at him as if to say *'What the fuck is up man?'*

Brandon looked at Trevor as he took the phone from his ear, "Man we bout to be paid and free from this bullshit. My girl said that the location was switched so all you have to do is be where those dirty FBI boys told you to be on Friday and the surprise will be on them."

Trevor was happy to hear that shit because he was not trying to be involved in no bullshit like that from the beginning. The less he knew the better. Trevor had a sigh of relief he would show up at the spot and If Brandon did not show up, the Feds couldn't say that he had anything to do with it because there would be no one at the spot.

Trevor listened to Brandon get all the details of the transaction from Shelia and by the time that they were off the phone, Trevor was parked in front of the Fox and Hound on Tryon Street.

Trevor said, "Brandon, we haven't seen or heard from each other. Call me only if the shit goes sour."

"Cool, Trevor, oh by the way, I am out of the country after Friday so you really won't be hearing from me no time soon."

Brandon jumped out of the SUV and slipped into the darkness.

Trevor pulled off and headed down Tryon Street, came to the stop light at E. Trade Street and turned right headed towards 77N. Trevor turned up the radio and let his mind run, thinking about Friday and everything that had taken place in the course of the night. Trevor called me on his cell phone but he got my voicemail, so then he called the house phone.

I answered the phone in my 'I-am-sleeping-who-in-the-hell's-calling-me' voice. "Yeah?!"

"Paris it's me. I was just calling to let you know I was on my way home."

"Trevor is everything okay? You sound like you have something on your mind."

"I am good baby, I will tell you about it later. Go back to sleep Paris, I will be home in about 10 minutes."

Trevor hung up the phone and in less than ten minutes, he was pulling into the garage. The garage door closed and across the street in the shadows stood a man in a black hoody with dark blue jeans. He watched Trevor pull into the garage and he flicked a lighter with his thumb as he watched the flames grow higher each time. It was Stefan. But Trevor didn't know it at the time. Stefan stood there for another ten minutes and he walked down the street to the empty house two doors down from where Trevor and I lived.

Stefan thought aloud, "Trevor I am going to kill you, and you are not going to know what hit you. And then it will be *me* coming home to Paris because you don't deserve her."

Stefan had always planned to kill Trevor after he found out that he was the one who leaked the information to the mob where the safe house was located. They had his sister and two other FBI agents blown up in that house and there was nothing but dental records to show proof of the bodies founded in the rubble. Stefan had to bury his sister in a closed casket, and he promised on her grave that he would get Trevor for what he had done. Stefan sat in the all black tinted windows of his SUV for an hour, finishing the final plans on how he was going to make sure Trevor breathed his last breath on Friday.

Chapter Ten

July 9, 2004. Friday morning, Trevor's eyes opened as he sat up in the bed. He looked over at me and I was fast asleep. He admired my hair cascading over the pillow I slept on. He had always thought that my hair was beautiful. Trevor reached over to give me a kiss on my forehead.

"I love you," he whispered as he gently pulled back the covers to get out of the bed.

Trevor jumped in the shower, and in 5 minutes he was drying off and getting dressed. Trevor put on a Sean John navy blue jogging suit with white Forces and a white Sean John ball cap. Trevor grabbed his keys off the dresser and headed for the garage.

He drove his Honda Accord to the same spot he had met the Feds earlier in the week. Trevor was sitting in the parking garage waiting for the FBI to arrive when he saw two black Suburbans pull into the garage. Knowing that they did not know his car, Trevor got out and stood in the middle of the road.

The Suburban stopped right in front of him and the driver let down his window, "Glad to see you made it back from Miami. Get in!"

Trevor told the driver, "Fuck you! Let's just hurry up and get this shit over with."

The driver said, "Watch your mouth because you're not in the clear yet, so get yo black ass in the truck."

Trevor got in the back seat next to another one of them Alphabet Boys. He was looking at Trevor with a little smirk on his face.

"What the fuck's your problem?" Trevor said with that, *'if I wasn't in this truck I'd whip yo ass'* look on his face.

The man did not say anything. He just smiled at Trevor, which was pissing him off even more.

In less than five minutes, the SUV stopped across the street from the spot where the deal was supposed to go down, but it was quiet. Too quiet. They sat in the truck for an hour before the man in the front seat of the other truck got out and walked back to the truck Trevor rode in. The federal agent in the front seat rolled his window down and as soon as he did, the house that they had under surveillance blew up. The sound was like that of a scene from a Mission Impossible movie. The man that was standing at the window was thrown to the ground and the SUV shook as all the windows shattered.

Trevor grabbed his head and put it between his legs to keep from getting glass in his face. When the blast was over, everyone got out the truck. Calls were being made left and right.

"Get the fire truck and ambulance out here now!" one of the agents yelled into his cell phone.

People were running out of their homes to see what was going on and all Trevor could see was smoke. He jumped out of the SUV with just a few minor scratches. He stood in front of the truck looking at the house and watched as the Firemen jumped from their trucks to put out the blaze.

Suddenly, one silent shot was fired to his chest, and as Trevor's knees buckled beneath him, another shot hit him in the head. Trevor's body fell to the ground in slow motion, blood running from his forehead and chest.

His life slipped quickly by him. As he felt the life leaving his body, all he could think about was me, and how sorry he was that he never told me the truth about his life and the people he represented as an attorney.

He was dead.

By the time, the FBI agent saw Trevor falling to the ground it was already too late, because he was dead before the agent could get to him. The shots seemed to come from out of nowhere. Now the FBI had a real mess on their hands—no witness, no Brandon, no weapons and no money.

The Feds never caught Hans or the people he was meeting and the explosion was the second part of Hans plan so that he could make the exchange and leave with the money. Brandon cut a deal with Hans to get him and Gina out of the country, so they both got over like fat rats. Brandon and Shelia were sitting in first class on there way to Greece a lot richer. But as for Trevor, his fate was death.

The news of the explosion spread fast. It was on every channel of the 11pm news. I had received a phone call from Jackie, one of my friends that attended church with me. I answered the phone and after I heard Jackie say that Trevor was dead, I did not believe her. I grabbed the remote from the dresser in my room and when I turned on the TV, I saw the explosion. There were pictures of the FBI agents. Then I saw them taking a man away on the gurney and the newsperson said, "A stake out gone bad. One man shot in the chest and head was pronounced DOA. Defense Attorney Trevor Tripple was gunned down in the street after the house that was under surveillance blew up. We will have more deals as we get them in. Stay tuned for updates."

The TV had Trevor's picture showing saying that he was the man that was dead, and as soon as I saw that, I dropped the phone and fell to my knees. I was crying harder then I had ever cried in life and I couldn't stop the tears from flowing down my face. I just kept sobbing, "Why, why, baby what happened to you?!"

I rolled myself in a ball, like a baby, and rocked back in forth. I couldn't pull myself together. Jackie was still on the phone trying to get me to pick up, but all she could hear was me wailing in the background.

Jackie clicked over and dialed Lolita's number.

"Hello?" Lolita answered.

"Hi, Lolita, this is Jackie, and I don't know if you have heard the news yet but—"

Before Jackie could finish her sentence, Lolita was asking her, "Is it true, is Trevor dead? I just saw the news, where is Paris?"

Jackie told Lolita that she had me on the other line, and that I was crying and would not pick the phone up. So Lolita told Jackie to meet her at my house.

Lolita hung up the phone, grabbed her purse and ran downstairs, and opened the door to the garage. Lolita drove the Porsche to my house. It usually took 30 minutes to get there, but it only took her ten. When Lolita arrived, I was still in my bedroom crying and holding a picture of Trevor and me. I was crying so hard until Lolita started to cry too.

The doorbell rang and Lolita wiped her tears and walked downstairs to open the door for Jackie. Now, Jackie was a very spiritual woman, and she was a lot older than I was. But she was always there to pray for me or just give me encouragement.

Lolita had tried everything to get me to stop crying long enough for them to deal with the situation, not to mention the phones where ringing off the hook, which was not helping at all. Everyone was calling to see if what they heard on the news was true, because Trevor knew so many people in Charlotte. He was like a celebrity.

Jackie walked in the room, put her arms around me, and held on tight. When Jackie started praying the Lord's Prayer, I started to calm down a bit. Then Jackie reached in her purse and pulled out a small bottle of oil. She put the oil on my head in the symbol of a cross.

"In the name of the Father and the Son and the Holy Ghost, Jesus please give Paris peace in this moment of tragedy in her life. Give her your peace that passes all understanding. Bless her Lord and help her to stay in her right mind, in the mighty name of Jesus, AMEN!" Jackie said.

I opened my eyes and looked at Jackie with such sadness in my face. Lolita stood in the background, tears flowing down her cheeks, because her friend was hurting, and she could not do anything about it.

I had to get myself together to go to the hospital morgue to identify Trevor's body. I had to call his parents and tell them the news of their son's death. I had so many questions in my mind that I did not know the answer to. I just was so hurt, but I had to make sure everything was done correctly for Trevor's burial.

I went to the hospital to identify Trevor's body, but when they pulled the tray out, and I saw Trevor's lifeless cold body laying there like a slab of meat, I fell to my knees wailing and crying so hard until my eyes were swollen and red. Lolita held my hand, as I nodded my head letting the coroner know that it was Trevor Tripple laying there dead.

***

Saturday morning had come too fast for me. I had not had much sleep the night before because I was hoping that it was all a bad dream, but when I turned on the TV, the news showed Trevor's face again, and the telling of his death seem to be on every channel. I pulled myself together and called Lolita on the phone.

"Hey Lolita," I said in a low, painful voice.

"Hey girl, you okay?"

"No Lolita, I'm not, but I will do what I need to do for Trevor."

Lolita sat up in the bed and shifted the phone to her right ear. "Paris, I am going to get in the shower and I will be over there as soon as I get dressed. I will call you when I am on my way."

I told Lolita that I was going to pull myself together so that I could make the funeral arrangements for Trevor. I had called the funeral home in Huntersville where Trevor had jokingly bought us a plot. I never thought I would be the one to arrange for his death. I always thought I would go first.

Jackie made all the arrangements for the funeral at University Life Christian Church were she attended in Rock Hill, SC. I had visited the church a while back, and I really enjoyed the preacher. I had always wanted to go back, but I never thought it would be to bury Trevor.

I finally made it home around ten o'clock and as soon as I walked in the house, the phone was ringing.

I walked into the kitchen and reached for the cordless phone, "Hello?"

"Paris, I was waiting for things to settle before contacting you. I heard the news about Trevor, and I am sorry."

"Stefan, how did you know? I thought you were out of the country?"

"I was, Paris, but when I came back to the states I heard the news from your friend Jackie. She and I used to belong to the same church. Paris I'm coming over to see you, because we need to talk," Stefan said.

"Stefan, this is not a good time for me, because Trevor's funeral is on Tuesday, and I need to finish packing his things to give to his family."

"Listen, I know this is hard for you, and that is why I want to be there for you."

"Maybe after the funeral, but not now, I just can't see you now." I hung up the phone before Stefan could respond, and he was upset that I did not run to him the way he thought I would.

But he was a very patient man.

Stefan thought to himself, 'Tuesday is the funeral. I think I might go pay my respects and be there for Paris. After we put that bitch ass nigga in the ground, I will have her all to myself.' Stefan looked out his window and thought about his sister, and how good he felt that she could rest in peace, now that he had made the nigga responsible for her death pay with his life.

No one ever saw Stefan at the scene because the explosion had everyone's attention, even Trevor's. Trevor never knew what hit him until it was too late. Stefan thought aloud, "I guess you do reap what you sow!"

Chapter Eleven

Tuesday morning I heard the alarm going off and I did not want to face the day. Trevor's funeral was at 10 am. Thoughts of him filled my mind, and the tears began to flow down my face.

"I really miss you baby, but I know you would want me to be strong," I whispered.

I pulled back the covers of the bed in the spare bedroom where I slept every night after the death of Trevor. I could not bear to sleep in the bed that we had once shared, knowing that he was never coming home.

I took a shower and got dressed in my black dress with the black hat and veil to match. I was in mourning, so I was dressed like a Greek Orthodox woman. My hair was pulled back in a bun, and I wore small diamond earrings with a tiny diamond watch. My eyes were swollen from all the crying, and I covered them with big movie star black shades.

Paris Love

The doorbell rang, and it was the limo driver ready to take me to the church. I opened the door and the tiny grey-haired man said, "Ms Love, are you ready to go?"

I grabbed my purse and turned to face the house that Trevor and I shared. With tears in my eyes, I looked at the "For Sale" sign in the front yard and with that, I turned and got into the limo.

Lolita was sitting in the back seat when I got in, and hugged me as I cried. Lolita rocked me like a newborn baby until I was calm. Lolita and I were silent the rest of the way until the limo stopped in front of the church. There were cars, which seemed like for miles, and people were lined up to get inside of the church. Some were standing across the street from the church looking with signs the read "We love you Trevor, rest in peace!"

I said, "Wow, Lolita I didn't know Trevor knew so many people. Look at them all lined up around the corner to get in the church. Girl I don't know if I can make it through the day without crying. Lolita I have never cried this much in my life."

"I know Paris, but you have to be strong so that you can stand up in front of the church and say your goodbyes to Trevor. Don't worry, I will be standing right next to you."

The limo driver opened the door and I tried to straighten up my face before getting out of the car. I lifted my sunglasses from my eyes and wiped my tears. As soon as I stepped out of the limo, the cameras were snapping. The media were asking me questions about Trevor's death, and Lolita was pushing them away from me.

Lolita snapped, "She doesn't have a comment, please let her grieve in peace!"

I just wanted to scream.

People were coming up to me from everywhere. I saw a group of men standing at the entrance of the church. One of them walked over to me.

In his thick Italian voice, he said, "Ms. Love, we are sorry about the loss of Trevor. He was my brother's lawyer and he got his case thrown out of court. He could have spent ten years in prison if it weren't for Trevor. We are here for you if you need anything. Here's my card, call me for anything."

Once we got inside of the church, I saw the casket sitting in front of the pulpit with Trevor's body laying there. At first, I thought it was a dream, but my reality hit me hard when I saw my baby lying dead in that casket. He was in a nice cream suit with a nice blue shirt with a royal blue, light blue and cream tie. His hair was cut low and perfectly shaped. He looked peaceful and so handsome. Even dead, the man looked good.

I was still trying to take it all in, as I stood there and cried, looking at my baby. He was gone, and I did not know what I was going to do without him. I knew that the pain would ease, but it just hurt so badly and I could feel my legs start to buckle under me. I had Lolita and Jackie holding me up as the tears flowed like a river. I bent over in the casket and kissed him on the forehead, "I love you Trevor, and I will always love you."

I turned to walk to my seat and after two steps, I fell to my knees, sobbing hysterically. It took three of the ushers, Lolita and Jackie to get me to my seat, and all I could do is weep and rock back and forth. The choir started singing, "I need you now, Lord." The whole church was crying and the pastor walked up to the microphone.

"Dearly beloved, we are gathered here today to celebrate the home going of Trevor Tripple. He was an outstanding citizen in the community and a great lawyer. We are going to start with another section from the choir, and then we will hear a few words from friends and family."

The pastor sat down and the choir began to sing another selection, "Amazing Grace." The whole church started to shout and get happy.

Trevor's aunt stood up and cried out, "Lord why did you have to take him!"

The people were crying all over the place and both Trevor's mother and father were crying. I was just wishing it were all over, because it was so sad, and I could hardly breathe in there. I just wanted to go home, close my bedroom door, and get away from everybody.

Finally, the singing stopped and one of Trevor's good friends got up to say a few words about him. The man was a little short dark-skinned man with curly grey hair. He spoke on how Trevor helped him and his family when their son was in trouble and how Trevor would do anything for you. After that, two other people came to say a few words and then his co-workers and fellow lawyers spoke.

I got up to speak and when I reached the microphone, I felt like a peace had come over me. I looked out at all the people that were in the church and standing in the hallway. I cleared my throat and spoke softly, "What can I say about a man that I loved for over ten years of my life. He was my lover, my friend, my confidant, we knew so much about each other and we loved each other dearly. I miss him. I know by the looks of all the friends and families that have come to his funeral, each one of you miss him too. Trevor was a good man, of course, he had his issues as we all do, but for the most part, he was a good man. I remember one time we went out to one of his dinner functions and Trevor and I danced and laughed all night. He was very entertaining and he would keep a smile on your face. I know that he is in a better place now. His 'sweet Paris.' That is what he used to call me when he was being playful. I will always miss him."

I returned to my seat and the pastor stood at the microphone and began the closing eulogy.

Three hours had passed, and Lolita was so happy that the homegoing service for Trevor was finally over, with all the people that wanted to say a few words, and me crying my eyes out when it came time for me to speak, which was more then enough emotions for Lolita in one day. We left the church first to get into the limo, and the pallbearers carried Trevor's body to the car. Our limo pulled out with the police escort. There were so many cars lined up behind us, you could have sworn that the President was being buried. We got to the gravesite that Trevor had jokingly brought for us to share. We all stood around and watched them bring Trevor's body to the grave.

The pastor said, "Ashes to ashes and dust to dust." He then closed with a prayer for the family, and I laid the last rose I had in my hand on top of the casket.

"Bye my love, I will always remember you and keep you close to my heart," I said.

I turned to walk towards the limo when I felt a strong arm around my shoulder. It was Stefan. And he was dressed in a dark suit with dark shades to cover his eyes.

Stefan said, "I thought you could use a friend today, so I came to be a strong shoulder for you to lean on."

I looked at Stefan with tears in my eyes, gave him a hug, and just stood there for a few minutes allowing Stefan to hold me tight in his arms. "Thanks so much for coming Stefan, I know that you didn't know Trevor but I appreciate you being here for me."

"No problem Paris, you know that you will always be my girl, and there is nothing I wouldn't do for you right?"

"Yeah, I know."

Stefan and I walked towards the limo. The driver opened the door for me, and I gave Stefan a kiss on the cheek and got inside the car.

Stefan watched as the limo drove away and he could not help but think how he could make me happier than Trevor ever did, and soon he would get his chance.

The limo driver drove Lolita and I back to the house for the homegoing dinner, and all of Trevor's colleagues, friends and family stopped by to comfort me. This would be the last gathering in the house that Trevor and I shared, because I could not bare living there without him.

Chapter Twelve

Leland had wanted to open a barbershop of his own after working in one for six years, but he did not have enough money to fund the project. He did have half, though. Leland knew that he could get the other half from Lolita because she had always looked out for him, but he also knew that before he could approach her with his proposal, he had to have his shit together. There was one thing about his sister, and that was she did not play when it came to school and running a business. Leland could remember many occasions where he got his ass whipped by Lolita for bringing home bad grades, so she was not the one to play with.

Leland had worked hard on getting his half of the money saved for his shop. He had checked out all the details as far as location, cost for the equipment, and the furniture. He had it all on a PowerPoint presentation that he was going to show his sister, so that she would give him the rest of the money to fund his business.

Leland called Lolita on the phone and when she picked up, she sounded a little down.

"What it do lil' bro?" Lolita answered.

"What's up big sis," Leland said with a nervous tone in his voice.

Lolita said, "Nothing, you heard the news about Trevor being shot and they still don't know who shot him?"

"Yeah, I heard that it happened during the explosion of some house they were watching and that the shots came out of nowhere. What's the latest news on Lucky?"

"Well it is all still under investigation and they still don't have any word on Lucky's disappearance. We just know that its foul play, but we don't know any details. Bro this day has been so hard for me, and it was so sad watching Paris cry everyday since Trevor passed away. She has the house up for sale and everything. Let's change the subject, what's on your mind? Why you calling me at 12 midnight?"

"Well sis, you know I have always wanted to open my own shop and now I have everything together. I wanted to see if you could help your little brother out by giving me the other half of the money," Leland said.

"Hmmm, you know what I require when you are asking for money like that don't you?"

"Yes. That is why I have my proposal on PowerPoint and ready for your review. Can we meet tomorrow for breakfast?"

"That's my baby brother, your sister taught you well!" Lolita was smiling for the first time in a couple of days. "Bring your presentation and we will have breakfast at the Waffle House on Harris Blvd. Be there at 10 am, and don't be late!"

"I won't, because I know what that means too—be late, no deal!"

"That's my baby, boy I am proud of my work!" Lolita said.

Leland smiled on the other end of the phone as he hung up to get all of his stuff together to meet his sister in the morning. He pulled out his suit and his business briefcase. He knew how Lolita liked things to be in order, and he was going to act has though he was meeting a lender from a bank. That would impress his sister and make her want to give him the money he needed.

Lolita's phone rang again and this time it was the detective on Lucky's case, "Miss Marcus?"

"Yes, this is she."

"This is detective Ryan, the officer on Lucky's case. I was calling you because we found Lucky's car on Bettie Ford Road behind the Excelsior, and we found fingerprints on the passenger side of the car and in the back seat, which are being ran by CSI. I just had one question for you, and that is did you know anything about Lucky's involvement with a Ty or Tanya?"

Lolita told the officer that she knew Tanya who was Lucky's assistant but she didn't know who Ty was, but she did know that Tanya was acting very strange when they had returned from Miami. She also told the detective that Tanya was the one who picked Lucky up from the airport. The detective told Lolita that he would be in touch once the fingerprints were ran, and he would call back if he had any more leads. Meanwhile, he told Lolita to call him if she thought of anything that might help them find out what happened to Lucky.

When Lucky opened her eyes, it was morning, but she was no longer tied to the chair. She was lying in the bed with bandages on her face. Somehow, the bleeding had stopped, but she still could not move her arms freely. Her wrists were duct taped together, and she could only feel her face with the tips of her fingers.

The bedroom door opened and it was Ron standing there. "Good Morning Sunshine, we almost lost you last night. Aren't you glad I was here to save your ass? Not to say you would have done the same for me, but nevertheless, you're still here for now."

Ron pulled Lucky up into a seated position and he scooted her to the edge of the bed. He picked her up in the Fireman's rescue position, throwing her body over his shoulder, as he carried her out of the bedroom. Ron put her back in the chair in the front room and he then duct taped her legs to the chair. Lucky just sat there with her head hanging down towards her chest. Every time Ron would tell her to look at him, she would just roll her eyes in the back of her head. Her neck was so weak; it was as if she was a newborn baby trying to hold her head up for the first time. This made Ron mad, because he felt as if she was doing that on purpose just to ignore him.

He was screaming at her, "Bitch hold your head up, it wasn't a problem for you when you where treating me like a piece of shit after all I've done for you! Hold your damn head up and look at me, you ungrateful bitch!"

The front door to the cabin opened and it was Tanya coming in from outside. It was six o'clock in the morning, and she had a look on her face as if she had seen a ghost.

Ron looked at her. "What's wrong with you?" he asked.

Tanya told Ron that she had went to the car, was listening to the radio, and heard the news about Paris' fiancé dying in some stakeout, and that Lucky was missing for two weeks without a trace. Tanya told Ron that the FBI found her car parked behind the Excelsior, and they were naming her as a suspect. There was a warrant out for her arrest, and she needed to leave the country.

Ron knew that Tanya would try to leave him holding the bag, and that is when he flipped on her.

"Bitch, I know you ain't trying to leave me here to take the blame for this whole thing! You are the one that wanted to kill Lucky, so you are going to finish the job and stick to the plan."

Tanya looked at Ron and she told him that she was not trying to leave, but she knew that she could never go back to Charlotte once this was all over.

Ron acted as if he did not hear her talking and walked back into the cabin. Lucky's body slouched over in the chair with her arms tied behind her back. Ron walked over to her and lifted her head, and she looked at him with the saddest look in her eyes, as tears rolled down her face.

Ron taunted her, "You want me to let you go don't you?"

Lucky just looked at him and he could read in her eyes that she was scared, so he told her that he could never let her go because she was the reason his life was so fucked up, and she had to pay for that. Surely, she knew she had to pay.

Tanya was thinking that she had made a huge mistake in helping Ron kidnap Lucky. She had just wanted to make Lucky suffer because of Ty, but did she really had not wanted to kill her. Tanya thought maybe if she helped Lucky escape, that she could get a lighter sentence for what she had done, but she didn't know how she would do that without getting herself killed in the process.

Tanya had her cell phone in her pocket. While Ron was talking to Lucky, Tanya went outside and tried to call me on the phone.

The phone rang and I picked up the other end. "Hello?"

Tanya wanted to speak, but when she tried to open her mouth, she couldn't.

I held the phone to my ear. "Lucky is that you, where are you? Just tell me and we will come to get you! Lucky? Lucky!"

Tanya hung the phone up. She was so nervous and didn't know what to do, because Ron had planned on killing Lucky and burying her body deep in the woods of Black Mountain. Tanya thought she could do that, but it was killing her inside, because every night since they had kidnapped Lucky, Tanya would have dreams of Ty asking her why she was doing that to Lucky. In the dream, Ty would say that it wasn't Lucky's fault, she didn't have anything to do with her death. The dreams seemed so real to Tanya. She could see Ty standing in front of her talking to her as if she was alive, but she knew that she was dead. Tanya thought that she was going crazy, and she would try to stay awake as long as she could because the dreams would occur as soon as she closed her eyes.

Tanya knew that she had to get Lucky out of there, but how? Ron was crazy, and she didn't know how she could get her away from him.

Tanya left the cabin for awhile to sort things out in her mind. She told Ron that she was going in town. She figured that since their pictures where not on the news, it was safe for her to be seen. Ron just waved his hand at her, as he sat at the table drinking whiskey and smoking a joint. He was looking at an old picture of him and Lucky on his birthday. They were so happy then, but she didn't love him anymore, so she had to die, in his eyes. The alcohol and the joint started to take effect and Ron was feeling good. He looked at Lucky and decided that she was going to make love to him again before she left this earth. He was horny as hell, and could feel his dick getting hard just thinking about fucking her.

Ron got up from the chair he was sitting in and walked over to Lucky. He pulled the duct tape from her mouth and before she could say a word, he was kissing her. Lucky tried to fight him off by moving her head back and forth and closing her mouth, but Ron just forced his tongue down her throat. He had her duct taped to the chair, and she couldn't move her arms. Ron took the duct tape from around Lucky's legs so he could spread them open. He pulled her panties down to her ankles and pushed her skirt up around her hips. Lucky was squirming in the chair but she was helpless against him. No matter how hard her body fought, she could not stop what was about to happen to her.

Tanya drove to Kings Mountain. She stopped at a gas station along the way. There were not a lot of people around, so she got out of the car and went in the station to pay for the gas. Tanya had used cash the entire time she was in Black Mountain because she did not want the police to trace her credit card and find where they were keeping Lucky. She reached into her purse and pulled out her phone, and started to dial my number again, but she knew I would recognize her voice, so she called the Mecklenburg police station. When the officer picked up the phone, Tanya froze, because she didn't know what to say to keep herself out of trouble.

"Damn it!" Tanya said, as she quickly pushed the end button and put the phone in her pocket.

Tanya needed to think about how she was going to get word to Lolita or me without Ron finding out she was the one that told us where to find Lucky.

Then it hit her, "I will just leave now and call the police once I am out of the country to let them know where Lucky is."

Tanya smiled to herself because this was her opportunity to leave, and she did not have to go back because she had plenty of cash on her. She had an extra bag clothes in the trunk of the car. She finished pumping the gas and got back in the car, and as she headed towards the highway, it dawned on her that if she didn't return to the cabin, Ron would think she contacted me or the police and would kill Lucky before she had a chance to let anyone know her whereabouts.

Tanya sat at the red light, and for the first time, she cried about what she had done and how far she had let her hatred for Lucky go. She thought she would feel a sense of relief by killing Lucky, but she only felt sadness. Tanya realized that she had to go back to the cabin to help Lucky, because Ty would have wanted her to do the right thing. It wasn't Lucky's fault that Ty killed herself, and Tanya finally could see that.

By that time, a car had pulled up behind Tanya. The light had turned green, but Tanya did not move. The driver in the car behind her started to beep his horn. Tanya drove off. While looking in her rearview mirror, she saw the driver behind her cussing and throwing up his hands. She just kept going because she did not want to cause any problems that would bring attention to her.

Tanya turned down the dirt road that led to the cabin, and when she got out of the car, Ron and one of his crackhead friends were sitting on the porch.

"Where the hell have you been for two hours?" Ron said, looking at her with those blood red eyes.

Tanya could tell he was high and she did not want to go there with him, especially since she had decided to turn herself and him into the authorities.

"I went to the store and put gas in the car, that's all, why?"

"Bitch don't you get smart with me or you will get the same thing Lucky ass got. Matter of fact, seeing that you don't like men, maybe me and old Rich need to show you what the fuck you been missing!"

Tanya looked at him with the biggest frown on her face. She walked up to the steps and looked at Ron and Rich with the meanest look she could, but deep inside, Tanya was scared as hell.

Ron yelled, "Bitch I don't care about you mean mugging me because I will take that pussy and do to it what has needed to be done to it for years, FUCK IT!"

Ron and Rich started laughing and Rich said, "Yeah, we need to give that bitch some dick, 'cause she's been sucking on pussy way to long."

They laughed even harder and Ron told Rich how she wanted to get revenge because Lucky had the bitch Tanya was dealing with nose wide open, and they laughed some more.

Tanya went into the cabin, and she slammed the door so hard it shook the windows. She could still hear Ron and Rich on the porch laughing and talking shit about how Lucky took her bitch from her. She could have killed them both, but she wanted to help Lucky escape. Tanya was so mad, but when she looked at the chair, she saw that Lucky was not tied to it. Tanya went into the bedroom and she saw Lucky lying on the bed in the fetal position with her arms, legs and mouth duct taped. When Tanya turned her over, Lucky had a bruise on her cheek and her thighs had bruises on them too.

"What did Ron do to you Lucky?" Tanya asked with sincere concern.

Tanya could not believe it, but Ron had raped Lucky. She felt like if she had not left her and went to the store, none of that would have happened. The guilt was taking over, and Tanya was willing to risk her life at that point to safe Lucky. Tanya hated Lucky for what she thought she had done, but now she felt guilty, because she realized it was the pain of losing Ty that had driven her to seek revenge. She had let her anger build up over the years, and everything had now escalated out of control.

Chapter Thirteen

It was ten o'clock on the dot, and Leland was sitting in the Waffle House waiting for Lolita to get there. Just as he looked at his watch, she walked through the door.

"I can't believe you beat me here!" Lolita said as she gave her baby brother a big hug.

"I know, and I can't believe you are late. I just put our order in so your pecan waffles should be ready soon," Leland said, embracing his sister.

"Ah, look at you trying to get brownie points already. I'm not mad at you, do what you got to do!"

"Well you know I've learned from the best business woman in the family!"

"Anyway, boy enough of the ass kissing, whatcha got for me?"

"Damn Lolita, some things never change!"

Leland pulled out his business proposal as Lolita sat across the table watching her little brother present his proposal to her. She could not but help think of how proud he made her, but it had not been easy raising that boy on her own. She had to whip his ass on many of days.

Leland wanted to open the shop on WT Harris Blvd, in the shopping center next to Chick-fil-A. The cost for the design that he wanted was 100,000 dollars. Lolita looked over the plans, and she noticed that the design for the shop was state-of-the-art, all computerized and shit. Leland was smart as hell, and it cost Lolita a lot, fucking niggas she wouldn't normally give the time of day, to pay for her little brother to attend Hampton University. But he graduated with honors, so to Lolita, all of her struggles were worth seeing him walk across that stage.

Leland went through his business spill and explained in detail the design and the floorplan. He also had planned a barber school next door to the building. Lolita agreed to give her brother the money as an investor in the business so that he would have a back-up, just in case he needed someone to step in for him. Lolita would only own 10% of the business, and she would allow her brother to make all the major decisions. She would only be there on paper.

By the time Lolita finished looking over the paperwork, their had food arrived. Lolita told Leland that she was starving, so business was over and it was time to eat.

"Leland, what is going on in your social life, and how many of them tricks are you fucking with these days? Make damn sure you wear a condom, because I am not trying to be an auntie to none of them stank ass hoes' offspring."

Leland just laughed at Lolita and said, "Now sis you know your brother don't get down like that, and right now I am trying to get my business off the ground so 'em bitches better get in where they fit in! I wear my shit, so don't you worry, 'em hoes will not be sneaking no baby in on me. And besides, I don't fuck with hood rats!"

They both started laughing. Lolita was just so proud of her brother, and in the mist of the laugh, she told him that. He wanted to make her proud of him because she had sacrificed so much so that he could be a successful young man. Now he would be opening his own business in a couple of months, which made Lolita smile even harder.

Lolita and Leland had finished breakfast when Leland's phone rang.

"Hello?" Leland answered.

It was his cousin Renay, and Leland did not want Lolita to know that she was on the other end. They had a perfect breakfast, and he did not want Renay to ruin it. He knew that Lolita was going to ask who he was talking to, and he could not lie to her, because she had taught him that if he told one lie, he would have to continue lying to cover up what he said before. Besides that, she could always tell when he was lying, and he never could figure out how, but she always knew.

Leland listened to Renay on the other end of the phone tell him her sob story on why she didn't have any money and could he give her 200 dollars. Leland remembered giving her 100 dollars the week before, and now she was begging again. Word on the streets was that his cousin was a crack ho, and he was giving her money to supply her habit. He never told Lolita that Renay asked him for money, because he knew that she would find Renay and whip her ass.

Leland remembered when he was ten years old and Renay talked him into letting her suck his dick. Even though he didn't know any better, he would let her suck it on occasion. When they were growing up, she used to tell him to give her three dollars and she would suck it. The first time was free. That never got back to Lolita, and if she had known that Leland did that, she would have beat the shit out of both of them. Renay told him often that she would tell Lolita that he paid her to suck his dick, if he didn't help out. Leland was so afraid of disappointing Lolita, until he never told her. He would just give Renay the money, but knowing what that bitch looked like right then, he wouldn't let her suck a dog's dick, nonetheless his.

Renay was still talking and Leland said, "I will call you back!"

Lolita looked at her baby brother and knew exactly who he was talking to.

"Is that your bitch ass cousin Renay? Why the fuck is you talking to her? That bitch keep calling me! I am going to find her and kick her motherfucking ass! Let me speak to that bitch!" Lolita grabbed the phone from Leland, "Bitch why do you keep calling my brother? I told you to stop calling him and not to call me. I see I am going to have to kick your ass to get my point across!"

Renay called Lolita a 'bitch' and hung the phone up in her face.

Now Lolita was mad as hell, and she told Leland, "If you talk to that bitch again and I find out, I will not be giving you shit for your business! I told you that bitch was no good, and you think I don't know that bitch was sucking your dick when you where young. Oh I found out, so you can stop trying to cover for her funky ass!"

Lolita was livid. She hated Renay's guts, and she vowed she was kicking that bitch ass on sight. Leland told Lolita that he was sorry but he was scared to tell her what had happened between them a long time ago. Lolita could not talk to him because she was too mad.

Lolita said, "I will call you later because I can't talk to you right now about that bitch. But I promise you better not let me catch you talking to her again, you hear what I am saying to you boy?!"

Lolita was the only person that could talk to Leland like that and get away with it, because he was not the type of nigga to fuck with. But his big sister wasn't no joke, and her ass was crazier then he was.

"I'm sorry!" Leland said.

"Whatever Leland, I will call you later."

"I love you, Lolita!"

"I love you too Leland!"

Lolita got in the car and she couldn't calm down for nothing. Just the thought of Renay infuriated Lolita, and she was going to make it a point to find that bitch and beat the brakes off that ass. Lolita sat in her SUV for a good ten minutes trying to get her thoughts right. She turned on the gospel station and prayed to God asking Him to help her get her temper under control.

Lolita sat in the parking lot of the Waffle House for another ten minutes when she heard her phone ringing. She quickly grabbed her purse from the seat and got her phone, "Hello, hello?" Lolita said into the receiver, and she heard a voice from her past on the other end.

"Hello Lolita, long time no see. What's been going on baby?"

Lolita had the look of fear on her face, because the voice she heard on the other end was someone that she thought was locked away for years. She wondered how this person got her phone number. Lolita never told anyone about him, not even Leland.

Still sitting in the Waffle House, Leland could not believe how a perfect breakfast could turn into hell with just one phone call from Renay. Leland had not seen his sister that mad in a long time. Only Renay could bring out the worst in Lolita, and Leland knew he should have told Lolita that Renay was calling him and asking him for money. He just could not understand why he allowed her to continue to manipulate him as she did so many years ago.

Leland dialed Renay's number and waited for her to pick up the phone.

"What's up Leland, did big sister kick your little bitch ass?" Renay said.

"Naw, Renay it's nothing like that. Unlike your raggedy ass, my sister loves me and only wants what's best for me. I just called to tell you that I am not giving you another dime and for you not to call me anymore because I am no longer afraid of you telling my sister about your nasty trick ass. She already knows what you did."

"Well haven't we grown some balls in the last hour! I tell you what Leland, we will see if you stop me from seeing you because you know you still love me and you can't say 'no,' especially when I put my mouth on you."

Leland thought about how he and Renay had been sleeping together since he was ten years old. It just started out as experimenting, but she coerced him into going further and she did things to him that he had never had done to him before, even until that day.

Leland sat on the other end of phone and thoughts of Renay ran through his head about all the times he would sneak and see her, keeping it from Lolita, because if she found out, she would kill Renay and beat the shit of him.

"Leland! Do you hear me talking to you, we are never over and I will be coming by there tonight!"

Leland hung the phone up in Renay's face and he was going to make sure that it was the last time that she called him. The tears flowed from his eyes like big drops of rain and Leland knew he had no choice, because Renay had turned into a crack ho, and he did not want her to ruin his chances of starting a new business.

He made one last phone call, "Yeah, this Leland man, I need you to do me a favor. Yes, tonight!"

Chapter Fourteen

August 2004, it had been weeks since Stefan saw me, and he decided to stop by my office on Monday morning to bring me breakfast. It was 9 am in the morning, and I was in the office early. I had just finished putting the final touches on the big event for the promotion of Urban Lite and given Palmer my itinerary to type up. My trip to St. Thomas was scheduled on the Friday evening that Trevor died, but of course I had canceled my flight, so the musical guest had to postpone playing the event. It seemed as though everything was going wrong that day, and by the end of the day, I knew why. God had a way of delaying plans, especially when life-altering events took place. We never really understand the reasons why we are late or forget to turn off the iron and end up being delayed another ten minutes. But in those few minutes, we miss death or something else tragic happening to us.

I sat at my desk listening in on a conference call with Mr. Minami, as the last details of the promotional tour arrangements were made.

Mr. Minami said, "Paris, could you go over the details of entertainment for this event, because last time they canceled. Are we still using the same band and DJ for the party?"

"Mr. Minami let me say this, we have given our deposit and had the contract signed for the DJ and the band. Everyone is aware of his/her position and shall be at the destination on time ready to perform. I have also arranged for the best chefs, waiters, and waitresses to work the event. All areas are covered, and we should have a great success in St. Thomas," I said.

I knew that Mr. Minami was a thorough man, and everything had to be done correctly, without error, because this promotion of Urban Lite had to be fun for the whole family. There were events all during the day for the entire family, and at night there was a concert and dancing for the adults.

My flight was leaving at 1:45pm, and since I was going to be leaving for St. Thomas within two hours, I had to finish the conversation with Mr. Minami and make it to the airport in time to catch my flight. I finally hung up the phone and was about to make a phone call when my intercom buzzed.

"Paris, Stefan is here to see you," Palmer said.

"Palmer, show him in!"

I really wasn't ready to see Stefan again, because we had that flame between us, and I was trying to keep myself busy with work so I would not think about him or Trevor for that matter.

I said to myself, "Damn! I am not going to get all hot and bothered over this nigga today. Besides, I have to be at the airport in two hours and I am not missing my flight!"

Stefan walked through the door with his fine-as-he-want-to-be self. That shit didn't make no sense. How in the hell could one brotha be so damn sexy and good looking? Shit, that was why I couldn't be with his ass on a serious level, 'cause I would've had to kill a bitch over that nigga.

I sat in my chair facing the window, when I heard him say, "Hey baby," in that deep seductive ass voice of his. I spun that chair around so fast I nearly broke my neck. I did not know why I still had those feelings for him, because it has been a long time since we were together as a couple, not including the sexual encounter we had at the grand opening of the club.

Stefan stood there in his faded ragged jeans with a crisp white button-down shirt and some black square-toed Kenneth Cole slippers on, with the big silver buckle KC black belt. Damn he looked good and smelled even better. I did not know what he wanted from me but if he kept that up, he was going to get it!

"Paris, are you going to sit there and stare at me all day, or are you going to let me take you to lunch?" Stefan asked.

"Not today Stefan, I have to catch a plane in two hours to St. Thomas, and I will be there until Monday night."

"Well Miss Lady, can a brotha take you to the airport and arrange for you to have lunch on the way?"

"Well I guess there's no harm in that. Let me make a couple of calls and I will be ready."

Stefan stepped outside of my office and called to have a limo pick he and I up. He told the person on the other end what he wanted—the limo stocked with Hypnotic, wine, GreyGoose and Hennessey. He also ordered blackened chicken with creamy mushroom pasta, salad, and dessert. Stefan ordered a dozen roses and asked if he could have them delivered with the limo. Stefan wanted to have me to himself, and he was prepared to do anything it took to make that happen. He knew that I was still missing Trevor, so he had to be careful and not seem to be inconsiderate of my feelings. Stefan knew if he just played his cards right, he could have me, but he had to move slow and do little things to win me completely over. He really could care less about Trevor, because he wasn't shit in his eyes, and Stefan felt that Trevor never should have been with me in the first place. Stefan was determined that he was going to be with me, and he was going to get rid of anyone that got in his way.

I sat in my office and made a few calls. My last call was to Lolita. The phone rang several times, and then the voicemail came on, "This is Lolita Marcus. Sorry I am unavailable at this time. Please feel free to leave a message and I will get back with you as soon as possible. Have a great day!"

"Damn Lolita, girl Stefan got his fine ass in my office and he is taking me to the airport. I need to talk to you because I am trying my *best* not to get involved with him. I got to go, call me later!"

Just as I was hanging up the phone, Stefan walked back into my office.

"Hey are you ready to go?" he asked.

I grabbed my purse from my desk drawer and looked around the office to make sure I did not forget anything. I had my suitcase packed and in the closet in my office, so I had Stefan to carry it for me.

I said, "Palmer, please call Lolita for me and give her my flight and hotel information. She is supposed to come out this weekend, so make sure she calls me and let me know what her plans are. Thanks Palmer."

Stefan and I left the office, and he told me that he had sent for a limo to take us to the airport. As soon as we walked outside, the limo was waiting for us.

I got in the car and there were a dozen red roses on the seat. I looked at Stefan and he just smiled at me with those white teeth of his and said, "Just a little something to say 'congrats' on the Urban Lite tour."

"Thanks Stefan, I know you are really trying to help me move on with my life and I appreciate that. Trevor was a good man and I miss him so much."

Stefan just smiled at me because he didn't want to say anything to me just yet, but one day he was going to tell me about my sweet Trevor, the man who helped kill his little sister. Stefan only used being Trevor's new-found buddy as a pawn to get close to him, and now that he was dead, he would continue to do whatever he had to make me his wife.

Stefan got into the limo, and the driver put my bags in the truck. Stefan had soft jazz playing as he poured me a glass of white wine. He handed the glass to me and while I took a sip, he opened the silver covers. The food that he had ordered for the two of us was hot and fresh. I was surprised that he had such a spread laid out for us.

"I didn't know you had ordered us food. This is so nice!" I said.

After we finished eating, and I had one more glass of wine, the back seat of the limo started to get heated. Stefan leaned in for a kiss. He took his time by caressing my breast and kissing my neck, with slow, soft kisses, and then he moved to my face, kissing my cheeks and then small soft kisses on my lips.

"I am trying to be good, so please stop!" I said. I could not get myself together because his kisses were feeling so good to me. I just wanted to grab him around the neck and press my body and lips up against his.

Stefan sat back in his seat and turned to look out the window of the limo. "Paris I love you, and I have loved you for a long time. Why can't you see that?"

I was shocked at what I just heard from Stefan, because I always thought it was just lust between us, and never once did I think he really felt that way about me. I just sat in silence for a moment because I did not know how to respond to him. I was not over Trevor's death, and I did not want to lead Stefan on. I just wanted a friend.

We arrived at the airport and the limo driver got out of the car to get my bags. I gave Stefan a kiss on the cheek, "I really appreciate the ride and the lunch Stefan. Thanks so much for everything, and just give me a little time to work through my loss, because I really need your friendship."

Stefan sat in silence. He was not happy with the reaction he was getting from me. Things between us were not going as he had planned, and that was something that Stefan was not used to. He was determined to be with me. I was going to be his woman, and nothing was going to stop that from happening.

Stefan sat in the limo and watched me get out and take my bags to the curbside check-in at US Airways. I waved goodbye to him, and he just looked at me. I did not want to ask him if he was mad because it was obvious that he was.

After all the check-in stops and bag checkpoints, I finally boarded the plane. By then, I was ready to order me a glass of wine to relax during the flight. I sat in first class, ordered my dinner and drink, read a couple of magazines and took a power nap. When I opened my eyes, we were landing in St. Thomas. I could hear the pilot over the intercom telling the passengers that he hoped we enjoyed the flight and the weather in St. Thomas was beautiful and sunny in the mid 90's. I quickly put my seat in the upright position and grabbed my mirror from my bag. I had to check my eyes for evidence of sleep and to ensure my hair and make-up were fresh for departure. I did not want to scare the people when I walked through the airport, even though I was fine as hell. I finished straightening myself out, gathered my belongings, and waited to hear the Captain say, "Please remove your seat belts and check your overhead compartments before you leave the plane."

I was so ready to get off the plane and get to my bungalow at the Marriott's Morning Star Resort. That place was beautiful, and it had a spa that I had planned to pamper myself at for all the days that I was there, because I knew I was going to be stressed dealing with that promotional tour. I did enjoy putting events together and mingling with the people, but it could be stressful at times. I had my itinerary planned to the tee, and I was ready to take a shower and change clothes before I met Mr. Minami for cocktails at the resort.

I arrived at the gate and finally deplaned and headed towards the baggage claim area when I saw Mr. Minami's assistant Kim.

"Kim, I didn't know you were picking me up, Mr. Minami never mentioned that to me when we were on the phone," I said.

"Hello again Paris. I know that man can be forgetful at times, but he asked me to pick you up after he got off the phone with you."

I said, "I am glad we saw each other and I didn't have you waiting for me."

"Well let's get you to your hotel suite so that you can freshen up before you meet with Mr. Minami."

I finally got my bags and headed outside with Kim. She had the limo driver waiting to take us to the resort. On the way over, I called the office to check to see if Palmer had spoken to Lolita.

"Palmer had you spoke to Lolita? I want to make sure she is not coming so I can give her room to one of my clients that decided to come out to St. Thomas at the last minute."

173

"Paris, I tried to call her several times and I left her a voice message to contact you as soon as possible."

"Thanks Palmer, I don't know what that child is up to, but she will have to make her on arrangements if I don't hear from her crazy ass soon."

I sat in the limo thinking about the rest of my evening and all the shit I had to do first thing in the morning to ensure everything was in place for this promotional tour. I thought about Stefan, and how he had just poured his heart out to me in the limo before I left, but I just could not give him the response he was looking for. But I would have loved to taste those sexy ass lips of his again. Damn that man was fine as hell, and any woman would love to have had him by her side. But I just could not shake my thing with Trevor, because I did not get a chance to hold him in my arms before he died, so it was just hard for me right then. My thoughts were running all over the place while riding in that limo and I thought I was experiencing what the Buddhist called "monkey brain," because my mind was all over the place. I had to focus, and I needed a drink bad, so when I spotted a bottle of Hypnotic in the limo, I took a couple of shots to hold me until I got to the suite. Kim was sitting across from me rattling on about something. My mind was somewhere else at the time, and I really did not hear a word she was saying. I just said 'uh,' and she kept on talking.

We finally got to the resort and the driver pulled up in front of the resort. It was so beautiful and surrounded by the prettiest crystal blue water I had ever seen. I walked inside of the resort to the front desk and the clerk checked me in and handed me the key to my room. When I got to my suite and opened the door, to my surprise the room had a comfortable bed, with a loveseat, coffee table, and desk, with a large and sparkling bathroom. The bellhop told me to reach the private beach; I had to take a glass-enclosed elevator. He took my suitcase in the room and the king-sized bed was so inviting. I wanted to lay my black ass down right then and there. I knew if I even touched that bed with my body, it would have been lights out for the kid. I just gave the bellhop a 100-dollar tip, poured myself a drink, and jumped my ass in the shower. I knew that I had to be ready to meet Mr. Minami for drinks by 6pm and it was already after five.

Just as I was getting ready to get into the shower, I heard a knock at my door. I was not expecting anyone to be coming to see me, so I was wondering who in the hell would be at my door. I went to open the door,

"Who is it?!" I asked.

I stood there. No one said anything, and I started to walk away when I heard the knock again.

I said, "Who the hell is playing games because I am not in the mood for this shit!"

I heard this damn giggling behind the door and I knew immediately who it was. I opened the door and Lolita's dumb ass was standing there in her fucking swimsuit.

Lolita said, "Hey girl, what took you so long to get here? I've had a couple of drinks at Coco Joe's waiting on you. Hurry up and change clothes, I got some new friends at the bar waiting for us."

I looked at that crazy as girl and said, "Nigga, I have a meeting at 6pm so you will have to play with your new-found friends by your damn self until I am done getting everything ready for tomorrow. Tonight's kick-off is a jazz concert on the beach at 10pm until, are you coming to the show tonight or are you hanging with your new friends?"

"Paris, girl I will be at the concert for a little while and then I am going to find me a hip-hop reggae spot, because all that jazz makes me sleepy."

"Whatever Lolita, just bring your almost white ass by for a little while so I can introduce you to my colleague. Now get your drunk ass out of my room so I can get in the shower."

Lolita left the room and headed back to the bar with her new friends. She looked at her cell phone and saw that she had ten missed calls. Her brother was one of them, and two calls were from a blocked number. Lolita had gone to St. Thomas to get away and take her mind off the phone call she had had earlier with a person from her past whom she didn't want to bring back into her future. Lolita decided to turn her phone off and not think about her past mistakes. Besides, she could see the two cute Italian men sitting at the bar waving at her to come back over there, so she put on her million-dollar smile and danced her little ass back over to where they were sitting.

    Mr. Minami was wearing his business causal attire when I walked in the bar and saw him standing there with Kim by his side. He looked relaxed, so I figured everything was going as planned.

I walked over and we shook hands. "Mr. Minami, it's a pleasure to see you again, how are things?"

Mr. Minami was a gracious little Asian man. He nodded his head to me and we walked over to our table. I sat across from Mr. Minami and Kim. We discussed the events for the next two days with Sunday being the last day. We were going to have a big Carnival type party with the whole animals and fire shows—the works. Kim had checked on the band and the DJ to make sure that they had arrived and the rooms were to their liking. I was relieved that everything was going so smoothly and according to plans.

We finished discussing business and ordered drinks. By that time, I was hungry again so I ordered some food from the menu. I had a couple of Incredible Hulks and I was feeling really good. Mr. Minami was laughing and joking with me, and if I had not been feeling that last drink, I would have sworn his little ass was trying to push up on a sista.

I got my tipsy butt up from the table and told both of them that I would see them at the jazz concert. I got my phone out of my purse and called Lolita's ass. Why did that bitch phone go straight to voicemail? I walked out to the bar and there she was sitting in her swimsuit with her new-found friends.

I walked up to the bar where she was sitting and said, "Lolita! Why you still sitting out here? I thought your drunken ass was coming to the party."

"Hey girl, I am having a good time, this is uh...what are your names again? Oh yeah, Tony, and this is his cousin Alex. Boys, say hello to Paris!"

"Hello Paris, you are a beautiful woman!" Tony said in a thick Italian accent.

I said, "Thanks. Lolita let's go so you can shower and change clothes for the jazz concert on the beach. It starts in one hour, so we need to leave now!"

Lolita said, "Nigga, I said I was coming, now let me say goodbye to my friends and we can go to the room."

I stood there and watched that drunk ass nigga say goodbye to her two Italian friends and then we headed to her room. I waved goodbye to Tony and Alex, as I grabbed Lolita by the hand and pulled her little tail away from the bar before she started talking again. We made it to her room and I went in the bathroom to start the shower while Lolita got undressed. I was looking through her bags to see what she could put on, and she told me that she was wearing a coral halter-top with some white shorts and her flip-flops. It was a cute outfit for the beach, so I waited for her to get dressed.

My phone rang, "Hello, hello?"

I heard breathing on the other end of the phone but no one said anything. I hung up the phone and was thinking about the call that I had earlier in the week. It was the same background noise like it was outside by a river or something. I did not know who was calling me but I thought about Lucky and I knew that the call had something to do with her, but I did not know what. It just felt weird.

When she got out of the shower, Lolita asked, "Who was that Paris?"

"Girl I don't know, but I got a feeling it has something to do with Lucky."

"It probably was one of your niggas playing on the phone. It might be Stefan's crazy ass, and girl I am telling you, something ain't right with that boy."

"Shut up Lolita and bring your drunk ass on. I am ready to mingle with the people on the beach, and I need a couple of drinks to get my buzz back," I said.

Lolita and I went to the concert on the beach and it was off the chain. The band I hired was from Boston, and the music was jazz mixed with some R&B, funk and neo soul. I had two poets that did the spoken word at the concert, and the crowd was going crazy, snapping there fingers and all of that. We had a good time laughing and I introduced Lolita to Mr. Minami and Kim. Mr. Minami was dancing trying to shake his little ass to the music. That shit was funny as hell, and I jumped up behind him and we were dancing and laughing, having the time of our life.

Mr. Minami was praising my name because the turnout for the promotional tour was a big success on the first night. Saturday was the big day party, we were going to give out samples of Urban Lite and have a dance contest. The winners got a chance to appear in our first commercial for the soft drink. We danced all night long and the band played an extra hour. What was supposed to be jazz turned into a neo soul party on the beach. People were drunk, but in a festive way. Everybody was having a good time and it was drama free. I danced with everyone from women to men and we were all on the beach just wildin out.

I saw Lolita dancing and just smiling, so I made my way to where she was and tapped her on the shoulder. When she turned around all I could see were teeth.

I said, "Damn girl, I thought you were leaving the party soon, looks to me like you are having a good time."

"Whew! Paris, girl this party is off the chain! The band is sooooo good for jazz, but they mixed it up with funk and neo soul. I like that!"

"I can't call it, girl you are so crazy. Let me go find Mr. Minami, I will be back in minute," I said.

"Okay girl, I will be right here. I think I need another drink."

I heard the dude Lolita was dancing with tell her to get whatever she wanted to drink and it was on him. I guess he didn't realize who he was dealing with. Not that she needed him to buy her a drink, hell she could buy the whole damn bar if she wanted to, but she was going to let him be the man he was perpetrating to be, that was for sure. I just laughed to myself and went in search of Mr. Minami.

I spotted Kim getting her dance on. Damn, I didn't know Miss Thang could move like that! She was winding and grinding all up on some dude. We made eye contact and I mouthed the words, *'where is Mr. Minami?'* She gave me the 'I don't know' shoulder hunch, and I continued to look for him. I walked over to the outside bar by the band and there was Mr. Minami talking to a couple of the business partners for Urban Lite.

I walked up to them and Mr. Minami turned and said, "Hey Paris, do you remember Mr. Charleston and Mr. Thompson?"

I had met the men briefly in the first couple of meetings when we were launching the product. "Yes, I remember meeting Mr. Charleston, but I haven't had the pleasure of meeting Mr. Thompson. Hello Mr. Thompson, it is good to meet you. I have seen you in a couple of meetings in the past but we were never formally introduced."

Mr. Thompson said, "I am glad to see that everyone is having such a good time Paris. I love the band, and everything is just lovely."

"Thanks Mr. Thompson, I am glad that everything is to your liking. I hope your rooms are comfortable as well," I said.

"Oh, Paris they are very nice. Mr. Charleston and I have wonderful accommodations, and the services couldn't be better."

Mr. Minami and I excused ourselves and walked down towards the beach.

I said, "Mr. Minami, I am scheduled to meet with everyone involved with the day party at 8am will you be joining me?"

Mr. Minami said, "Paris I am going to sleep in and this is the first time in a long time that I have the opportunity to do that. I will let you handle everything and I will meet you for lunch during the festivities."

"Mr. Minami I am very grateful for this opportunity to lead this tour and I want you to know that I appreciate you believing in my work," I said.

"Paris I knew the day that I first met you that you had a great talent working with people and entertaining them with all of your creative ideas. I am very proud to have you on my team."

"Thanks, Jim!" I said with a smile.

Mr. Minami and I laughed about that because no one called him Jim, and when I said it, he took it as if I was his friend. That made me know that he really meant all of the things that he said to me. Women have to be careful, because men are always trying to hit on us and we have to know when a man is genuine in his comments and when he is just being a dog.

"Paris I want you to lead all of the events for the product and once we get this soft drink moving, we will branch out to other things so keep up the good work, and we will have a long relationship together."

"Thanks Jim, I am looking forward to great success in the future with Urban Lite."

Mr. Minami told me that he was going back to his hotel room and that he would see me around noon on Saturday.

I went back to the party, looking for Lolita. When I got to the dance floor, I saw her dancing with the two men from the bar.

I asked, "Hey Lolita, are you having fun?"

"Paris, where have you been? I was looking for you, because Alex wants to dance with you," Lolita said.

"Yes, Paris, you must dance with me," Alex said, holding his hand out waiting for me to accept.

I took his hand and we danced to the reggae music that the band was playing. I was swaying my body, feeling the music and the summer breeze from the ocean. I closed my eyes, just let the music take over my body, and then I felt Alex's hands running up and down my waist. I put my hands on his hands and we just moved to the rhythm of the music. It was if we had become one with the music, and we moved together like dance partners in a competition.

"Alex, where did you learn to move your body like that? You can really dance."

"Paris, in my country we dance and have parties and family over all the time. I was dancing since I was a little boy."

Alex and I danced two more songs, and by that time, it was 3am in the morning and the crowd was starting to dwindle down. I told Lolita that I was going back to my room because I had an early morning, and I left her hanging out with Tony and Alex. I walked back up the beach towards my room and I saw a man coming towards me from a distance. It looked like Stefan, but I wasn't sure, because I only had the light from the moon to guide me. I had the key to my room in my hand and I put it between my fingers in case I had to protect myself from this man I saw coming towards me. I got close enough to see his face, and it wasn't Stefan. The man scared me when he asked if I could tell him where the jazz concert was, because he was going to meet his friends there. I was scared as hell, and I was nervous because I thought Stefan had followed me to St. Thomas.

When I finally made it back to my room, I was so tired, so I took my clothes off and slipped on a t-shirt and shorts. I checked my phone to see if I had any calls while I was out. I had a couple of missed calls and three messages. One call was from Johnny Case. I hadn't spoken to him in awhile. He left a message asking about the promotional tour because he was thinking about coming out on Saturday. I definitely needed to call him back. The other two calls were the same as earlier, I just heard outside noise in the background.

I finished checking my missed calls and saw that Stefan had called me four times. I was going to have to sit down and talk with that boy because he couldn't be blowing up my phone like that.

I called Johnny and his phone rang three times before he picked up.

"Hey Paris, how's things in St. Thomas?" Johnny was half sleep but it sounded like he was trying to sound as if he was awake.

"Johnny I am sorry to call you so late but I just got your voicemail. Are you still coming out in the morning?"

"Paris I wanted to see if it was okay for me to come, because I know you are busy with the tour and all, but I wanted to be able to spend some time with you as well as enjoy the festivities."

"Yes Johnny, it's fine with me. What time does your flight arrive?"

"I will be there at 11am. Will you meet me at the airport?"

"I have some last minute things to go over but I will meet you at CoCo Joe's. Just call me when your flight gets in," I said.

"That's cool, Paris. I will see you tomorrow, sweet dreams."

"Goodnight Johnny!" I hung up the phone and got in the bed and before I could count sheep, I was fast asleep.

Chapter Fifteen

    Tanya hung up the phone because she didn't know what to say to me. She had called both Lolita and I, but each time, she didn't say a word. Tanya stood on the porch of the cabin and tried to think of a way to get Lucky out of there. She didn't want Ron to become suspicious of her, so she had to play it cool. It was a cool night in the mountains. Tanya could not sleep, and she was still haunted by Ty every time she closed her eyes and saw her face. Tanya lit up another cigarette and sat on the porch in the old rocking chair as she blew smoke circles. She could hear Ron moving around in the cabin. Tanya wondered what he was doing in there because it was 3:30am and he had passed out at midnight from drinking.

    Tanya got up from the chair and when she walked into the cabin, Ron was standing there looking at her with that shit-eating grin on his face.

Ron said, "What the fuck have you been doing, and why are you still up? I thought you were going to bed a long time ago. I hope you weren't thinking of no stupid ass plans, because you will find yourself headed down the river with Lucky's ass. Don't fucking play with me!"

"Ron, I couldn't sleep, so I was on the porch having a smoke. Is that okay with you?"

"Bitch don't get smart, because you got yourself in this shit. I could have done this without you, but you insisted on helping me to revenge your bitch's death."

"Whatever Ron, I am not trying to blame anything on you, so shut the fuck up and leave me alone."

And before Tanya could say another word, a quick hard slap came flying across her face.

Tanya grabbed her cheek, "What the fuck you hit me for, Ron?"

"That's for always talking shit, you don't run nothing, you hear me bitch! I am in charge, and I tell you what the fuck to do and when to do it!"

Tanya went into the room to check on Lucky, and found her lying on the floor. And when she bent down to help her up, she felt a sharp pain in her stomach. A couple more jabs in the kidneys and Tanya's body fell on the floor next to Lucky's. Lucky had stabbed Tanya with a steak knife that she'd found in the drawer in the bathroom. Ron had let her go in the bathroom to wash up, and when she opened the drawer, it was an old steak knife in there. Lucky hid the knife under her shirt, she planned to use it on Ron, but Tanya became her first victim. The funny thing about it was Tanya did not even scream. Tanya did not want Ron to hear her so that Lucky would have a chance to get away from him.

When Lucky looked down at Tanya she heard her whisper, "Lucky I am so sorry for everything." Tanya took her last breath and closed her eyes. Her body was still, and she was dead.

Lucky had used the knife to cut the duck tape from her legs. Her hands were already free, because Ron allowed her to wash up in the bathroom. She didn't think she was going to have to kill anyone, but it was life and death. Lucky knew if she didn't do something that they were going to kill her soon, because Ron had told her that when he raped her.

Lucky heard someone coming in the bedroom, and she thought it was Ron, so she pretended to have fallen on the floor. Lucky quickly got up and ran in the bathroom to wash the blood from the knife, and she paced back and forth in the bathroom trying to think of a plan to escape from Ron. Lucky went back into the room and turned Tanya on her back. She searched her pockets and found a cell phone. Lucky quickly dialed my number, "Come on Paris, please pick up, pick up!" she whispered with intense anxiety.

The phone rang four times, and then Lucky heard the voicemail pick up, "This is Paris Love, sorry I can't come to the phone right now, but please leave a message and I will call you soon as I can."

Lucky left a message for me, "Paris this is Lucky, I am in a cabin somewhere in Black Mountain and I can hear a river running near. I am thinking it is close to one of those whitewater rafting areas because I heard people on the way up here to the cabin. Please send help! I have killed Tanya and I don't know where Ron is, but I am scared, and I don't know how much longer it will be before he discovers that I have cut myself loose from the duct tape!"

Lucky hung the phone up and tried to call Lolita, but again, she got her voicemail. She hung the phone up and started to panic, "What the fuck am I going to do now? Ron will be in here soon I have to escape from him, damn!"

Lucky sat on the bed and started to cry. She was talking to herself, "Pull it together girl, you can do this, think, think."

The door to the room slowly opened. Lucky jumped behind the door and then the door closed back. Lucky caught her breath, because it felt like her heart was going to jump out of her chest. She heard two other voices in the room, so she put her ear closer to the door so that she could hear the people in the room talking. The men were from the ranger department for the mountains, and they had received a report that a woman was seen in town that fit the description of the woman that police in Charlotte were looking for. Apparently, the woman in question was Tanya, and Lucky knew that moment was her chance to escape.

Lucky knocked over the lamp that was on the nightstand and when it came crashing to the floor, she heard the police asking was there anyone in the bedroom.

Ron started to panic, and the rangers could see that he was getting uncomfortable the more they questioned him about the noise. The door to the bedroom was still cracked open because Ron was going to check on Lucky right before the rangers arrived. Lucky could see movement in the room, and she saw one of the rangers with his hand on the gun moving towards the bedroom door. The other ranger stood there and was asking Ron more questions, but when he turned to say something to his partner, Ron rushed him. The ranger and Ron struggled and Ron tried to grab the gun from his holster. His partner ran over, grabbed Ron's arm, and twisted it behind his back. Ron tried to swing on the ranger, and one shot was fired from the other ranger's gun that struck Ron in the back.

Lucky heard the gun shot and ran out of the room crying, and the ranger grabbed Ron and put him in handcuffs while his partner checked on Lucky. The officer asked, "Miss, are you okay? Are you Lucky Blue?"

Lucky nodded.

The ranger said, "We were looking for you ever since Tanya was spotted in town at the local gas station. Apparently, she had stopped in the store for gas and after she left, the clerk noticed her from the picture sent by the Mecklenburg police department. We had her followed back to this cabin, but we were waiting to see if she had anyone with her, and that is when we saw a man described as a possible suspected in your kidnapping standing on the porch. We called for backup before we approached the cabin and they should be on the way now."

Lucky sat in the chair and cried. She held her face in her hands and she could feel the scars that were on her face and the bruises on her legs. The dried up blood was on her clothes and her hair was in a matted ponytail.

The police and the ambulance arrived at the cabin. The news media was all over the place, and they showed Lucky getting into the car, and Ron Brown's ass in handcuffs. Lucky had a look on her face that was so sad and yet relieved that it was all over.

The coroner took Tanya's lifeless body and put it into the truck. Cameras were snapping everywhere, and the news of Lucky's kidnapping was all over the television. The police notified Lucky's brother that she was found, and he tried to call Lolita and I, but he still got our voicemails.

It was 8am in the morning in St. Thomas and I was just getting up because the carnival festival was starting at 10 am. I heard my phone beeping and when I looked at it, there were five missed calls and three voicemail messages. Thinking aloud, I said, "Who the hell been blowing up my phone?"

When I checked my messages, I fell on the bed. Immediately I called Lolita, "Hello, Lolita girl they found Lucky!" With tears in my eyes, I told Lolita about the phone call and voicemail messages I had. I told her the details of what the voicemail said. "Lolita we need to find out what hospital she is in and find out if she is okay. We will have to catch a flight back to Charlotte *now*, so please make the arrangements for us so that we can get back quickly."

With the news of Lucky's rescue, I could not finish the rest of the promotional tour. I immediately called Mr. Minami's assistant Kim.

The phone in Kim's room rang several times before she finally picked up. "Hello?"

"Kim, hi this is Paris, I have an emergency back in Charlotte. Do you remember the news about Attorney Lucky Blue being kidnapped? Well they have found her and the only information I have now is that she is on her way to the hospital for examination. I have to leave immediately, so could you have Mr. Minami call me and I will go into details with him? Can you please make sure the rest of the tour goes well? I have arranged for everything to be in place so there should not be a problem. I have three event coordinators who know exactly what needs to be done for Saturday and Sunday. Lolita is working on getting us a flight out right now so I should leave in the next half-hour."

Kim said, "Paris don't worry, go see about your friend, we will take care of everything here."

"Thanks so much Kim, and please let Mr. Minami know that I apologize for the inconvenience."

"Girl please, he is already raving over the party from last night and he is pleased with the set-up for the rest of the tour. Don't worry about him, just go see Lucky."

Lolita and I left St. Thomas at 10am. When we got to Charlotte, it seemed like six hours on the flight, and I was so nervous about seeing Lucky. I was praying that she was alright.

The plane finally landed and we grabbed our carry-on bags from the compartment above our seats. Lolita and I were both worried, and we just prayed for Lucky, because something like that could have pushed her over the edge, and we knew she could have a nervous breakdown. I had called her brother before we left St. Thomas to find out if he had any more information than we did, but he could only tell me that Ron was in custody and Tanya was dead. I was wondering how in the hell did Lucky escape.

"Lolita, I had always knew that Tanya's ass had something to do with Lucky's disappearance, because she was acting so strange when we called her about Lucky being in LA."

"Yeah Paris, I knew she was involved somehow, but we will find out the details as soon as we get the hospital and speak to detective Ryan."

Lolita had driven her car to the airport so we had transportation when we arrived in Charlotte. She drove us to the hospital. They had bought Lucky back to Charlotte, and she was in the Presbyterian hospital on Randolph Road. When we arrived at the hospital, there were news media outside of Lucky's room, and the detective on Lucky's case was talking to her brother. Lolita and I walked over to find out more details about her rescue.

Lucky's brother, Kelley, said, "Hello Lolita and Paris, I am glad you are here. Detective Ryan was just telling me how they caught Lucky's abductors."

Detective Ryan said, "Ms. Blue and Ms. Love, it is good to see you ladies again and I am sorry that we had to meet on this sad occasion. But at least Lucky came out of it with her life. Lucky was kidnapped, because Ron felt she owed him something, and Tanya felt that she was responsible for her former girlfriend, Ty's death. We questioned Ron and found out that Tanya had asked him if he wanted to get revenge for what Lucky had done to him because she was responsible for the death of her life partner. Ron told us that she had made all of the arrangements for the kidnapping but I guess she had a change of heart, according to what Lucky told us."

"Who the hell is Ty?" Lolita looked at me like I knew the answer, and I just shook my head as if to say *'I don't know who that is, I never heard of her.'*

The detective told us the story about how Lucky was a stripper during her college days and how she was working at a lesbian bar when she met Ty. The two of them became involved, but when Lucky didn't want to keep the relationship going, Ty killed herself, which caused Tanya to blame Lucky for her lover's death.

I was standing there with my mouth hanging open. I knew Lucky was a freak, but I didn't know she was into women. I thought she only liked men, and Lolita was about to pass out when she heard the detective say that Lucky was a stripper. Not Miss Prissy, she was too conservative for that.

We finished talking with the detective when the doctor came out and told us that we could see Lucky for a little while because she was still a little shook up.

We walked into Lucky's room and she had bandages on her cheeks, and her arms had bruises on them. The doctor told us that she had scars from the knife cuts; apparently, Tanya didn't cut deep enough into her face to where she would need stitches. She looked good for the most part, but I could see in her face that she was still shaken by the whole ordeal.

I asked, "Lucky, hey, how are you feeling sweetie?"

Lucky spoke in a low shaky voice, "Paris I am so glad that I was able to escape, because I was so afraid." With tears in her eyes, she asked, "Did the doctor tell you that Ron raped me?"

I said, "Oh Lucky, it's okay, we are going to work through this thing together. Just thank God you made it out with your life; we can get therapy for your emotions."

Lolita said, "Yeah Lucky, don't worry, because you know we are here for you. Girl, Paris and I are going to do whatever we can to make sure you get back to your self."

Lucky smiled and said, "Paris and Lolita I am glad the two of you are here. I was trying to think of what to do, but I couldn't get loose until Ron let me wash up, and that's when I discovered the knife in the drawer in the bathroom."

I said, "Girl that was brave of you to try to get away. Just think what would have happened if you didn't find that knife."

"I know. I am so tired. Are y'all coming to see me tomorrow? The doctors want me to stay overnight, and they are going to release me in the morning."

I sat on the bed beside her and said, "Lucky we will come back tomorrow and pick you up. Just call us when the doctor releases you and we will have your room clean and ready for you when you get out."

"Thanks girls, I love y'all." Lucky said.

Lolita and I said, in unison, "We love you too Lucky."

Lolita stood there with tears in her eyes and I saw Lucky was about to cry as well, so I said, "Let's get out of here and let her get some rest."

Lolita and I left the hospital and headed toward TGI Friday's to get something to eat.

Lolita said, "Girl you know I wanted to ask her about Ty and this lesbian stripping thing, but I didn't want to upset her. So I will wait until she is feeling better, because I will get the details on that shit soon."

I said, "Lolita shut your crazy ass up, but you right, I wanted to know about that shit myself!"

We laughed and walked towards the elevator to the parking deck. Lolita handed me the keys, "Here you drive, I am just ready for some food and a drink cause a nigga is starving."

"Girl, who said I wanted to drive? Give me the keys, ol' punk!"

"Anyway, stop acting like that. I will pay for your food and drinks okay. Now let's go!"

We drove to Friday's on Harris Blvd and it was crowded in there. We had to wait for 30 minutes to get a booth. We started to sit at the bar, but it was too much smoking going on, and I didn't want to smell it while I was eating.

Our names were finally called and we sat in a booth in the center towards the back of the restaurant. We immediately placed our orders, because we both knew exactly what we wanted. The waiter was a nice young dude who made jokes the entire time he was waiting on us. I guessed he wanted to make sure he got a good tip. We sat in the booth and I saw the white girl that Ron used to mess with come in the restaurant with two other black guys who looked like some straight up hood niggas.

"Lolita, girl is that the trick that Ron used to be with? The one that was in the parking garage waiting for Lucky."

"You know what Paris, I think that *is* that bitch. Damn she looks like she had been suckin on that glass dick for real!"

The girl was skinny as hell, her hair looked a hot mess, and I was wondering why in the hell were those guys with that crazy looking bitch. Lolita told me that she probably owed them some money, and they were going to make her trick off to get it. I was tripping, and I started to kick that bitch's ass, but she look like her life was fucked up enough. Me kicking her ass would probably have been like I gave her a gift.

We continued to eat our food. Lolita and I just shook our head at that shit. My phone rang, and when I picked up, it was Stefan's ass on the other end.

"Paris, how are you doing? I heard the news about Lucky, how is she doing?" Stefan asked.

I sounded dry as hell. "Hello Stefan, Lucky is doing okay, and she just has a few bruises and cuts and is still a bit shook up, but she will be released from the hospital on tomorrow."

"That's really good Paris. I am glad that they found her, because two tragedies in one year would be too much for one person to stand. I know how close the three of you are, and I heard that they caught the guy, which is even better."

"Thanks Stefan. Can I call you back? I am in the middle of eating my dinner."

"That's fine Paris. I will talk to you later."

I hung up the phone, and continued to eat and talk to Lolita.

I said, "Damn girl, I like Stefan, but that nigga is starting to be a bug-a-boo."

Lolita said, "I told you something wasn't right with that man. You better be careful before you end up on the front of a milk carton."

"Please, I wish a nigga *would!*"

We both laughed at my comment, but in the back of my mind, I was wondering if that nigga was a stalker for real.

After we finished eating, we got up to leave the restaurant when that stupid white bitch spotted us.

She screamed out my name, "Paris, come here girl, Paris you remember me? Ron's woman! Come here!"

I tried to ignore that bitch, but she was making a fucking scene. So I walked up to her and whispered in her ear, "Bitch if you don't shut the fuck up in here right now, I am going beat your crackhead ass in this piece."

I grabbed her by her shirt and pushed her back into the bar, and one of the people she was with said, "What's up Ma, you got beef with ol' girl?"

I said, "Naw, but you might want to calm that bitch down before we do have a problem in here. She don't know me like that!"

Lolita started pulling me away from the girl and that bitch was getting loud, and I was getting mad as hell, "Bring your low life ass outside bitch, so I can beat your ass for Lucky, you stupid dirty bitch!"

Now I was livid at that bitch, but Lolita told me to calm down and not to worry about that bitch, because eventually, she would get hers.

And with that, we walked out of the restaurant, but that bitch had the nerve to follow me out to the car calling behind me as if she was crazy, so I turned around and busted that bitch straight in her mouth.

"Now what bitch, you done brought your ass out here now I am going to beat the brakes off that ass! I told you to stop fucking with me, now you have done let that glass dick get your motherfucking ass whipped out here!"

Lolita was crying laughing, because that bitch couldn't even fight her way through a wet paper bag, and she was trying to hit me and fell on the ground.

Lolita ran up and kicked the bitch in the stomach, "That's for Lucky!"

We got in the car and left that bitch on the ground, holding her ribs, because the bitch didn't have a stomach. She was skinny as a mother.

"I LIKE THAT!" Lolita's crazy ass said, as she drove to my house.

I said, "Girl I could have stomped a hole in that bitch, and it wouldn't have taken much, because she was already a malnutrition looking bitch."

We were so hyped, and it was so funny, because I usually didn't get mad like that, but that bitch pushed my buttons, calling me like she was a damn fool in public.

We pulled up to my house, I got out of the car, and Lolita's ass was still laughing at me. Lolita said, "Girl bye, I will call you in the morning."

Lolita pulled out of the driveway and I walked in the house. I could still feel Trevor's presence in the house, but I still slept in the guest room. I could hardly go in the master bedroom without crying. His death was so hard for me, and I was trying to keep busy so I would not think about it. I had the house up for sale, but I did not have any offers as of yet, and I was just about ready to go stay in a townhouse until the house sold. I just wanted to try to get on with my life, and sleeping in that house was not helping at all. Trevor's memories were so strong sometimes, that I could hear him calling my name. I prayed that I was not losing my mind, but I missed my baby. I had to take sleeping pills at night so that I would not dream of Trevor, because it just seemed so real and I could not wake up every morning with bags under my eyes because of lack of sleep.

My cell phone rang and I saw it was Stephan calling again. I just let the phone go to voicemail, because I didn't want to talk to him. I took off my clothes and jumped in the shower, when the phone rang again. It was Johnny.

"Hi Johnny, how are things in H-Town?"

"Hey Paris, I called yesterday to your room in St. Thomas and was told that you had to leave on emergency, is everything alright?"

"I thought you would have heard by now, especially since your boy was kinda sweet on Lucky. She was found yesterday, and she is in the hospital with cuts on both cheeks and bruises on her arms and legs."

Johnny said, "I didn't know, last I heard she was still missing and Jackson was worried about her. He didn't want to call you because he thought it would just upset you even more. I am glad that she is okay. I am sure Jackson already knows about it, but I will call him tonight."

"Thanks Johnny, that would be nice, and I would love to see you again. How's business?"

"Paris, business is great, and you know playing football is my first love, but I am trying to get some other avenues lined up so I can retire before I get all broken up."

"I heard that, shit just let me know if you have any business ventures you think we can both make some money doing," I said.

"You're crazy Paris!"

"I know, but I am for real. So tell me, what have you and the twins been up to lately?"

"Nothing much, just working hard. We are going to get together and come out to see you all. Maybe we can meet at the beach or something. I think it would be good for Lucky to be around her friends, having a good time. I believe she will need to feel safe again, so she can move on with her life."

"You know Johnny, you are the sweetest man I know, and we would love to hang out with y'all again. We had such a good time when we came to Houston."

"Then it's a date. We will give Lucky some time to recuperate, and then it's on!"

"Works for me, let's make a plan to do that in a couple of months."

"Okay Paris, we will do that!"

"Cool, now I am getting off this phone with you because I got to go to bed. A sista is tired."

"Have a good night, Paris."

"Good night Johnny!"

I got in the bed and took two sleeping pills so that I could rest the entire night without waking up after dreaming about Trevor.

I said to myself, "Tomorrow is another day, and at least I will be able to face it a little better now that one person I love is still alive."

⋄⋄⋄⋄⋄⋄⋄⋄⋄⋄⋄⋄⋄⋄⋄⋄⋄⋄⋄⋄⋄

Stefan stood outside on the street looking up at the window to my spare room. He had never been inside, but he imagined himself in bed with me lying in his arms. Stefan saw my lights go out in the room and he got in his SUV, which was parked outside of my house. He sat there and kept watching.

"Paris, if you only knew how much I love you and want to take care of you, then you wouldn't push me away. But soon you will understand, because we are going to be together forever."

Stefan started the engine and pulled off slowly, watching the house as he passed it. His patience was wearing thin. He wanted me to be with him, and he was tired of playing games.

Chapter Sixteen

Three months had passed since Lucky's rescue and she was back at work with a new assistant. My assistant Palmer recommended him. Lucky vowed that she was never hiring a female assistant again, and we were supposed to go on a trip with Johnny, Jackson and Jaylan in a couple of months to help her get back to her normal life.

Lucky was excited about the trip, and we had a party to attend on Sunday. Lolita's brother Leland was having a grand opening of his barbershop/school. He had his first ten students signed up for classes, and he was going to introduce both them and his staff on Sunday.

Lucky had been in therapy everyday ever since her rescue, and her therapist told her that it would be good for her to get out and spend time with family and friends. Lucky sat in her office and decided that she was going to look for a puppy at the pet store. It was Saturday afternoon and she didn't know why she was still sitting in her office, when she could be out enjoying her day.

Lucky looked through the yellow pages and found a pet store. She picked up the phone and dialed the number, "Hello, I was wondering what time you closed today? I am interested in purchasing a small dog and wanted to stop by to see if I could find one."

"Miss, we are opened until 8pm today and I am sure there is a perfect dog here waiting for a good home. Why don't you stop in and see us?"

Lucky said, "Thanks I am going to do just that."

Lucky hung up the phone and told the security guard that she was leaving for the day. Lucky got to the parking garage and her car was parked in the VIP section right next to the elevator. Lucky reached into her purse and put her hand on her gun. She never left home without it, and she practiced daily at the gun range, just in case a nigga wanted to test her. She had her keys in the other hand and hit the button to unlock the doors, let down the window, and started the car.

Lucky paid more attention to her surroundings and was extremely cautious about being in any place alone. She got in the car, pulled out of the parking garage, and headed to the pet shop. Sometimes she had flashbacks of the time when Ron's woman was waiting for her in the parking deck garage, and she would shake her head and vow that shit would never happen to her again.

We had planned the perfect Sunday afternoon, and I decided to drive my brand new Mercedes CLK 550 coupe to the party. I was picking Lucky and Lolita up at Lucky's new house; she had

Paris Love

bought a house off Mallard Creek Road. Lucky sold the house that she had before her kidnapping, and she was starting to feel like herself a little more each day.

We were all there for her, and we were looking forward to having a great time at Leland's grand opening. I arrived at Lucky's house around 12:30pm. She and Lolita were sitting at the island in Lucky's kitchen, sipping wine and snacking on cheese and crackers.

I said, "Damn, you bitches couldn't wait to get to the party to eat and drink. Shit, where is my glass?"

Lucky said, "Paris, you know how Lolita's ass has to have something to eat before we get to the spot, because she hates to wait for all the introductions and hoopla to be over to get fed."

I said, "Yeah, you're right about that Lucky!"

With her hand on her little hips, Lolita pointed her finger at us and said, "You bitches are just mad because I don't be sitting there starving to death waiting on those slow ass people to finish giving their tired ass speeches. My stomach is straight full."

I said, "Shut up Lo, and let's go before we are late for your brother's opening."

I grabbed her by the arm and started pulling her. Lucky grabbed their purses, and we headed out the door.

I didn't tell the girls about my new whip, so when they got outside, they started trippin when they saw it.

"Damn bitch, this you? Who's dick you been sucking?" Lolita said, as she walked around the car looking at it from all angles.

I said, "Yo' daddy's, and that motherfucker came so hard he almost had a heart attack, now what?"

"Paris that shit ain't funny, you know the story about me and my pops, why you got to go there?"

"Bitch please, you know I'm playin with yo' stupid ass."

Lolita started laughing, "Damn Paris you such a Mark, I had you believing that shit."

"I hate you, Lo!"

"Yeah, but I love you girl!"

Lucky was laughing her ass off, so I had to crack. She was having too much fun at my expense.

I said, "Lucky what the fuck you laughing at, I had your pops last week, and that nigga was calling my name like he was saying his fuckin ABCs."

Lucky said, "Paris please, my dad wouldn't even look twice at your stank ass."

"Whatever, he was looking at more then my ass last week, he had his eyeballs all between these thighs."

Lucky gave me that 'yeah right' look and said, "Whatever nigga!"

Lolita said, "Come on let's go, y'all some dumb ass bitches. Paris open the damn doors so we won't be late, while you out here playin the dozens."

Lucky said, "Yeah, bitch, because if you had said some shit about my *momma*, we would have had a problem."

Lolita put her two cents in, "I know that's right Lucky. We don't play that momma shit, talk about daddy's ass all day, but don't you say shit about my momma."

I looked at both 'em bitches and said, "Let's go, damn!"

Lolita opened the door and jumped her fas' ass in the front seat, and Lucky got in the back. Lucky was back there checking out all the features.

Lucky said, "Paris, this shit is tight, you did the damn thing girl."

"Thanks Lucky!"

We left Lucky's house. When we got to the party, people were everywhere. The shit was mad crowded. I guessed the whole hair stylist community was there, because you saw all kinds of hairdos, from crazy ass colors to hair that was stacked to the top, and low cuts with designer styles cut into them. It was sick around there.

I really enjoyed watching the fine ass brothers showing off their skills on those haircuts. In addition, there were a couple of sistas putting it down on some haircuts and hairstyles. I saw one brother cut this chick hair, and I thought he was using a razor blade. His hands were moving so fast, until I thought the bitch was going to be bald about time he finished with her.

We walked around looking at all the different hairstyles. Then we went inside the school and saw that Leland had that shit hooked up. He had the black, white and red colors going, the classrooms were huge, and the black boards had electric projection screens. Leland had the latest state of the art computerized shit in that school. I was so impressed with the whole set up, and you could tell that Lolita was very proud of her little brother's accomplishments.

We walked through the entire building, and when we came back to the front entrance, we spotted Leland giving one of his students some instructions on where they were going to come out from, when he introduced them.

I peeped that chocolate fine ass and said, "Lolita you see your baby brother over there? Damn how long has it been since I seen him? He is looking like a full, grown ass man! Damn why didn't you tell me it was like that?"

Lolita said, "Bitch, don't make me kill you, don't even think about fucking with my little brother, he ain't even ready for no cat from your wild ass."

I said, "Girl it is probably what the little young nigga needs, some *real* cat in his life! Shit better me then these money hungry bitches, because you know Paris got her shit and don't need his. Is the little nigga packin or what?"

"Paris, shut the hell up, 'cause you know you ain't about to be fucking my little brother."

Lucky was standing there checking Leland's ass out too, and she said, "Well shit, let me have his ass if you are so worried about Paris!" Lolita said, "How 'bout both you bitches take that shit somewhere else, 'cause I ain't trying to hear it!"

"Come on Sis-in-Law," I said, laughing my head off at Lolita, 'cause that bitch was looking at me like she wanted to slap the shit out me.

"I ain't playin Paris, go 'head with that shit."

Leland walked up to us and said, "What is going on over here? Y'all enjoying the show, food, and drinks? I hope y'all like everything."

Leland asked that question like he knew we were talking about his fine ass. I couldn't remember if Leland was ten or five years younger than me, but that motherfucker was so fine standing there with that pretty ass chocolate skin glistening in the sun, shit I wanted to take a bite out of that sweet ass chocolate and see if it tasted just as sweet as it looked.

"Paris, are you enjoying yourself?" Leland asked, while looking me up and down like he was hungry. "How long has it been since I seen you?"

I said, "Boy I don't know, I think the last time I saw you, you were still a baby."

"I am not a baby no more, so you need to go to lunch or something with me."

Lolita chimed in, "Paris is too busy to be hanging out with your young ass boy, she used to change your diapers."

"Well I don't wear diapers anymore and I can handle my own, thank you big sis," Leland said. "Paris, think about what I said, you know how to reach me. Now I must go and get ready for the introduction and ribbon cutting."

Leland walked away, and that man even looked as good going as he did coming, and Lolita was giving me the eye like *'don't make me hurt you'*. I just laughed, but I was seriously thinking about calling that young brother to see if he really could hold his own. I was thinking it, but I had other shit to worry about, with Stefan's ass following me around like a damn puppy. It was no wonder I didn't see his ass out there. I was going to talk to that man when I got home that night.

Lolita looked at me and said, "Come on let's go, they are about to start, and my brother reserved seats for us at the front."

The stage was set up in front of the building in a T-shape with tables and chairs on each side of the middle line. We watched the models come out in the latest styles of hair and clothes. There was a 'cut off' contest with five barbers who worked in the shop with Leland. He had them do their own style of cutting, and it was just amazing to watch the men at work. The men modeled their hairstyles, from dreads to low cut Caesars with the deep waves. I loved that look. The men were built and came in all flavors, between deep chocolate to light, bright and damn near white.

In the grand finale, all of the stylists and models walked down the runway first and stood on each side of the stage. Leland walked out in this hot ass linen shirt and pants; it looked so good against that chocolate skin of his. The entire place was standing to their feet and clapping for that nigga like he was the Pres. I looked over at Lolita, and she was clapping and smiling so hard, I thought the girls teeth were going to fall out on the ground.

With excitement in her voice, Lolita cheered for her brother, "Y'all look at my baby, he looks so good and I am so proud of him!"

I thought Lolita was getting ready to cry, but instead, Lucky was standing there wiping away her tears.

I said to Lucky, "What the hell you crying for, I thought this was Lolita's brother?"

Lucky said, "Shut up Paris, you don't have any feelings!"

"Girl, I am happy for the young man and he is fine on top of that, shit I am ecstatic!" I said.

Lolita said, "Paris, you had better stop talking about my brother like that, 'cause the two of you will not be getting together."

I said to myself, *'that's what she thinks so we will leave it like that 'cause her brother was checking a sista out.'*

We waited around for the crowd to leave and then we said our goodbyes to Leland, and when I gave him a hug, he held me extra tight and long.

Lolita said, "That's enough of that. Damn baby brother, what are you trying to do, squeeze the life out of Paris?"

Leland said, "Naw, sis, I was just letting her know how good it was to see her again, that's all."

"It better be boy, come here." Lolita put her arm around his shoulder. "You know I am so proud of you, this was a very nice grand opening and it looks like I made a great investment."

"Thanks Lolita, I just wanted to make you proud of me."

Lolita said, "And you have!"

Lucky walked up to Leland, "Little brother you have made me proud. I have only known you for a little while, but you have accomplished so many great things as a young black man. Keep trying to do the best you can, because your sister has worked very hard so that you could have the best in life. Don't forget that."

"Thanks, Lucky. And I will always do my best because I want my sister to all ways be proud of me."

Lucky said, "Whew, whew, group hug."

Lucky grabbed everyone and started her touchy-feely-love-everyone group hug. We all hugged, laughed, and cried, except me on the crying part, of course, and then we headed to the car.

I drove Lolita and Lucky home and then I headed to the Pier 1 in Birkdale.

◇◇◇◇◇◇◇◇◇◇◇◇◇◇◇◇◇◇◇◇◇◇◇

Lucky walked into her new house. She had four bedrooms and a basement. She had not put furniture in the formal dining room or the master guest room, but all the other rooms were done. She had put pictures on the walls and bought all kinds of floor plants. Lucky was keeping herself busy so she would not have time to think about Ron's ass. Even though he was in prison for a long time, she still had to face him one more time when she went to court.

The date was six months away and Lucky was wishing that they would give his ass the chair, but knowing the court system, she knew he would not probably get a long sentence for his crime. Lucky wanted death, and she thought about him being executed. That was the only satisfaction she saw, Ron dying.

Lucky walked into the master bedroom on the first level of the house and saw the note to call Jackson when she got in, because she had spoken to him earlier in the week and made a note for herself to call him. Lucky laid on her bed and reached for the phone from her nightstand and dialed the number. She heard it ring three times, and as she started to hang up, she heard Jackson's voice on the other end.

"Hey stranger, how are things going? I started to call you again today because I thought you had forgot about me."

"Hey Jackson, how are you? I didn't forget, in fact that is why I am calling you. I made a note to remind me to call you when I got home. Are we still on for the reunion gathering?"

Jackson said, "Of course we are, and I am just waiting to hear from Johnny to get the details of where we all are going to meet up this time."

"I think Paris said something about going to Cancun and just having our own party for the weekend or maybe a week this time."

"I would love that Lucky, because I had been waiting to see you again, seeing that I didn't get a chance to come to the grand opening of the club. And since all the things that have happened to you. I just wanted to give you time to get back to your normal routine."

"I know, I am still a little shaken, but my therapist has helped me sort out many things, not just the kidnapping. I have searched deep inside and found many things that I really did not deal with growing up and the 'cleaning house,' so to speak, is the best thing that I can do to get my life back to normal. I could use a good friend to help put a smile on my face from time to time. You think you can handle that?"

"Girl you know I got you, and we are not going to think about any of the bad times. We are going to focus on the good ones to come, because I plan on being around to keep that pretty smile of yours shining."

Lucky was standing in her master bedroom looking in the mirror at the scars on her cheeks. They were healing, but you could still see them. Lolita had ordered some special cream to put on them that was supposed to remove the scar. It cost like 100 dollars a tube. Even with the scars on her cheeks, though, Lucky was still pretty. Sometimes she would put cover-up make-up on them, which made them barely noticeable.

"Thanks Jackson, I really need that. Lolita and Paris have helped me get it together, because I was trying to stay in the house all locked up but they wasn't hearing that. Them heifers were in my face every time I opened my eyes."

"Yeah, that's what good friends do. But I know that you want to get back to work and all, so how is that going?"

"I went in the office a couple of days ago and I hired a new male assistant, because I wasn't letting any female get that close to my personal life again. Tanya had me fooled, I can say that. But she was sorry towards the end, which I did see in her eyes. But it was too late, because I had already stabbed her, and I couldn't take that back. I was just trying to protect myself, but it still was somebody's life. That is the hardest part of therapy, to talk about the feelings I had when I killed her. I just was scared as hell, and she had already cut my face, so I didn't know if she was coming to finish the job or not."

"Damn Lucky, I am so sorry you had to experience something like that, people are just crazy these days."

"I know but I am going to be much more careful about the way I do things now, that's for sure."

"I know that's right. But listen, I have another call coming in that I have to take, so I will get with you this week and see how the plans are going for the trip. Take care Lucky."

"Bye Jackson!"

Chapter Seventeen

Lucky went into the kitchen to make her some tea before going to bed; her bedroom was on the first level towards the back of the house so the kitchen was only a few steps away. Lucky really enjoyed the new house. It had a certain peace to it the first day she walked in it so she didn't waste anytime purchasing the house, because she needed to have all positive good things around her.

Lucky heated up the water in a coffee mug in the microwave. When the beeper went off, Lucky removed the cup and dropped a tea bag in the hot water. She sat at her kitchen table dipping the tea bag in and out of the cup. The house was silent, and Lucky sat there thinking about everything that had happened to her.

Paris Love

She started to cry and the phone rang. That scared her and caused her to jump. "Hello, who is this?"

"This is your brother, is every thing alright?"

"Yes, the phone ringing just startled me because it's so quiet in the house."

Kelley said, "Sis, maybe you should get a dog, and that way you won't feel alone in the house. It will be good for you."

"I did go by the pet store on Saturday to look at the dogs, but I didn't see one that I liked. And besides, you know I don't like dogs like that, but maybe I can check into getting a small one."

"That would be nice sis, just a little Jack Russell Terrier or something small like that."

"Well I'll check it out, but I know I didn't see a Jack Russell at the pet store on Saturday. They had a few poodles and some other larger dogs, but nothing I wanted to bring home."

"Well try one of the larger pet stores because I am sure they would have them. Or check the internet for breeders."

"Okay I will."

"So how have you been feeling sis, everything healing okay?"

"I guess. The scars on my cheek are looking better but you can still see them. Lolita brought me some cream that is supposed to remove the scars. I am going to make me a doctor's appointment tomorrow because my stomach has been a little upset in the mornings, and I don't know what the problem is. It could be because I am stressing trying to get my work and life back on track. It has been really hard for me, especially at night, because I am the only one here."

"That's why I am telling you to get a dog, it will take away the loneliness and you will feel better, trust me."

"Okay, I am going to look again, but I am still calling the doctor."

"Good, try to get some sleep. Call me tomorrow and let me know how the dog hunting is going."

"Okay, I will call you tomorrow."

"Good, I love you girl!"

"I love you too, bye!"

Lucky finished drinking her tea and headed to her bedroom. She turned on the TV and watched the news before she dosed off to sleep, leaving the lamp and TV on.

I was sitting in my office when Palmer came in to tell me that I had a package that UPS dropped off for me, and when he gave it to me, there was some company's name on it out of San Diego. I opened the box and it was a small red velvet box inside. When I opened that box, there was a diamond engagement ring setting surrounded by the pretty velvet tissue. I did not see a card or anything attached to it, but when I looked in the bottom of the box, I saw a card with a heart around it and with Stefan's name in the middle. I thought to myself *'what in the hell is he up to now? I told him that I wasn't ready for all of this and he is sending me a damn engagement ring.'* I had to have a serious talk with him because we had a misunderstanding and it was starting to get crazy.

I picked up the phone in my office and got Lolita and Lucky on the phone. When we were all on the phone I started the conversation, "Y'all ain't going to believe what this crazy ass man done today!"

Lucky was the first one to say something. "What crazy man, who are you talking about Paris?"

Lolita didn't wait for me to respond. "She is talking about that crazy ass Stefan, he is stalking your ass. I know he is, you don't even have to tell me."

I said, "Girl you were right, 'cause this fool done sent me a diamond engagement ring through UPS!"

Lucky said, "Paris, girl what is going on with you and Stefan? See Lolita, I told you her ass fucked him in Miami when she was acting like it was nothing going on."

"Whatever, I also told him that I just needed a friend and he is still trying to make me be his wife. What the fuck is going on!"

Lolita said, "All I know is you had better watch yo' back, and please give him that ring back before he thinks you have accepted his proposal."

"Lolita I am going to give the ring back today, because I am calling his ass soon as I hang up from y'all."

Lucky said, "Paris, Lolita is right, he is acting a bit crazy and after what I have been through, you had better start carrying your gun with you. Girl I am at the range everyday, 'cause I'm shooting first and asking questions last."

I said, "Shit you ain't said nothing, I keeps my shit with me!"

Lolita said, "Girl I knew when that nigga showed up at your office before you went to St. Thomas he was a fool, and I tried to tell you that when we were in St. Thomas, but you didn't listen to Lolita, naw. Now you see what I was talking about, don't you?"

I said, "I am a little worried about this whole thing between us, and I am going to talk to him about it soon."

Lucky said, "Paris make sure when you talk to him you speak soft and chose your words carefully, because if he is as crazy as Lolita thinks, then he might hurt you if you say the wrong thing or if he thinks you are trying to leave him."

"Yeah okay, but I don't think he is *that* crazy. Besides we've known each other for a long time, he is really a sweet person. I don't know where this obsession for me is coming from."

Lucky said, "I don't either, but I am going to have my friend do a background check on him because after dealing with Ron's ass, I don't trust anybody."

"Thanks y'all, now let me get back to work because I have some events coming up in six months that I need to put together. I will call y'all later tonight."

In their valley girl voices, Lolita and Lucky both said "Bye!"

I hung up the phone and started to think about Stefan, but I immediately started making phone calls to check the hotels and convention center for upcoming events, just to keep my mind off the big ass diamond I had sitting in my drawer. I knew that this was going to be a problem, but I was hoping he would understand that I was still grieving over Trevor, and I was not ready for a serious relationship. Especially marriage.

The phone rang and I picked up quickly because it startled me, "Paris Love!"

"Hello Paris, this is Kathy Daily from ReMac Realty, we have a couple that's interested in purchasing your house. They have put their bid in and they agreed to your price of 250,000 dollars with you paying their closing costs."

"That's great Kathy, and what about the house that I was looking at, have you contacted the people for me yet?"

"Yes Paris, I did. Are you interested in meeting with them, or do you want to go ahead and bid on the house?"

"I think I am going to look at it again, because I am not sure if I want that one or the one I saw on Lake Norman. I will call you on tomorrow, because I have to make a decision soon, now that I have a buyer for my house."

Kathy said, "I will look forward to speaking with you on tomorrow, and I will let the Woodlocks know that you have accepted their bid."

"Thanks Nancy, I will talk to you tomorrow, bye."

I was finally selling the house that Trevor and I shared. It was going to be a big change in my life, because we shared that house for a long time, and his memories were in every room. But selling the house was the only way that I could move on with my life. I loved him, but I had to get passed his death and start my life fresh without him, because he was not coming back.

I called Palmer into my office to take some notes and set up new files for my new clients. I was still running my personal assistant company, but I didn't do much of the work anymore. I had actually hired a crew that took care of all of that, and Palmer was now over them as well as still my assistant. I kept that boy busy, because he could get into trouble if I didn't.

Palmer came in my office in his nice baby blue gator shirt and khaki pants, with a nice brown belt and shoes to match. He had his hair all fresh and pulled back, with the neatest twist set that I had ever seen on a man. Palmer was very good looking but he was bi-sexual like a mother.

"Palmer, come take a seat, I need you do a few things. First we need to get new files set up on these five people. I want you to personally make sure that everything they need is done right, and then you give it to Darren. He is the best one I have out of the crew."

"Paris, Darren is so freaking anal until he gets on my damn nerve. Can't you give the job to Carrie instead?"

"No Palmer, I want Darren to take care of it, because these are some very important business clients and their shit has to be on point. And I know Darren won't drop the ball, and besides, didn't you use to date him? So he couldn't be that bad."

Palmer looked at me and rolled his eyes, "Anyway Paris, that's why I don't want to work with him—because I used to date him.

Can't you at least let me try to get over our relationship before you put us on such a huge project together."

"Palmer! This is your job not 'As the World Turns' so pull it together and just do your job!"

Sucking his teeth Palmer said, "Okay! But I don't have to like it!"

We finished going over all the details and other things that I needed done. I gave that boy enough work to keep him busy for the next week.

I dismissed him from my office and turned my chair towards the picture window. It was pretty outside, and I could see all of uptown from my window, all the way down Tryon Street. I looked at all the new buildings that were going up left and right. The city was growing and moving faster by the day. I sat back in the chair and just closed my eyes for a brief second when my office phone rang. I could see the red button lighting up on the phone, but I didn't hear Palmer's voice come over the intercom. I figured he had gone to make copies or something, so I answered it myself.

"Paris Love speaking, how may I help you?"

The voice on the other end was so deep and seductive, "Well let's see, you can help me out a lot if you will join me for dinner tonight."

I didn't recognize the voice so I played along to see if I could figure out who was calling me. "Well that depends on where you are trying to take me, because I don't just eat anywhere. I have to know if the place is a legitimate place or not."

"Well let's see, what about Morrison, do you like steak?"

"Hmmm, that sounds like a nice restaurant, I heard the food was excellent there." I still couldn't figure out who the hell I was talking to and I didn't want to give up the fact that I didn't know, but his voice wasn't one that I was used to hearing.

"Paris, you don't have a clue who you are talking to, do you?"

I just busted out laughing, "I sure in the hell don't, so who is this?"

"Girl you was going to ride this shit out to the end. This is Leland, Lolita's brother."

My damn mouth dropped in my stomach. I knew we flirted a little bit here and there at the grand opening, but damn, I didn't think he was going to call me. Shit, I didn't remember giving him my number.

"Leland, hey, I am surprised to hear from you."

"When I told you I wanted to take you out, did you think I was joking? I know you wondering how I got your number, but I just dialed Information. It's not like you are not listed. Besides, I couldn't ask my sister for it, because I would've had to hear about how you were older than me, blab, blab blab."

I said, "I know, right. I told her that we would be cool together, but she wasn't trying to hear all of that, and I am not about to listen to your sister's speech about messing with you either. So why are you really calling, to piss her off or what?"

"Naw, I just want to spend some time with you and talk over dinner. Is there something wrong with that?"

"Well I am going to have to think about this, so I will call you back on tomorrow. What is your phone number?"

"Oh, so that's how you going to play a brotha? What are you going to do, call my big sister to get permission to go out with me? That is some BS Paris, and you know you were feeling me just like I am feeling you. I am not the little brother or baby you knew back then, so stop tripping and let me take you out. If you don't like me after that, I won't bother you again, how about that?"

"Damn boy you are persistent, just like that damn sister of yours. But don't you breathe a word of this to her, 'cause she ain't even ready."

"Okay, what time shall I pick you up?" Leland asked.

"Let's make it around 8:00pm, is that good for you?"

"Yeah, whatever time you wanted me to be there is good. I don't have a problem with that."

"Okay Leland, I will see you tonight."

I hung up the phone, and thought about that fine chocolate brotha and smiled, but soon after that, images of Lolita's face popped in my head. I could hear her saying, "Bitch I will kill you!" I just laughed to myself.

I looked at the clock on my desk to check the time. I was meeting with my decorator in an hour. I pushed the intercom button and called Palmer. "Palmer, are you back in the office?"

He did not respond, so when I walked out of my office, I saw that his computer was still on and his jacket was on his chair. I wrote him a quick note and headed towards the elevator.

When I got to my car, my phone rang. "Hello?"

"Hey pretty lady, did you get my package?"

"Stefan, how or better yet *why* would you send me an engagement ring through UPS?"

"I just thought it would make your day, and I was just trying to get the thought in your head before I actually, well *officially*, asked you to marry me," Stefan said.

"Well that is not the way I would want to be proposed to, even if I was looking to get married. That was not romantic at all! I told you after Trevor's death that I just needed a friend, and I didn't want a relationship. I'm still not over his death, but you don't seem to care about what I said, because you continue to make advances towards me with this 'marry me' shit. Please stop, or I am not going to continue being friends with you," I snapped.

"Damn Paris, I got your point. But I just can't help it if I love you and want to make you happy. I wasn't going to tell you this, because I know you thought Trevor was such an angel, but he wasn't shit, and he helped so many of them damn drug lords get off too, it wasn't funny. He didn't give a damn about them selling drugs to little kids or the mothers being strung out on crack, he just wanted to get paid for his high-priced lawyer services, no matter if his clients were guilty or not. Paris you deserve so much better than what that bastard could ever give you, and his death should have been a fucking celebration."

Stefan was so mad that he didn't realized what he was saying to me. Even though it was true, he shouldn't have approached me like that. I knew that I would never marry him now.

Stefan continued, "I am sorry Paris, I didn't mean to get so upset, but you didn't know the real Trevor, and I did. He didn't know me, but I knew all about him and the company he kept every since he had my sister killed."

I was sitting in silence and thinking all sorts of things, because for one, how long had he been following Trevor? And when did he have his sister killed, what was he talking about? I knew he was crazy, then, because my baby did not kill anybody.

"Stefan, why are you lying on Trevor? He is not here to defend himself, and I am not going to listen to you shit on him like that. If you are mad because I am not trying to get into a relationship with you, that's one thing, but don't lie on Trevor to make yourself look better, because it's not going to work. I am returning your ring and I want you to stop calling me, because you are acting crazy."

"Paris this is not over. You are just mad now baby, but I will call you later, okay? I love you."

Before I could say anything else, Stefan hung up the phone, and I was sitting in my car with tears in my eyes. I wondered why he would say those things about Trevor. And I never knew he had a sister who he claimed Trevor killed. I wanted to call him back, but I didn't do it, because I was not ready to bring up Trevor, again. Especially when I was trying to get over his death.

I turned on the radio and listened to the Michael Baisden show to take my mind off that conversation I had with Stefan. I wanted to slap the shit out of him for trying to make Trevor out to be a monster, when he was nothing but good to me. And I didn't get into what he did with his job, because Trevor never brought that stuff home with him. I just could not believe Stefan; he was acting as if *he* killed Trevor.

I called Lucky to see if she had spoken to her friend about doing a background check on Stefan, which was going to be hard because his ass worked for the DEA.

"Hey Lucky, girl, why did Stefan call me tripping? He went slap off on me because I told him that I wasn't looking for no relationship because I wasn't over Trevor. But he didn't want to hear that, he started to tell me how Trevor got his sister killed and that Trevor wasn't shit, girl it was crazy."

"Paris I told you to be careful because he sounds like Ron's ass, and I am never going to get put in that kind of predicament again. You have to look at the signs because they are there. Since I been going to the therapist, I realized that the signs were there about Ron's insecurities, but I didn't see them. I thought I was so in love with him and he tried to kill me. Girl I still have nightmares about that. I am getting better, but it is still a problem with me when it comes to trusting a man."

"I feel you Lucky, but I just can't believe that Stefan hated Trevor like that, and he was acting as if they were all buddy-buddy at our grand opening. He sounded so hateful, and he said that it should have been a celebration when Trevor died. It was horrible, and then he told me that he loved me and he would see me later."

"Paris, girl that's a fool, and I am telling you, if you have not been to the range to practice shooting that new nine of yours then I suggest you start tomorrow. I will be going in the morning around 10am if you'd like to join me."

"I might take you up on that, I will call you in the morning."

"Okay, be careful girl, I love you."

"I love you Lucky. Get some rest and don't think about that dumb ass Ron, because that ass is locked away for a long time."

"I will try not to. It's hard to get to sleep at night but I am working on it. I am thinking about buying me a dog tomorrow."

"Well that might be just what you need to keep you company."

"Yeah, that's what my brother said, so I think I am going to get one."

"Okay, my other line is beeping so I am going to call you in the morning."

"Okay, Bye Paris!"

I clicked over to my other line to answer the phone, "What it do!"

"Girl what do you know about that, you know that's my sayin'. Don't try to be like me."

"Whatever Leland, you don't know who you're messing with."

"Oh look at you, now you recognize my voice. Damn, so all a brotha got to do is offer to take you out and you know who he is all of sudden? What's up with that?"

"Nigga please, what do you want, 'cause I don't have time to be playing with you on this phone."

"Paris don't make me spank you girl, now are you going to be ready on time, or are you going to have a brotha waiting hours for you to get dressed?"

"I will be dressed and ready to go, so you just have your fine ass here by eight o'clock on the dot."

"Okay. Now remember, don't mention this to my sister because we don't want her to have a fit just yet. Give me some time to put my mojo on you first."

"Boy you are crazy! But we will see, because I got my own special Paris Love dust that most men can't resist, especially a young man like yourself."

"Girl I am telling you that I am not that young. I am only five years younger than you, so don't trip."

"Oh you're just a baby. I might have to make you a bottle to bring along on our date."

"Ha ha, we will see if I will be needing that bottle, because I promise you will be the one that needs changing when I get through."

"You are a little nasty something, but it's all good, because if you can get me wet like that, then you are the shit. But you know talk is cheap."

"Well time will tell. I will see you at eight sexy."

"Bye Leland, I will be ready!"

Chapter Eighteen

    Stefan was sitting in my neighborhood for an hour before he saw me coming around the corner turning onto my street. I pulled into my driveway and hit the remote to open the garage. As I was pulling into the garage, I looked in my rearview and I saw Stefan's SUV parked across the street. I thought to myself that his ass was really starting to act foolish and he needed to stop stalking me. I knew that he could do some dirty shit because he worked for the DEA, so I had to outsmart that motherfucker. I wished I knew the nigga had gone off on the deep end before I gave him some pussy, because now I couldn't get rid of his ass.

    I pulled into the garage and turned the car off. I had to play that shit off because I was getting ready to start recording that nigga's every move, and then I was going to call Johnny in the morning, because he had a detective friend that I could hire to watch that nigga watch me. I couldn't afford to have no shit go down with me that went down with Lucky. I was going to put Stefan's ass on notice, 'cause the po-po's wouldn't be finding my ass in the trunk of that nigga's truck, that was for damn sure.

Stefan walked up to my car window, "Hey baby what took you so long to get home? Did you have a good day at work?"

Now I was thinking to myself, *'what the fuck is wrong with his ass,'* but didn't I tell him that. "Stefan, I had to work a little longer than I thought. What are you doing here? I did not remember us having a date tonight."

"We don't have a date, can't a brotha come and check on his future wife and fix her a nice warm bath?"

Okay, that nigga was acting like one flew over the cuckoo's nest, and I was really starting to get scared. I was thinking shit, Leland's ass would be over soon to pick me up, and what I could say to get rid of that nigga without him going off on me. Just as I was getting ready to give him some excuse why he couldn't come in, his cell phone rang.

"Yeah, this is Stefan! Man, right now I am at my girl's crib. Oh all right, I will be there in 20 minutes." Stefan looked at me and said, "I am sorry baby, but something has come up in the office and I have to go. We can go out tomorrow night or catch a movie."

Stefan gave me a kiss on the forehead and walked across the street to his car. I had a big sigh of relieve and sat in my car for a minute watching him get in his car and pull off. I could not believe what had just gone down. When I came back to my right mind, I hurried up and closed the garage door, went in the house, locked the doors and set the alarm.

I thought Stefan was such a levelheaded man, and I had known him for a long time. He always had plenty of women chasing behind him, so why was he tripping? I got upstairs to the spare bedroom where I now slept, took my clothes off, and laid my gun on the dresser. I was about to run the water when I heard my cell phone ringing.

I grabbed my phone from my purse, but I missed the call. From the Caller ID, I saw it was Leland calling me. I called him back and when he answered, I started telling him about Stefan.

"Damn Paris, you must have really put it on that nigga to have him acting a monkey like that. I am scared of you girl, shit you might be too much for me. But on a serious note, you had better watch him, 'cause he sounds like he is crazy, and that nigga is DEA, too. Shit he is probably capable of anything."

"I know, right. Lucky asked me to go to the gun range with her in the morning, shit I might need to do that."

"Well I think you need to take her up on her offer because you want your skills to be tight just in case you need to defend yourself."

"Well let's hope I won't need to do all of that. I don't want to talk about Stefan anymore, how long will it be before you get here?"

"Calm down Paris, I will be there in 20 minutes, and I bet you are not even ready."

"That's 'cause I been on the phone talking to you!"

"Well let me let you go so you can be ready when I get there."

"Thank you! I will see you when you get here."

I quickly turned the shower on and as soon as the water got hot, I jumped in and washed the 'goods' giving myself a quick military shower. I grabbed the towel and dried off. I stood in my walk-in closet and looked for a pair of jeans. I grabbed the faded low-rider jeans and a cute red top, put my red matching Vickie's

Secrets bra and thong set on, threw on my jeans, top, and my red leather wedged heeled pumps. I pulled my hair back into a ponytail and fixed my face. I was just getting ready to put my earrings on when I heard my phone ringing.

"Hello?"

"Hey Paris, I am in your driveway," Leland said.

"Okay I am going to come down and let the garage up so you can pull in, and I will open the door for you."

"Alright!"

I looked in the mirror and finished putting on my Tiffany earrings with the matching necklace and bracelet, grabbed my purse and ran downstairs. I let the garage door up so Leland could pull in, and I stood in the door and watched him.

When he got out the car, I could smell his cologne. He was so fine, and I never remembered him being that good looking. Then again, I never paid him any attention before then. He was so tall and chocolate like a black ass Hershey bar, damn that was a fine brotha. Leland had the prettiest light chestnut brown eyes and the thickest black shiny eyebrows. They looked as if they were drawn on with an eyebrow pencil. *'Why in the world ain't none of these young girls up on this nigga,'* I thought, because he had it going on! *'Unless that nigga has something wrong with him, like a little ass dick or something.'* Damn I didn't see why his ass was still single.

Leland was young, fine, educated and owned his own business. He was the cream of the crop, and I was going to at least find out why he was interested in me. Not that I wasn't the shit myself, it was just that I was older than he was, and not to mention, his sister's best friend.

Leland stood there looking like he was a damn oak tree with all them damn muscles, and all I could do is smile. That was the first time in a long time that any man other then Trevor had my full attention, and it wasn't about sex. I was interested in getting to know Leland.

"Damn Paris, I am surprised you are ready. I like the red on you, it looks really good."

"Thanks Leland, I didn't realize you were this fine, damn boy you got a sista leaking!"

"Go head with that, you stupid as hell!"

"For real boy, you think I'm playin?"

"Whatever Paris, you ready to go to dinner?"

"Yeah, let's go, but first can I get a hug?"

"Oh my bad, I thought I would keep my hands to myself 'cause you are looking so good, I didn't want to get carried away by hugging you too tightly."

"Well I know your sister raised you right so a hug would be just a friendly greeting, so hug me and shut up!"

"Okay Ma, I am sorry for not showing my good home training skills."

With a fake smile on my face, I looked at Leland and said, "Funny! Let's go!"

Leland was sporting a black BMW coupe, with tan leather interior. He said that Lolita bought it for him when he graduated from college. That girl had spoiled the shit out of him, but I guessed as hard as they had it growing up, she only wanted to give him the best.

I opened the garage and we backed out onto the street. Leland was driving the shit out of that BMW, and I was just sitting in the passenger seat enjoying the view.

He was playing some rap old school, Biggie, Pac and that Jay Z song he recorded with Foxy Brown. I was bobbing my head to the music, and Leland was singing every verse in all of the songs that he played. He was extremely good looking and his hair was so pretty. He had a low cut Caesar with the deep waves. That seemed to be the style those days for the brothas that were trying to look professional.

His jeans were dark blue, almost black, and he had on a Sean John button down light pink shirt. He looked handsome and very confident for a young man, which I really liked that about him.

We arrived at The Palm, and I was shocked because I didn't think he was into that type of restaurant where you ordered the main dish and the sides were a la carte. But he did mention going to Morrison's so I guessed this was on the same level.

"Damn Leland, so it's like that huh? I didn't know you hung out in Phillips Place, or are you taking me here because someone told you about it?"

"A brotha can't get no credit these days, Paris. I am not some old busta ass nigga, I have been to all of the fine dining places in Charlotte and Lake Norman, so I do know where to take a woman that I am really feeling on a date."

"I didn't mean it like that, but I see you do have class about yourself and I really like that."

"Nothin *but* class. But don't get it twisted, 'cause a nigga can go get it if he got to. I still got some street in me, and my sister spent good money on martial arts and boxing lessons so a nigga can defend himself too."

"Well I just got myself a straight hood, gangster ass business-man. I ain't mad at you, do your thug thistle boy!"

Leland turned into the Phillips Place parking lot and drove in front of The Palm. The valet guy opened my door first and walked around to the driver side. Leland handed him the keys and we walked towards the restaurant.

Leland said, "Paris you know you are crazy right?"

"Yeah, I know!"

Leland slipped his arms around my waist, and it felt so comfortable. I didn't know if I should pull away from him or just enjoy the moment. I was thinking about Trevor and how it wasn't that long ago that I had buried him, but I was enjoying being with Leland. Was I wrong for what I was feeling? I just knew that I felt as though he was my angel of comfort. Jackie always said that God had a ram in the bush, meaning he always had something better waiting for you. I thought Leland was the comfort that I needed. He made me laugh, and he was such a gentleman. I just couldn't believe no one had snatched him up, because he was so gorgeous.

"Paris, are you okay, what are you thinking about? You look like you are a million miles away."

"I am okay, I was just thinking about Trevor. I really miss him Leland, but I am glad that you are here, because for some reason you make me feel comfortable when I am around you."

"Thanks Paris, I think we can be good friends starting out, because I know that it's hard for you to think about a relationship right now. I am not here to pressure you, because I really want to get to know you, and we can take our time doing just that."

We walked into the restaurant and the waitress showed us to our table. Leland pulled out my chair and before he sat down, he gave me a kiss on the forehead, which sent a chill through my whole body. I thought, *'what the hell was that and where did it come from?'* That nigga was sexy as hell and I was damn near melting in my chair.

Leland ordered from the menu for both of us. "Paris you don't mind if I order for you do you?"

"No, let's see if you can order what I would like."

"Okay, if you don't like it, you can order for yourself, because I want you to be happy."

I gave him the *'Negro please'* look. "Whatever Leland, just order the damn food!"

Leland looked at the menu. He chose the wine first and then our meals and I just sat and listened to him place our order. I heard the waiter say, "Good choice of wine sir." I smiled at Leland, because he had chosen everything from the menu that I would have chosen for myself.

What didn't this man know? He was so well-rounded and we sat and talked for hours about him and Lolita and how they struggled to make ends meet. I had a wonderful adult conversation with this man, and he could talk about anything.

By the time we finished our meal, we both were good and tipsy. I didn't want to be fas', but I was horny as hell. It was probably just the wine, but I looked across the table at Leland's fine chocolate ass, and I wanted to fuck the shit out of him right there at the table.

Leland asked, "Why are you looking at me like that Paris, do I have food stuck in my teeth?"

"No, you just look like a big chocolate lolly pop, and I want to get to the chewing center."

"Paris, be a good girl. That wine has you trippin and believe me, once you go there you are not going to want to go back. Not that I wouldn't want you to, but we are supposed to be taking our time, remember?"

"Yeah, I remember. Can't I just imagine being on top of you, riding like a cowgirl into the sunset?" I said.

Leland said, "I would love that, but I want to make sure you are not drinking when I lay you down, because I am playing for keeps. I will provide all the high you need when I am between those sexy soft ass thighs of yours, and I need you to be fully alert when I do."

"Alright now, boy! I am really going to enjoy getting to know you. Now let's get out of here and go do something fun, before I start undressing you with my eyes and mind again."

"Come on, let's go. Waiter, can you please bring me the check and have valet to bring the car around?"

Leland pulled my chair out, and when I stood up, he grabbed me and kissed me. I think my freakin toes curled up as if I was in one of those love story movies. I promise my ass was 'bout to nut!

Leland said, "Damn Paris, I am glad we are going to be friends for right now."

"Yeah, me too!"

We walked outside, and the valet had the passenger side door opened for me, so I got in the car. Leland walked around to the driver's side and the valet handed him the keys. We started to go to the movies, but we headed to South Park mall instead.

I didn't need anything, but we just were going to walk around and look in the store for a while and talk. We got to the mall and Leland had them valet park his car, and I was thinking this nigga was spoiled, because he couldn't even park his own car at the damn mall.

Leland said that he used valet when they had it, because he hated looking for a parking space when he didn't have to, and he didn't have to remember where he parked when it was time to go. I was okay with that, if that was what he wanted to do, but I just as well would park my own shit. But it was cool, because we were right at the door of the mall.

We stayed in there for about an hour. I bought a purse out of the Coach store and a leather wallet to match. Leland bought a couple of Timberland shirts and a pair of boots to match one of the shirts. I was ready to get out of there, so we stopped at Victoria Secrets and Leland brought me a whole bunch of shit out of there to save for when he 'laid me down', as he would say.

We left the mall and waited for the valet to bring us the car. When we got in the car, Leland said that he wanted to stop by his crib, since we were on his side of town.

We turned onto Sharon Road going towards Uptown. We went through two lights and turned on Wendover, and then we pulled into this driveway with this big ass half-circle cobblestone road. The house had the big landscaped trees and colorful flowers, and it was a three-story house with a basement and three-car garage entrance on the side.

What the fuck was Leland's young ass doing with a house like that, and on the Southside too? That shit had to be in the 300,000 dollars, tops. I knew he was doing it big, but damn, not that big.

"Paris I know what you're thinking, why do I need a house this big? But this was Lolita's first house when she opened her spas in Europe and it's paid for. Lolita didn't want to sell it, so she told me that she was going to give it to me, along with the car, for doing so well in college. I graduated top of my class, and that made my sister proud. She has worked really hard and I didn't have any money to buy her a lot of nice things, so I just did my best in school to make her proud. I stayed out of trouble and kept positive people in my corner at all times, but I mostly spent time around older cats that knew the game, and listened to their mistakes so I could try to do better and be a better man than my father ever was. I want my wife to be proud of me, and I want to love her to death, not beat her to death like my father did my mother."

I almost started crying listening to him talk about his past. I didn't know that Lolita had gone through so much. She had told me some of it, but I didn't know how deep things really were. Leland was just so proud of her; you could hear it in his voice when he spoke of his sister. The truth of the matter was that she loved that boy to death, and she was equally as proud of him and all that he had achieved.

"Leland I am sorry that your father did that to your mom, but you are not like him, so you don't have to worry about treating anyone like that."

"Thanks Paris. I'm sorry, I didn't mean to go on about my sad story. I hope I didn't bore you to death, I just feel so comfortable with you like I can tell you anything and you won't judge me."

"Like my friend Jackie would say, 'Ain't nobody perfect but Jesus.'"

"Amen! Let's go in the house for a minute, you don't mind do you?"

"Well seeing that you drove your black ass over here without asking, I guess I don't."

"Paris get yo' smart ass out the car for I whip you with my belt."
"Please, don't threaten me with a good time!"

We started laughing and walked onto the porch of Leland's house. Once inside the foyer, there was all-marble with cream and brown swirls. There was a winding staircase in the middle of the room, with a huge chandelier hanging from the ceiling. On the left, there was a family room with a big screen TV, and Leland and I went in that room and sat on the plush leather sofa. We sat there and talked, and then he began rubbing my back and I laid my head on his lap, because it was feeling so good.

I closed my eyes for a moment and when I woke up four hours had passed. I looked at Leland and he was sleep too.

"Leland wake up, you need to take me home."

Leland laid there and in his sleepy voice he said, "Paris why don't you stay here tonight? I will take you home in the morning."

I didn't know why I agreed to staying with him, but I did, and we got up and walked across the hallway to the other side of the foyer to the Master bedroom. Leland gave me one of his t-shirts to sleep in, we got in the bed, and that shit felt like I was laying on clouds. Leland gave me a kiss goodnight, and we just snuggled up next to each other. I fell asleep as soon as I laid my head on his chest.

※※※※※※※※※※※※※※※※※

Lolita was laying in her bed, thinking about her little brother, and how all her hard work had paid off, when she heard her cell phone ringing. She looked at her watch and it was 11pm at night. "Who the fuck is this calling me from a restricted number?" she said aloud. When she answered the phone, that same voice that had her shaken spoke into the phone.

"Hello Lolita, this is Raymond. Why haven't you returned my calls? I told you that I wanted to see you, now that I'm out of jail. You know it was a rough life in there for the past ten years."

"Raymond, what the fuck do you want? I can't believe they let you out after all the shit you did, from selling drugs, running hoes, gambling, stealing, you name it. Your ass should have gotten Life. Now what the fuck do you want with me?"

"Now Lolita, is that any way to talk to yo' baby daddy?"

Those words hit Lolita in her soul like a fucking ton of bricks. "You fucking bastard, how dare you bring that shit up to me! I was fucking fifteen years old, you fucking pedophile. Your ass should have got Life in that fucking prison."

"Honey, calm the fuck down. Do you want to know where your little girl is or not?"

Lolita sat there with tears welling up in her eyes, and she thought to herself, *'This shit is so fucking wrong, but I knew it would resurface, just as things were going so good with Leland and now this fucker wants to ruin it.'*

Raymond repeated, "Well Miss 'rich girl,' do you want to know or not? It will cost you 25,000 for the information, but you can afford right?"

"Go to hell Raymond, I haven't known this long, so what makes you think I give a fuck where she is now?"

"Oh come on Lolita, this is big Ray you talking to, and I know you thought about it several times. But just like you do everything else, you pushed it deep in the back of your mind. You want to know, so meet me, and I will give you the information."

"Raymond, why should I believe you know anything about where she is? You are such a bastard, just leave me alone."

"Meet me tomorrow at the Hilton in University area, and I will give you a copy of her adoption papers. Don't forget to bring the money."

Raymond hung up the phone before Lolita could respond to him and she sat there with the phone in her hand and cried like a baby. She decided to meet him and just get the information to check to see if her baby girl was being taken care of, and not in some fucked up family. She at least owed her that.

Chapter Nineteen

Stefan had been on a stakeout all night and he was ready to get out of there, because he wanted to see me, and he didn't know why I wasn't answering my phone. Stefan left the stakeout and drove by my house to see if my night light was on in the guest room I slept in. When he arrived, he saw that the entire house was dark, except for the light over the garage.

"What the fuck! Where the hell is Paris, and why isn't she at home?"

Stefan stood in front of my house talking to himself, and then he walked up to the side door and took a small key from his pocket. He turned the key once, and the door opened. Stefan walked inside of the house and he quickly turned the alarm system off.

He had gotten the password by watching me put the code in. I guessed he learned that shit in DEA School.

Stefan walked around the house. He went through my nightstand drawers, and when he looked up at the light, he saw the small camera he had planted in the button on the lampshade.

"Good it's still in place. Let's see if she had anyone in her bedroom." Stefan checked the actives recorded on the camera, and he only saw me in the room alone, but he still wasn't convinced that I wasn't seeing somebody else, when the fact was, I really wasn't seeing him either.

Stefan looked in the bathroom to see if there was any evidence of another man being there, but he didn't find anything, so he decided to leave. He had to get back to the stakeout before he was discovered missing from his post and besides, his boy was covering for him, and he didn't want to jeopardize his friend's job.

Stefan put everything back to the way it was. He then looked at the picture of Trevor and I that he found in the nightstand drawer.

"I am glad that I shot you, because you should have never spent any time with Paris. I love her, and she is going to my wife."

Stefan put the picture back in the drawer and left the room. He was mad as hell that I wasn't home, but he promised himself that he would not let anything stop him from being with me. Stefan set the alarm to the house and went out the same way he came in. Once in the car, he noticed his phone was beeping. The message light on the phone was lit, so he opened the message. It was his boy telling him to hurry back because their supervisor was coming to the stakeout location in 30 minutes.

Stefan started the car and headed back to the stakeout point. He dialed his partner's number and when he answered the phone, he told him that he would be there in 15 minutes. Stefan put the red siren light in the window and sped down the street.

Cars pulled over to get out of his way, but he still had thoughts of me in his mind.

"Tomorrow I will confront her about not being at home. Better yet, I will just wait in the house for her to get home."

◇◇◇◇◇◇◇◇◇◇◇◇◇◇◇◇◇◇◇◇◇◇

Tuesday morning, Leland was in the kitchen cooking breakfast and he thought to himself, *'Damn I haven't cooked breakfast for a woman in a long time, especially one that I didn't get no ass from. What the hell is really going on?'* The phone in the kitchen rang, so Leland put the pan on the back eye of the stove and walked over to pick up the phone. "What's good man, you calling 'cause you took care of that little problem for me, or what?"

"Leland man the shit is done, and you won't see nor hear from that trick ass cousin of yours again. She is living in little Tijuana with my boy Lupe, and she is really getting her trick on now, 'cause Lupe will beat a bitch ass if she don't bring him no money."

"Fo' sho nigga, that's good man. You did your boy right on that tip, 'cause that bitch was trying to ruin a good thang me and big sis had going, and yo' nigga wasn't haven't that shit."

"I know man, but it's a done deal and that bitch don't have no identification to say she is a US citizen, so she can't ever come back here. I spotted her ass trickin' off on Statesville Road by the truck stop, just like you said she would be doing. That bitch didn't know what hit her when my boys and me pulled up. We snatched that ass in the car and deported that bitch with Lupe when he left. Lupe had that ass hyped up on drugs, and she didn't know what the fuck was going on. He took that bitch on a plane to Cali and that was all she wrote."

"Cool, I am glad you handled the biz for me, and you know I got your package for a job well done. Holla at your boy tomorrow for the pick-up spot. Alright man, I am trying to cook up some food so let me get at you later."

"Paris must be over there because that's the only woman I know you would be cooking for, especially since she got your nose all open." "Nigga you know I ain't gone even front, I am really feeling her. But she is sleeping right now, so I got to get off the phone with you and finish cooking breakfast before she wakes up."

"Boy yo' ass is whipped, and I bet you didn't even hit it."

"Whatever nigga, bye!"

I woke up and heard Leland talking on the phone. I smelled food cooking and it made me hungry. I got out of the bed and went into the bathroom, opened one of the drawers, and I found a tube of toothpaste and a three-pack of new toothbrushes. Now unless he just bought in bulk, he must have had company over often. I took one out of the package and used it to brush my teeth. I heard Leland in there singing some gospel song and I was impressed; he could sing. I finished brushing my teeth, still wearing the t-shirt he gave me the night before, with my hair pulled back in a ponytail. I walked into the kitchen, and I saw Leland cooking eggs, bacon, waffles and hash browns. He didn't notice me standing there watching him cook and sing. It was so cute, and he was so handsome standing there in his pajamas pants and wife-beater.

"Good morning, Leland!"

He turned around and looked at me with the biggest grin on his face.

"Well good morning Sunshine, did you sleep well last night? I thought you might be hungry, so I cooked you some breakfast."

"Yes, I slept like a baby, and I am very hungry. Thanks for cooking breakfast for me, that was very sweet of you Leland."

"It's not a problem, anything for you Paris, and I mean that."

"Well I am going to have to cook dinner for you this week. Would you like to come over to my place for a nice quiet dinner?"

"I would love that, just let me know what time is good for you, and I will be there."

"Okay, it's a date!"

"Oh so will this be our second date, Paris?"

"Yes Leland, this will be our second date."

I smiled at him, and as we sat down to eat our breakfast, his house phone rang.

"Excuse me Paris." Leland answered the phone, "Hello? Hey big sis, what's going on with you, and how's work?"

"What's up Leland, everything is good. What are you doing? I was thinking about stopping by to see you," Lolita said.

"Well sis I would love to see you too, but I got to run an errand first. But I will call you when I get home."

"Cool, I will see you later, and don't forget to call me either, 'cause you know how you do. I want to talk to you about something."

"Okay, I won't forget, see you later."

I asked, "Leland was that Lolita? Why didn't you tell her that I was here?" In my southern bell voice with my hands on my hips I said, "You shamed of me or something."

We both started laughing and Leland looked at me with this serious look on his face.

"Paris you make me feel like I've known you forever, and I don't know how to handle everything that is going on in my heart right now. I want to take off running with everything that is inside of me, because I feel like a schoolboy, as if it's my first time being in love. I am not even sure if I can say that, but it's the way I feel, and I am going to be honest with you, it's scary."

I stopped dead in my tracks because I was feeling the same way, but I felt like it was too soon, because Trevor was not even dead six months yet, and I knew people would talk. I didn't know what to say to Leland, because he just broke that thing down to me like no man had ever stepped to me before. And to admit to being afraid of love was turning me on even more.

I didn't know what kind of game he was trying to run but I was going to watch his actions from then on to see if he was being real with me.

I just gave him a hug and held him in my arms for a minute. "Leland, I am feeling the same way, and it's really tripping me out, because Trevor was the only man I had loved like that. So I just have to be sure this is real between us before I give myself to you totally."

"I know Paris, and that's not what I am asking you to do. I just want us to spend as much time with each other as we can before we let anyone else in our world."

"That's fine with me Leland."

"Cool, then that's what we will do."

I finished eating breakfast and had Leland take me home.

Chapter Twenty

Lolita was on her way to the office when her phone rang. "Hey Leland, what's up with you?"

"Nothing much sis, I was just calling you back as I promised I would do. I had an errand to run and now that I am finished, I was calling to see what your day was looking like."

"Well lil' bro, I am headed to the office, why don't you come out here and get you a spa treatment?"

"I just might do that, but I got to go to the shop and put in some time today, because we are very busy these days, and I have a couple of my boys coming to get their regular cuts."

"That's cool. What time do you think you will be done, because I got some shit I need to holla at you about?"

"What's up sis? You sound serious, do I need to cancel my appointments today or what?"

"Naw, it ain't that serious. I will get with you when you are done at the shop. I am going to go into the office and get some paperwork done, just call me later."

"You sure everything is alright, 'cause you know I could come right now if you really need me to?"

"Leland its cool, I am good, just call me when you done."

"Okay sis, I will, later."

"Later!"

Lolita hung up the phone with Leland and she was wondering how he was going to take it when she told him about the baby she had and how her boyfriend at the time sold her. She was hoping he understood that she didn't know any better at the time, because she was just young. Lolita had forgotten all about that shit. She had buried it so deep inside of her, but when that nigga got out of jail and called her, it brought back every memory of that delivery that she had thought was gone for good.

Lolita said aloud to herself, "What was I thinking, damn. It wasn't my fault this nigga had me all wrapped up in him and I thought I was so in love at the time. I would have done anything his ass said for me to do. He was twenty-five and I was fifteen. What the fuck did I know at that age? But circumstance will make your ass grow up quick, because after that shit, I made them niggas take care of me or get the fuck on.

"I wasn't fuckin for free, and my little brother and I had to eat and have a place to stay. I had us in a nice apartment and Leland went to a school that was majority white. Fuck that, we weren't going to stay in the projects, that shit was out, so I had to make it happen."

As Lolita drove down the street talking to herself, she was not paying attention to the speed limit. So when she looked in her rearview mirror, she saw the police turning onto the street that she was driving. He was sitting in the cut when she passed him doing 60 in a 35. He had already clocked her, and he was coming up behind her now with his lights flashing.

Lolita pulled over, and the office got out of his car and walked up to her window. When she let the window down, she handed him her license and registration.

"I'm sorry officer, I wasn't paying attention to the speed limit. I was thinking about my girlfriend, she's in the hospital, because her man beat her up, and I was trying to get there to see her."

Now Lolita knew she was lying her ass off, but she was trying to get out of paying another damn ticket.

"Miss, you were doing 25 miles over the speed limit, and this is a residential area. I understand that you are upset, but you will have to slow down. I am going to give you a warning this time, but you need to slow down and pay attention to the speed limit."

"Yes sir, thank you so much."

The officer went back to his squad car and wrote some notes, as Lolita pulled off slowly, trying to drive the speed limit, which felt like crawling to her because she liked to drive fast.

Lolita arrived at her office and when she went in the back room, she went in the safe, got the 25,000 dollars, and put it into a large black leather bag.

"I am going to meet this nigga, and if he has the information, I will give him the money, just like he don't mean shit to me. This money ain't nothing, 'cause I got a fucking money tree, and there is much more where this came from."

Money was never an object for Lolita, ever since she graduated from college, and even before she opened her first spa, she was stackin money. The only thing she promised herself was that she would never go hungry or without money again.

Lolita sat in the office at her desk and called Raymond. "I will be at the spot in two hours, have the documents and don't fuck with me, because I will have my nine with me."

Raymond said, "Now, Lolita, is all that necessary? And besides, who taught your ass how to properly shoot a gun anyway?"

"Raymond just *be* there, and don't fucking be late either."

"Okay, damn!"

Three hours had passed, and Raymond's ass still had not shown up. Lolita had sat there waiting for him, and she was so mad at the fact that she had to call Leland and let him know she was going to be late going to his place.

"Where is this nigga, I am going to kill him. I should have known better than to trust his lying ass to be here."

Lolita started her car and was getting ready to pull off, when she saw Raymond walking towards the spot that he told her to meet him. For the most part, he looked the same. He had aged some, but his body was still built. Probably because he had nothing else to do in prison *but* lift weights.

She saw him walking. He was coming across the bridge and a guy was jogging passed him when Lolita saw Raymond collapse on the bridge.

She thought to herself, *'What the fuck is he doing, now? Did he trip over something, or what?'*

People started walking towards him, so Lolita got out of her car and walked closer to the bridge. Then the woman that was standing there started screaming, "He's been shot, call 911!"

Lolita said, "What the fuck is going on," and when she got closer to him, she could see the blood running down the bridge like a river. Anyone could have killed that nigga, because he turned so many families' little sisters out on drugs and the streets. It could have been any one of them getting revenge on his ass.

Lolita looked, but she didn't see a package on that nigga, and he had a gun. So he wasn't planning on given her shit. That bastard was going to try to jack her.

It was daylight, and whoever shot him used a silencer. Lolita turned to walk back to her car, when the police arrived and started clearing the place out.

Lolita got in the car and thought aloud, "This nigga never knew where my little girl was, that bastard. He was just trying to get money from me."

Lolita sat in the car and gathered her thoughts. The tears started to roll down her cheeks. She couldn't help but cry, because all she could see in her mind was the day that her little girl was born, and how she only saw her when they first took her from her womb. The doctor didn't even put the baby in her arms, because Lolita was giving her up, and they didn't want her to become attached. Raymond never told her anything when she was released from the hospital, he just told her to act as if nothing ever happened, and she did.

Lolita wiped her eyes and called Leland on the phone. "Leland, hey, are you home? Because some shit just went down with me, and I need to talk to you about all of it. I need to tell you something that I have not told anyone. How long are you going to be at home? I can be there in 30 minutes."

"Lo, you all right, you sound bad, are you crying? Whatever it is, it will be okay. Just come over, and we will sort it out together like we have always done."

Lolita's voice was shaking as the tears from her eyes flowed like raindrops, "Baby bro I am okay, and we are going to be okay. And I will be there soon so we can talk."

"Okay, sis I will be here waiting for you."

Lolita hung up the phone and headed to 85S to her brother's house in South Park.

Chapter Twenty-One

    It had been three days since I spent the night with Leland, and we had been on the phone until three or four in the morning talking about everything from the foods we liked, to growing up and all the fears and pains of our childhood. It seemed like we were meant for each other, and it was strange, but I did not feel guilty about being with him. I thought about the upcoming weekend. We planned to have dinner together and watch some movies. Leland liked most of the same movies, and we enjoyed each other's company. I had not had sex with him; we had only kissed each other a lot. But he told me that he was sure he could satisfy me, and he would do his best to make sure I was pleased.

Now that was my kind of man, not selfish, and wanting to make sure his woman was taken care of. Oh shit, did I say 'his woman?' Boy, how in the hell was I going to tell Lolita that I was in love with her baby brother? She was going to kill both of us, but we were not telling a soul until the relationship was stamped with the official seal.

I was so excited about him coming over to have dinner with me. That was going to be the last time I would be having anything in that house, because I had sold it to the Woodlocks, and my new house right outside of Concord Mills was going to be ready in two weeks. I had started packing up things that I wanted to take to the new house myself, because I had a moving company that was going to pack up the rest of the house. I had given a lot of things away, and I gave all of Trevor's things to his parents and cousins.

I walked downstairs to put the boxes I had packed in the garage when I heard the phone ringing. I quickly sat the box on the kitchen table and I grabbed the cordless phone from the wall.

"Hello? Hey Lucky, girl what's going on with you?"

"Hey Paris, I was calling to see if you wanted to go with me to the gun range? I am going at noon, if you'd like to join me, and we can have lunch afterwards."

"You know what, that sounds like a good idea. I will meet you there at noon. What is the address? Okay…got it written down. I will see you there. How's things coming along, did you get a dog yet?"

"Naw, I am going to try to find a Jack Russell Terrier. I only went to one pet store so far, but I am going to look again this weekend."

"Cool, I think you will like having the dog around for company."

"Yeah, that's what everyone keeps telling me, so I guess I will see if that will help.

By the way, I spoke to Jackson the other day, and he said that we are going to Cancun or some place like that for a little reunion. Have you spoke to Johnny?"

"Yeah I did, and we are planning a trip, but I think we are getting a big suite, and they are getting one that connects to ours. I am going to call him tonight to get all of the details and let you know what's up. I think we are going in two weeks, so just be ready to have a good time, okay?"

"Well I have a few things to get done, and I will see you at the gun range."

"Paris, bring your 'A' game 'cause a sister been practicing. Shit, I can get a job with the FBI as a sharpshooter, that's how good I am." "Ain't that some shit, well I think I can put a bullet in a nigga's ass quick, but I am going to work on my skills too, so I will see you soon."   Lucky and I laughed at our conversation, but even though she was laughing, she was serious about learning self-defense. Lucky took self-defense classes every Monday and Wednesday nights. Detective Ryan had suggested that she go to the classes offered by the crime prevention department.

Lucky had learned so much and she was coping with the kidnapping everyday with sessions in her therapist's office. We were proud of her progress, which could have been much worse, given her family's history of women losing their minds.

I hung up the phone with Lucky and went to put the box I was carrying into the garage.

I was in the garage putting the box on the shelf, and I opened the garage door to put some trash out, and when the door came up, Stefan was standing there.

"Hey Paris. Why have you been avoiding my phone calls? You seeing someone else Paris, because if you are, I will fuck the two of you up."

I was scared as hell, thinking to myself, *'what in the world is wrong with this nigga?'*

"Stefan what are you talking about, I told you that I had to go out of town on business, and I was packing some of my things because I sold the house. I am going to move in with Lolita for a little while until I find what I want."

Even though I was lying my ass off, I didn't want him to know the real reason I wasn't calling his ass just yet.

"No Paris! I think you are trying to leave me. Didn't I tell you how much I loved you?"

"Stefan, I know what you told me, but I am not over Trevor, and I asked for time, but you refuse to give it to me."

Stefan was so angry, because just the mention of Trevor's name had his entire facial expression change.

"I DON'T FUCKING WANT TO HEAR THAT NIGGA'S NAME AGAIN! I told you that he wasn't shit, but you still insist on bring him up to me. Can't you see he never loved you, and that's why he is dead, and I am standing here with you."

I turned and walked back into the garage to put the trash down, and I was looking around to see if I saw anything that I could hit that nigga in the head with, because he had gone off the deep end.

Just as I sat the trash bag down, Stefan grabbed my arm and twisted it behind my back. He looked deep into my eyes and I could see that he was mad as hell. I had never seen that side of him, and I was scared for real.

"Stefan let me go, what in the hell is wrong with you? Get your damn hands off of me."

Stefan pulled me closer to him. He stuck his tongue down my throat, and he tried to grab my breast with his other hand. I pulled away from him by twisting my body in the opposite direction, and he snatched my arm back and damn near pulled it out of socket.

Paris Love

Stefan yelled, "Come here! Why in the hell are you running from me, you act as if you don't love me anymore."

"Stefan what are you talking about, I told you several times that I wasn't interested in a relationship but you just won't listen. Just leave me alone."

Why in the hell did I say that? That nigga blanked on me. He grabbed me and started trying to kiss me and pull my pants down.

"I love you Paris, you belong to me, and that is why I had to kill Trevor. He walked around like his shit didn't stink. I played cards with him, and he was so fucking arrogant, until I couldn't wait to smoke his ass. You never should have been with him, and I am here to take care of you now. With him gone, I killed two birds with one stone. I revenged my sister's death and I took you away from him."

I was in shock because I did not have a clue that Stefan was that crazy, and he had just admitted to me that he was the one who shot Trevor. And he thought that I would want to be with him after that? He must've been out of his damn mind.

I wrestled myself away from him and ran towards the door to the house. I got up one-step, and I could feel Stefan's hand grab my foot and drag me back down the step. I flipped over and started to kick him in the face with my other foot. He grabbed it and slammed my back into the steps and he ripped my top.

I started to scream, so he put his hand over my mouth. I started kicking and kicked him in his nuts as hard as I could. He slumped over grabbing his nuts and I elbowed him to the side of his face. I jumped up and ran towards the street, when I saw the crowbar lying on the ground. I grabbed it and just as I reached the garage door, it started to come down. I turned around and I saw Stefan pushing the button to let the garage door down. I backed up against the garage door and Stefan came towards me. He tried to grab my arm, but I pulled away from him and swung around and hit him it the face with the crowbar.

He grabbed his face, "Paris no!" And before I knew it, I swung and hit him with the crowbar right across his temple. The blood gushed out onto my car window and I just kept hitting him over and over again. When I finally stopped, he was slumped down on the car with his head bashed and blood running down his face.

I dropped the crowbar and fell onto my knees. My hands were shaking and the blood was everywhere. I was screaming and screaming. I ran and opened the garage door, ran out on the sidewalk and yelled for help. "Somebody help, help me please, I think I killed him!"

My next-door neighborhood ran outside, "Paris what happened? I'm calling 911!"

∞∞∞∞∞∞∞∞∞∞∞∞∞∞∞∞∞

The police and ambulance arrived in front of the house. I sat on the steps crying and trying to tell the officer what happened. I told the police officer what Stefan had said and how he had been stalking me, and when they searched the house, they founded the camera in the button on the lampshade. I told them that he admitted to killing Trevor, and that he said Trevor had killed his sister by giving up the location of where she was staying. The police called Stefan's office at the DEA to check to see if Stefan did have a sister that was under the witness protection program. By that time, Lolita and Lucky had driven up and they were tripping.

Lucky said, "Paris, I waited for you to show up and I didn't hear from you. I called your phone several times and then I called Lolita. I told her that something was wrong, girl what happened?"

I just could not stop crying and the police told me that I would have to come to the station to give my statement. Lolita and Lucky followed us to the police station and waited for me.

Lolita said, "Lucky, I knew Stefan's ass was crazy, and when Paris told him that she didn't' want to get married, I knew he would be tripping."

Lucky said, "I knew that too!"

Lolita looked at her cell phone and saw that she had a missed call from Leland. "Lucky I am going to step outside and call my brother, come get me when Paris is done."

Lolita told Leland everything that happened and before she could finish, he told her that he was on his way to the station. Now when Lolita hung up the phone she was wondering why Leland felt the need to come to the station, but she just brushed it off because she figured he was worried about her, since she and I were like sisters.

When Lolita walked back into the station, Lucky and I were walking towards the door.

Lolita asked, "What happened Paris, did they take your statement?"

"Yeah they did, and when they called the DEA office and spoke to Stefan's commanding officer, he told the policeman that Stefan had some problems in the past of stalking and threatening his ex-girlfriend, but he had went to therapy for awhile and seemed to be doing much better. The police officer told me that they were going to check deeper into my story, especially about Trevor's death and the death of Stefan's sister to see if the two are connected. He told me that I was free to go, and that he would contact me if he had any further questions."

Lolita and Lucky gave me a hug, because I was still a little shaken up over the whole thing. I never knew that Stefan was that damn crazy.

Lucky said, "Paris, girl I told you that his ass was crazy, and I know how to spot crazy a mile away, believe me. Ron's ass had taught me a very valuable lesson, believe that!"

We left the police station and headed to Lucky's car, when I saw Leland pull up, and I was wondering why he was there.

I asked, "Lolita is that Leland parking his car over there?"

Lolita looked in the direction that I was pointing and she said, "Yeah that's him, how in the hell did he get here so fast?"

"'So fast,' how did he know I was here, and please tell me you didn't tell him what happened?"

"Well I did, because he called me while we were waiting for you in the police station."

I was thinking to myself *'how in the hell are we going to act as if we have not been seeing each other,'* because I could see the worried look on his face before he even got out of the car. I had told Leland about Stefan, but damn, I didn't want to tell him this shit.

Leland walked up to us and he looked at me with that *'Are you okay baby'* look on his face, and I gave him the *'Yes, and I will talk to you later about it'* look.

Leland gave each of us a hug and he said, "Are you okay, Paris?"

I said, "Yes Leland, but you didn't have to come to the police station. Didn't Lolita tell you what happened?"

"Yeah, but she made it sound like you had killed Stefan, is he dead?"

"I think so, but I didn't stay around to find out. He was rushed to the hospital in critical condition, but I don't know his status."

Leland said, "Well he had no business stalking you and trying to force himself on you. I am glad he didn't hurt you, because--"

Just then, I looked at Leland and shook my head. He was getting ready to say something that would have opened up a conversation that neither one of us was ready to deal with just yet.

Paris Love

Leland understood what I was telling him, and he just changed the subject, "So where you guys going now?"

Lolita said, "We are going to go to Paris' house because she has to get the rest of her things to bring to my house. She has Three Men and a Truck coming in the morning to pack up all her things and move them into her new house."

Leland said, "Well I am going to come with you guys to help get her things, if that is okay."

Lolita said, "That's cool, we will need some help with the heavy boxes. Lucky and Paris, y'all cool with Leland coming to help out, right?"

I said, "Lolita I don't mind, but I am feeling a little sad about this whole thing with Stefan. I tried my best to be honest with him but he wasn't hearing me. I shouldn't have got with him, and I wouldn't have had to attack him like I did."

Lolita said, "Paris please, that nigga was crazy before you got with him. You heard what the DEA officer said about that nigga having a past history of stalking women. Shit you *should* have beat his damn brains out, if you ask me."

I said, "Lolita you are crazy. But I still can't help feeling bad about what I did to him, but he would not let me go, and he was trying to rape me."

That made Leland mad, and he just looked at me with those pretty ass eyes of his. Leland said, "Paris don't feel bad, the nigga is still breathing, so he is lucky to still have breath. Because I would have killed him if I was there."

I said, "I know, let's just go, because this was enough drama for one day, and I just want to keep myself busy so I won't think about his crazy ass."

We got in the car and headed to my house to finish packing the things that I was taking with me over to Lolita's house. When we

Skeletons, Deceit to the Bone

got to the house, all of my neighbors were standing outside. I got out of the car, and they were all asking if I was okay. The man who lived two doors down from me told me that he saw Stefan going in my house, and he thought that I had given him a key, because he saw him go in the side door. Some of my neighbors were telling me that they saw Stefan's truck parked outside of my house on several occasions.

I was tripping, because that nigga had been stalking my ass for real, and I didn't even know it. And when the police officer said that they found a camera in the lampshade, it really scared me. All kinds of thoughts were going through my mind about that nigga.

Damn, you just never know people like you think you do. I was glad I found out before anything bad happened, and I was glad I hadn't invited Leland over, because it could have been a lot worse if that crazy nigga saw us together. Shit, I was so glad for that!

I finished talking to my neighbors and went in the house. Leland, Lolita, and Lucky were in the living room looking around for boxes that I had already packed.

I said, "The boxes that I am taking with me are in the guest bedroom and the majority of them are clothes and shoes."

Leland looked at me with that cute ass smile. "I knew you were going to make sure you took all your clothes and shoes, you never know what you might need to wear huh?"

I said, "Boy shut up!"

I could see Lolita looking at us strangely, and I knew she was wondering what the hell was up with us. But I just played it off and kept getting my stuff together.

About an hour later, we finally finished getting everything in Lucky's truck and me and Leland's car, locked up the house, and headed over to Lolita's crib.

Two weeks had passed and I was coping with a lot. As it turned out, Stefan suffered major brain damage because of the blow to his temple, but he didn't die, which I was happy about. I wasn't trying to kill the nigga, but I wanted to hurt him bad enough to get him off me.

The investigation concluded that Stefan had killed Trevor and he had a serious problem with reality. The police searched his apartment and found pictures of me in my bedroom that I didn't know he took and pictures of Trevor with the FBI on the night of his death. They also found the gun that was used in Trevor's death, which was hidden in the floor in Stefan's apartment.

The apartment was in someone else's name, because Stefan had a house that he lived in too. I guessed the apartment was where he did his dirt, but all charges against me were dropped, and because of Stefan's brain damage, he was unable to stand trial. So he served time in a nursing home.

I was ready for the whole thing to be over and besides that, I had a date with Leland. I had just finished moving into my new house and Leland was coming over for dinner. I had ordered Chinese, because I had not pulled the pots out of the boxes yet, and I was also tired from working earlier in the week. I called Leland on the phone to see if he had left the house. We had not left each other's sight ever since the shit that went down with Stefan, and Leland made me promise that I would call him whenever I got in the house, so he would know that I was okay.

I was in love with him, and I couldn't help myself. I had gone to Trevor's gravesite to place fresh flowers on his grave, and I told him all about Leland. I told him that I loved him and it seemed as though God had sent me a special gift to help heal my pain from my loss love with him. I told Trevor that I hoped he had peace and that he understood that I would always love him, and my memory of him would always live in my heart.

I wanted Trevor to be okay with my new love for Leland, and when I left the gravesite, I felt a peace come over me, and now I could love Leland freely.

The phone was ringing and Leland answered on the last ring.

I said, "Baby what you doing? I have already ordered the Chinese food so I hope you are on your way."

"Calm down Paris, I am in the car, and I will be there in 20 minutes."

I had a big smile on my face, "Well hurry up, because I miss you and I can't wait to see you."

"Okay baby, I will be there shortly. Just have my kiss waiting for me."

"I will have more than that waiting, so hurry up and get that chocolate ass over here!"

"Yes, Honey!"

We got off the phone and I started putting the final touches on everything. I had the Goose and juice and a bottle of Crown Royal, Gin and Peach schnapps to make a Royal Flush for Leland. I remembered one night Trevor drank that shit and his dick was hard all night. That nigga couldn't even cum, that's how hard his shit was.

Leland told me that the Hen made his shit hard all night, but I was going to try some new shit on him, and if it didn't work, then we were going to the Hen, because I needed a stiff drink and a stiff dick all night long.

I smiled to myself as I got my stilettos out of the box in the closet. I had on a black, see-through short robe with the black matching thongs underneath. I wanted that night to be extra special, because this was not just about fucking; this was fucking and making love mixed together, which was a hell of a combination.

That was our first night together sexually, and I was ready to make it the best we had ever experienced.

The doorbell rang, and it was the delivery boy with the food. I gave him the money, plus a tip. I had the table set up with candles and the whole nine. I had the drinks ready, the music playing in the background and the house smelling good, and my pussy smelling good too.

I was ready for that night. We had spent several nights on the phone talking about our likes and dislikes. We knew each others' goals and fears. We were so close, and now we were going to make this thing happen between us that no one could change. We had agreed to become close to each other without any outsiders being in our business, and now we were so close, until this was just the grand finale.

I heard the door bell ring, and when I opened the door, Leland's fine ass was standing there.

"What's up, Ma? Damn baby, you look sexy as hell. Shit, do we have to have dinner first, because I see what I got a taste for standing in front of me."

I gave him a deep ass kiss with my tits pressed up against his chest, and he put one hand around my waist and the other one on my ass. Leland gently squeezed my ass and I could feel my pussy getting wet. I looked up at him and that motherfucker was so fucking sexy, I could have fucked him right where he was standing.

That shit was unreal, because I could feel my heart racing and could see the love he had for me in his eyes, and I knew he could see that I loved him back. Damn, I could not believe I was having those feelings, because I thought that Trevor was the only man that I could ever love, but I was so wrong.

I stood there and we kissed for about 20 minutes before he actually came into the house. I took the bottle out of his hand and sat it on the kitchen table. I had the food on the table with the plates and I had the candles lit. I said, "Baby come sit down over here." I pulled the chair out for him and he sat down.

I walked passed him, and my ass was shaking in that black thong like two midgets were fighting, and I could feel Leland watching me, so I put a little more twitch to it for him.

"Damn, Paris you look so sexy baby, I am really not that hungry right now!"

I walked in the kitchen and poured Leland and myself a drink. I made it nice and stiff. When I handed it to him, he drank it down and sat the glass on the table.

Now I had Jagged Edge playing in the background, and he was already feeling his drink. I poured him another drink, and while he was drinking it, I stood behind him and rubbed his chest. I asked, "Baby how's your drink?"

"Paris, my drink is fine, and I am feeling really good. How are you feeling?"

I turned his chair around and I sat in his lap and started kissing him and rubbing my hot wet pussy on his crouch.

Leland started rubbing my breast and then he opened the split that was right down the front of my robe and started sucking my breast.

I was flexing my back and leaning my hips into his body. He started licking my stomach all the way down to the top of my pussy. "Hmmmm Leland, damn baby that feels so good. I thought we were going to have dinner first?"

"We are, but I am starting with my dessert first."

Leland picked me up and took me into the living room in front of the fireplace on the rug. He laid my body down on that rug and started kissing my neck and licking my nipples. My nipples were so hard and stiff, I could see them sitting up like the nipples on the disposal Playtex bottles. I arched my back off the floor, and he just continued to lick my stomach all the way down the line to my pussy, and then he pulled the thong to the side.

I had my eyes closed. I was licking and sucking my bottom lip because that shit was feeling so fucking good that I was about to lose my damn mind. I could not believe the foreplay was so fucking off the chain. That nigga stuck his tongue in my pussy and at first, I thought I was going to cum, but then he quickly removed his tongue, leaving my pussy throbbing like a motherfucker.

I was practically begging that nigga to come back. I started pulling his head towards my pussy and moaning like a damn infant in that bitch.

He moved my hands and whispered, "Paris let me do this, and I promise you will cum more than once. I love you, and I am not going nowhere, just let me take my time baby."

What the fuck was I supposed to say after that? Damn nigga, do yo' thang.

I moved my hands and that nigga went to work on a sista like a fucking artist. He was kissing and sucking on my inner thigh, and then he stuck his finger in my wet pussy. He fingered me while he licked my clit. That shit was feeling so good that I just closed my eyes and moaned that nigga's name over and over again.

He took his finger out of my pussy and sucked on the juices as if the shit was from Kentucky Fried Chicken. I just watched him and my pussy got wetter. He then started sucking on my toes, sticking his tongue between each of them, and sucked them one by one, and then he stopped.

I was laying there thinking *'what the fuck is going on.'* I could feel the juices running down my leg, because my pussy was wet as a motherfucking river up in that bitch.

"Leland, baby where are you going?"

He didn't say a word, but he went in the kitchen and came back with this fucking vibrator shaped like a big black dick, but it had balls going around inside of it, and this little clit tickler on the end.

I sat up off the floor. "Leland where the fuck did that come from?"

"Paris, you didn't see me sit the bag on the kitchen table when I came in? This came from my bag of goodies, now here's another drink. Don't worry, you will love this."

I drank the glass of Goose down quick, and I was feeling good and warm all over. That nigga started kissing all over my body and he licked on my pussy some more, and then he turned that fucking vibrator dick on, and them balls inside of that shit was going round and round, and the dick was going round and round too.

Leland licked on my pussy and stuck that fucking dick inside of me. I couldn't hold the shit no longer, I came so fucking hard. That shit had my whole body shaking. I could feel the balls in the dick, they were hitting the walls inside of my pussy. The dick was going in circles, and that nigga was licking the shit out of my clit and pushing that dick in and out of my pussy at the same time.

I came three times in a row. I was like okay, *that* was foreplay? Damn, I was scared to see what else that nigga had up his sleeve. I laid there in ecstasy, and he just kissed me all over and held me tight in his arms.

I looked at him and said, "Leland what about you, don't you want to cum too?"

"Don't worry about me Paris, we got a life time, and besides that, I am ready to eat now. Aren't you hungry?"

Paris Love

I couldn't believe that nigga. He had worked up an appetite and I was feeling so fucking relaxed. He helped me up off the floor, and we went to sit at the table in the kitchen. I sat down and he heated up the food and fixed our plates. We ate, talked, and had a couple more drinks.

I was looking at him talking to me, and then I started feeling horny again. I said, "Leland, it's your turn now."

"Oh is that right, Ma? So what, are you going to do to please your man?"

We had finished eating and I walked over to Leland, put my hands on his crotch and started to massage the tip of his dick head. He leaned his head back and started rubbing my breast while I rubbed his dick. I unzipped his pants, reached inside of his boxers, and pulled out the longest, fattest, and roundest dick I had ever seen.

That nigga's dick had to be every bit of 11 inches or more. I was stroking that big ass dick, up and down, while rubbing my thumb on that thick ass vein down the shaft of his long rock hard dick. I said, "Damn baby, this is a big ass dick. How did you hide all of this from me?"

"Just a little trick I learned from the old man in the neighborhood. Can't let you know the total secret, but I told you that you would be more than satisfied."

"You got that shit right, damn baby!"

I continued to work on that Anaconda like a pro', and gave it all the attention that it deserved. I licked it like it was a lollypop from the circus, and I sucked the head like a crawfish from a restaurant in New Orleans.

He was talking to me now, "Damn Paris. Shit, Paris, hmmmm Paris, whew!"

"Yeah baby you like that, you like how I make you feel don't you?" "Yessssssss, shit I love how you make me feel!"

I stood up and moved the chair away from the table and I straddled that big ass dick like a saddle on a 25-cent pony. I slowly lowered my wet pussy on top of that dick head and squeezed it with my muscle, and then I lowered my body more and more until the whole thing was deep inside of me. I rotated my hips and lifted my ass up and down until Leland grabbed my ass and started squeezing it and slapping it, and I rode that horse until we fell over in the chair.

Afterwards, we got up laughing our ass off. I took Leland's hand and we went in the living room and got on the floor in front of the fireplace again. I kissed him, and then I got on all fours and he was up on his knees behind me. And when he put that big ass dick in my pussy, I could feel every inch all the way to my fucking stomach.

Leland had a big ass dick, and he knew how to work every inch of that shit. He was pumping harder now, and the next thing I knew, he came so hard and he was holding my hips and pulling me into him so hard. My tits were bouncing back and forth so fast, until I thought they were going to swing into the damn fire in the fireplace.

We both collapsed on the floor. He wrapped his body around mines and we just laid there and talked. We fell asleep in front of the fireplace, and that was the beginning of our relationship.

Chapter Twenty-Two

It was 7 am in the morning and Lolita could not sleep. She had a dream about the delivery again, which she had been having ever since she went to meet with Raymond. Lolita had received a letter in the mail from him that she didn't open. It came a week after the day that she went to meet him in University area.

Lolita didn't know why she hadn't opened the letter, but she guessed it was because she was afraid of what was inside of it. She put it in the nightstand drawer next to her bed and decided when the time was right, she would open it. She knew she would have to face the fact that she had a daughter out there, and she needed to attempt to find her.

Lolita reached for the phone on her dresser, and she dialed Jaylan's number. When he answered, she started to smile.

Lolita said, "Hey baby, you miss me yet?"

"Now Lolita, you already know the answer to that question. We had such a good time together, and I have been trying to get with you ever since, but you keep me at a distance. What's up with that? I know you are feeling me Lo, so why you frontin?"

"Whatever Jaylan, I told you that I was digging you, so don't even try it!"

"Okay so what's up, can I be your man or what?"

"Boo, you live in Texas, and that's far."

"Boo, you are freakin' rich, and I am not broke, so we can see each other. And then when things get deep between us, we can decide what we will do about it."

"Okay smart ass, I guess we can do something, but we can't be telling everybody just yet. And then again, you know Lo got some skeletons in her closet, so you might want to find out what's in the closet before you start applying for a position."

"Girl, it doesn't even matter, 'cause yo' boy got some too!"

"Yeah I hear you talking. So what's up with the trip to Cancun? Has Johnny booked that shit yet?"

"As a matter of fact, he called me yesterday with some dates for two weeks from now, so what's up with the crew?"

"You know what Jaylan, let's do a conference call and see what's up?"

"Let me give you my 800 number and you get the girls on the phone, and I will call Johnny and Jackson."

"Oh look at you 'Mr. Businessman with the 800 number,' damn I want to be like you when I grow up!"

"Whatever Lolita, write down the damn number!"

"Okay, what's the number?"

It was about 8 am. Lolita knew that Lucky was up but me, I was another story, because I could be a bitch in the morning.

266

Lolita called me and said, "Hey Paris I am surprised you are up and sounding all chipper and shit, what have you been doing?"

I said, "Bitch get some business and stop worrying about what I am doing over here."

"What the fuck ever Paris, I am getting ready to call Lucky so we can get on this conference call with Johnny and the boys."

I didn't tell Lolita that Leland had just left and I was laying in my bed thinking about that fine ass chocolate nigga while Lolita dialed the number to get Johnny and the boys on the horn.

We were all on the call except for Lucky she dialed in later, and I could hear the phone beep.

"What's up y'all," Lucky said in her ghetto ass voice.

Everybody said 'hello,' and then Johnny told us about the dates for the Cancun trip in two weeks, and we were all available, so he went online and booked everything. We were staying in a big ass villa with six rooms and four bathrooms, so the shit was about to be crazy.

We all always had a good time together. Johnny and I were just friends, and now that I was with Leland, Johnny wouldn't be getting NO cat!

We all agreed on the dates and times for our flights. We would meet Johnny and the crew in Cancun at the airport; our flights landed at the same time. So now it was a matter of getting our shit packed and ready for a trip to Cancun in two weeks.

We all got off the phone and Lolita told Jaylan that she would call him later, and then Lolita, Lucky and I talked for a while. Lucky finally bought a dog, and she was so excited about her little Jack Russell. She named him "Mr. Peabody." She put a black tie around his neck along with a diamond dog collar.

That dog was spoiled already, and Lucky carried his ass around in her purse, because he was still a puppy. We were happy that she had a dog, because she needed to have a dog in that big house with her, so she would not go crazy in there at night by herself. She told us about how smart Mr. Peabody was and how he was just the best dog in the world; I mean she was acting as if the dog could talk. I was just tripping listening to her telling Lolita and I all this and that about the dog.

We finally got off the phone and I fell back to sleep watching TV. I had to go to the office on Monday, and I was not trying to be there all day, because I was meeting my baby to go to the movies that night.

Lucky got off the phone with Lolita and she took the dog outside in the back yard to do his business. When she came back in the house, she made some tea because her stomach was feeling upset, and she could feel herself becoming light-headed. She sat down in the chair in the kitchen, and when the water was ready, she stood up to put the tea bag in the cup. She had to sit down, because she felt like she was going to fall out. She went in the bathroom downstairs and bent down in front of the toilet, because she thought she was going to throw up, but nothing came out.

"What the hell is wrong with me, I been feeling like this for the last three months and I know I am not pregnant. Lord please don't let me be pregnant, because I don't know what I would do, shit!"

Lucky got up off the bathroom floor, went back into the kitchen, and got some crackers out of the kitchen cabinet. Her stomach started to settle and Lucky just figured it was just that morning. She may have eaten something that didn't agree with her system the previous night.

"Naw I can't be pregnant, ain't that right Mr. Peabody? You are the only baby that Lucky got."

Lucky held Mr. Peabody in her arms and then she went upstairs to get in the bed for a few minutes before she went to the office to catch up some work.

Chapter Twenty-Three

A few weeks passed before I knew it, and I had spent every waking moment with Leland. He was spending the night with me, and I was staying over his house. We went to lunch together, and we were having sex everyday. I was so in love with him and he was in love with me. We didn't see anybody, we spent most of our time with each other.

He would go play ball with his boys on Saturday mornings, and I would go to the gym and work out while he played ball. Then we would spend the evening together.

We would go to Greensboro sometimes for the weekend and just stay in the hotel and shop, and then we would go to Atlanta and do the same things, except we hit the clubs in Atlanta, because we both loved to dance.

One weekend, we came back from Atlanta, and Leland was acting strange, as if he wanted to tell me something or something was on his mind. But whenever I asked him, he would always say it was 'nothing.' He held me close to him and just looked at me and gave me little kisses on the forehead repeatedly.

I often said, "Baby you sure everything is okay, you know you can tell me anything, right?"

And Leland would say, "I know. We are good baby, I am good."

I would give him a kiss on the lips, and we often watched TV until it was bedtime.

It was Wednesday about 5pm, and I was getting ready to leave the office. Palmer was great, and he ran my business like it was his own; he made sure shit was correct when I was away. I had told him that I was going to make him my partner, so that he could just chill and hire someone to work for him.

I really enjoyed my job, and my clients were coming from all over. I finally started picking up more women, and I was giving them to Palmer and his gay friends, because the women seemed to love them and the work they did. Palmer knew how to shop for clothes, household stuff, and the finest restaurants in Charlotte. The boy was bad as hell and he knew it, but we worked well together and we had a great team.

I called Lolita and Lucky on the phone, "Are you heifers ready to go to Cancun and have some girl time or what?"

"Hell yeah," Lolita said.

Lucky sounded like she had a real baby, "Well I have to take Mr. Peabody to my co-workers house so she can baby sit him. She has a Jack Russell and I take Mr. Peabody over there sometimes to play with her dog. I am going to leave him with her since he is comfortable at her place, that way he won't miss his mommy too much."

Lolita said, "Lucky you are trippin but okay girl, make sure Mr. Peabody is straight so we will not have to worry about him while we are gone."

"Thanks Lolita, I knew you cared about Mr. Peabody."

Lolita said, "Girl don't get it twisted, I don't care that much!"

I said, "Lucky don't let Lolita tell you that lie, because she told me that she loved your dog."

"Whatever, I am not thinking about you bitches because I am going to take care of my baby. Isn't that right Mr. Peabody?"

I was tripping on Lucky; I was just sitting there waiting to hear Mr. Peabody tell her how right she was. Damn, she really loved that dog.

We talked about what we were taking on the trip and Lucky and I decided to ride with Lolita to the airport, so we were going to meet at Lucky's spot on Thursday at 7am; our flight left at 9am.

I got off the phone with them and I called Leland, "Hey baby, what are you doing? I want to see you before we leave, so are you coming to my house tonight?"

Leland said, "Yeah Paris, I will be there. Do you want me to take you to the airport?"

"Naw, I am riding with your sister, so you will have to be gone before she comes pick me up. I am going to tell her about us while we are in Cancun, is that okay with you?"

"Yeah, but don't you want to tell her together?"

I said, "Naw I will tell her first, and then we can talk if she wants when we get back. I just will soften the blow for you, okay?"

"That's cool, Paris, but you know I don't need you to do that, I could tell her."

"I know, but it will be okay baby, we will be okay."
"That's cool Ma, I will see you tonight."
"Bye baby!"

⸦⸦⸦⸦⸦⸦⸦⸦⸦⸦⸦⸦⸦⸦⸦⸦⸦⸦⸦⸦⸦

Lolita was in her office at Spa Margarita on the computer searching for her daughter. She put in the information of the date of her birth, but she didn't have a name, because Raymond told her it would be best if she didn't give her one.

Lolita had thought that memory would be one that would never come back, and she knew the only way to fight her demons was to face them. The computer people search didn't provide Lolita with any information, because she didn't know the girl's name or anything that could link her to her.

It was impossible for her to get information on a child that she knew nothing about, and she was wondering if she would ever find her. Not to interrupt her life, but to make sure she was taking care of, and that she had good parents.

Lolita turned the computer off and just said a prayer for the daughter that she had never knew. She grabbed her purse and headed to the parking garage to get her car. Lolita got in the car and headed to her house. She was going to go home and pack for the trip to Cancun and go through her mail and make sure she had everything she needed before we left in the morning.

It took Lolita 30 minutes to get home, and when she pulled up to her driveway, she checked her mail and opened the garage door to pull her car in. Once she got in the house, she went into the master bedroom and started packing her clothes. The phone rang and when she looked at the Caller ID, she didn't recognize the number, so she let the call go to voicemail.

Lolita finished packing her clothes, and when she opened the nightstand drawer, she saw the letter from Raymond in there.

She said aloud, "I am going to take this with me and let Paris read it to me, because I am just afraid to read it on my own. I will tell her and Lucky about my daughter, and they will help me deal with everything."

Lolita put the letter in her suitcase on top of her clothes, then she closed it and zipped it up. Lolita went into the bathroom and ran some bath water, put some Vickie's Secrets bubble bath in the water, poured a glass of wine, and lit the candles around the tube.

The bubbles in the tube rose to the top and Lolita took her clothes off, clicked the 'on' button on the remote, and the flat screen TV above the tub came on. Lolita got in the tub, put her pillow behind her head, sipped her wine, and watched the news.

◇◇◇◇◇◇◇◇◇◇◇◇◇◇◇◇◇◇◇

Thursday morning, 5am, I woke up to Leland looking at me.

I asked, "What's wrong baby, did you have a bad dream or something?"

He said, "Naw baby, I was up thinking about us and how everything was going. Paris I feel like I have known you a lifetime and I know it sounds corny, but this shit is like a fucking fairy tale. I want to wake up to you every morning, so Paris…will you marry me?"

I wiped my eyes and when I looked at him again, I saw that he was serious, and I wasn't fucking dreaming the shit.

He opened the red velvet box and inside was a princess-cut diamond engagement ring. It had to be every bit of 3 carats.

I was speechless. The tears just started rolling down my eyes and the next thing I knew, I said "Yes, yes, yes."

Leland grabbed me and kissed me all over my face. He jumped up and down in excitement. "Damn baby, I am so glad that you said yes! I wasn't sure if you would think it was too soon, but I love you so much, and I just didn't want to waste anymore time without you being my wife."

"Baby I feel the same way, but I just didn't know if I was thinking too far into everything. I was just waiting for you to tell me that you changed your mind about us."

"No girl, I could never leave you."

"Oh shit, shit, baby how are we going to tell Lolita this shit? I can't show her the ring just yet. Damn, maybe I will just wear it when we get to Cancun and then spring it on her, what do you think?"

"I don't know Paris, let's just wait until you all come back, and then we can take her to dinner and we will both tell her."

"Okay, baby I will wait, but it's going to kill me, because I want to wear my ring."

Leland put the ring on my finger and it was a perfect little fit. Come to find out, he had took one of my other rings to the jewelry store to get the size. I wanted to wear the shit right then.

Leland said, "I guess we are going to wait to tell everyone, but we can look at dates now if you want to."

"Okay, let's check the availability on the island first, because I don't want to do the church thing. I want to get married in Tahiti."

"Okay Paris, we will do all that when you get back from your trip, now come here and give me some of that sweet pussy before you leave me for 4 days."

It was 6:30am and Lucky had just came back from walking Mr. Peabody. Her co-worker was on her way over to pick him up, so

Paris Love

Lucky made sure he had his favorite toy and all of his food before she left to go to Cancun.

Lucky packed her toiletries and she put an EPT pregnancy test in her bag. "I will take the test while I am in Cancun, and if it comes out positive, I will have Lolita and Paris with me to help me decide what I want to do. But Lord knows I don't want a baby, especially by Ron's black ass."

Lucky had received several letters from Ron since he had been in prison, and she hadn't opened any of them. She decided to throw them in the bag too. She would let Lolita and I read them, and that would help her to deal with his ass still being able to breathe each day.

By the time Lucky finished putting everything in the bag, Lolita pulled up in front of the house and Lucky could hear her truck pulling up in the driveway.

Lucky had wondered which car Lolita was going to drive, because we all packed a lot of shit when we went out of town. It was good to get out of town and enjoy her friends; Lucky was looking forward to having fun and just talking with the crew again. It was also going to be good to see Jackson.

I jumped out of the truck and rang Lucky's door bell. On that day, I was so fucking hyped, because I was the happiest I had ever been in my life. I was in love, and damn it felt good.

I said, "Lucky, bring yo' ass out of the house, 'cause we are ready to go!"

Lucky came to the door with three bags, and she was smiling from ear to ear. "Bitch, I am ready so let's go!"

We put her shit in the truck and pulled out of the driveway, blasting the music. I was up and alert like a motherfucker, and usually my ass was not saying a word, especially at 7am in the morning. But I was too happy and I had my ring with me. I had to tell those bitches, 'cause I couldn't hold the shit. It was killing me that I had to wait until we got to Cancun.

We got to the airport and did our routine of giving the curbside baggage handler our shit and going straight to the gate. We did the check-in thang and got to the gate in time for the first boarding to start. And since we were sitting in first class, we boarded right after the old people, children and babies.

I was glad when we got to our seats. We ordered drinks and talked shit all the way there. We had first class hyped as hell, and we were just making all kinds of noise. My girls and I were headed to the warm weather in Cancun, and we were going to party our asses off when we got there. I was happy because we each had a successful business and our club was the bomb down in Miami, which we were going to visit after Lucky's trial was over. I looked at my girls, and we were together having a good time.

We were three blessed bitches and we were grateful for our lives and for Lucky being back with us unharmed. I could not wait until the plane landed in Cancun; we had all been through a lot and we deserved this vacation to get back to our normal lives of living, laughing, and enjoying our friends.

Jackson, Jaylan and Johnny were some down to earth brothers and we were looking forward to seeing them again. Johnny and I had a good working relationship and friendship and he knew all about Leland, but we were still cool, and we could talk to each other about anything. This trip was going to be the bomb!

Coming Soon!

Coming Soon

Skeletons, Part 2

Spring 2007

The plane landed in Cancun and we were all tipsy as hell. I looked out of my window, and I saw the flight crew driving the stairs over to hook up to the plane for arrival.

When we walked down the stairs, Lucky almost tripped over her big ass feet.

I was laughing my ass off, "Damn Lucky, you might want to pick your feet up before you go tumbling down this motherfucker."

Lolita was behind her laughing her ass off too. Lucky grabbed the rail on the steps, trying to steady herself so she wouldn't go tumble down and break her neck. "I know one thing, if I fall; I am going to sue the hell out of this fucking airline."

Lolita said, "Bitch please, they didn't tell you to get drunk on this motherfucker. I didn't hear the Captain say, 'Welcome aboard, my name is so and so, now get drunk and enjoy the flight.'"

"Ha ha, you are not funny Lolita. You *and* your friend Paris can kiss my entire ass."

I said, "I got this Lolita, now would that be the entire ass you don't have, because it won't take long to kiss that little bit."

Lucky gave both of us the finger and we fell out laughing. When we got inside the airport, Johnny and the crew were posted up like some straight gangsters. They spotted us and came over as if they were the shit.

Johnny said in his thug voice, "You ladies need some help with yo' bags?"

Jaylan and Jackson were standing there looking fine as hell, and Lolita and Lucky were cheesin' their asses off.

I said to Johnny in my hoodrat-gangster-girl-voice, "Yes we do, so what's up, y'all got us or what?" I looked at Johnny and we both busted out laughing.

Johnny said, "Paris yo' ass is stupid!"

When we got to the rooms, the shit was off the hook. Johnny, Jackson, and Jaylan were tripping because we each had a phat ass ocean view from the picture window in the living room. The villas were connected and sat right on the beach. We also had a private pool and Jacuzzi.

The furniture was plush, and the colors were beautiful tropical colors with matching rugs and curtains. The place was so nice, and everybody was happy with the lay out of the villa. You could walk out the front door right onto the beach.

All I could think about was Leland, and I couldn't believe how much I missed him already. I was thinking that he and I would enjoy being in a place like that, and just as my thoughts were getting deeper into my own world, Lolita startled me when she pushed me.

"What are you so deep in thought about?" Lolita asked.

"What? Oh girl, I was in my own little world. What are we getting ready to do?" I said, snapping back to reality.

Lolita said, "I think it's going to be girls' night and the guys are going to go bar hopping. Then we are all going to get up in the morning and go to breakfast."

I was glad that we were going to spend some time with each other before hanging with Johnny and the crew. We needed to spend some time just chilling and having some drinks, talking, and laughing. We had all been through so much and that vacation was going to be about getting our lives right and learning to let go of the bullshit.

The guys left and went to their rooms. Now I didn't know how long this 'the girls stay in one room and boys in another' shit was going to last but whatever. We all had our own rooms with doors that locked. Anyway, I had already discussed the arrangements with Johnny so we were cool.

We each went in our rooms and put our pjs on. We ordered some food and got our drinks out of our bags that we brought at the Cancun airport from the little Mexican dude.

Lucky went in the bathroom and she pulled the EPT test out of her bag. "I might as well pee on the stick to see if I am pregnant now and in a couple of hours, I will come back to check the results."

Lolita was in her room looking at the envelope she had received from Raymond. "Well this time is just as good as any other. Let me take this in the living room and open it with my girls."

I was in my bedroom talking on the phone to Leland and looking at the big ass rock on my finger. "Damn baby, I am not going to be able to hold this shit the hold trip, can I please tell them?"

Queen Pin

Summer 2007

Sunday morning, January 1997, LaShay heard the dogs in her neighborhood barking loudly outside her bedroom window were she slept with her two sisters. The two-bedroom apartment on 5th Avenue, right down the street from the Boys and Girl's club, was not the picture perfect home that LaShay had in mind. She often fantasized about living in a big beautiful home in San Diego or Houston were there was plenty of room and plenty of food to eat. She promised herself that she would one day escape the ghetto that her mother, with her bad choices in life, created for them.

LaShay was born in Gary, Indiana at Mercy hospital she was the baby of seven children. Her mother was twenty years old when she had LaShay and she had already had six other children, by four different men, before LaShay was born. Antonio was the oldest and then her twin sisters, Latoya and Lakeshia were a year younger then Antonio, her brother Kaylan was a year younger than the twins were, and then her mother had twin boys James and John. Lashay was born two years after the last set of twins and the doctors made her mother get her tubes tied.

Latisha Renay Brown was LaShay's mother she was a very beautiful woman, 5'7 dark brown with deep dark brown eyes, her hair was jet black and long, down to the middle of her back. She was gorgeous and she had a body that men would die for, but she was dingy as hell. Latisha dropped out of school at fourteen when she became pregnant with her first child, the father was Anthony Hill, he was a football player in high school which he never claimed to be the father or have anything to do with Latisha.

There were no DNA testing back then and everyone knew Latisha was an "easy" girl, that's what the old churchwomen would call them; nowadays it's just a straight up hoe. No one ever believed her when she told them that the baby was Anthony's so she ended up on her own and in the system.

Latisha continued to date men that weren't bout nothing, she would have babies by them and hoped that they would take care of her and marry her but they always left her holding the bag.

Anthony came to see Antonio for the first time when he was six years old and that was only because his family, especially his grand mother told him they didn't care what he said that baby was his. Antonio's father and LaShay's father were the only men that slept with Latisha that cared about their children; the other men just left her 'stuck like chuck' and never came to see neither her nor the children they fathered.

LaShay's father despised her mother but he loved his daughter. So he would come, pick her up, and take her to all the nice places in Chicago to eat. He would take her to the Taste of Chicago every

4th of July weekend and they would spend the day shopping, eating and walking around Navy Pier.

LaShay remember the story her daddy told her about how he met her mother, and why he did not marry her after she told him she was pregnant.

LaShay thought about Derrick not being her father, and how she would not have existed, and how there would be no chance for her to escape the jungle she now lived in. Just the thought of one of those other deadbeats being her father made her want to throw-up; at least she had a father that cared about her.

LaShay hated staying with her mother, she wanted to live with her father, but he couldn't have her around, especially with the type of people he kept company with. He would tell LaShay that it's not good for a girl to be around that type of environment and that she needed to stay with her mother.

Derrick Dolton was a Kingpin in Chicago Heights, he never touched the dope but he always collected his money, he also had several stores, car detail shops and four barbershops, which all made him good money.

LaShay's daddy was ghetto rich and he always brought the finest things for his baby girl, which happens to be is only child, so she was spoiled rotten.

Derrick knew that Latisha wasn't a good mother but he just couldn't take care of LaShay like he knew she needed to be taken care of.

He told LaShay that as soon as she tuned sixteen that he would let her come live with him. She was counting down the days because she would be sixteen in four months.

LaShay thought about her life and she remembered how she loved it when the holidays came around because she would go to stay in Chicago Heights with her father. His house was so big, there were several bedrooms, two were Master Bedrooms and one of them was hers.   She had a king size bed with a walk in closet and it was filled with clothes, shoes, coats, handbags all of the design things. When LaShay was thirteen Derrick took her to California to see the Oscars awards and they went shopping on Rodeo Drive.

LaShay felt right at home with her father but she would cry every time she had to go back to Gary to stay with her mom. "Daddy, why can't I stay with you?" She would say, with tears welling up in her eyes. "I can take care of myself; I have been taking care of myself since I was nine years old."

Her father would just hold her in his arms and tell her that it wouldn't be long until summer and then she could stay the summer with him and when she turned sixteen, she could say with him for good, but he just traveled too much for her to stay with him now.

LaShay didn't like it but she had no choice so she started focusing on the holidays and summer until she could leave her mother's for good.

LaShay sat in the bedroom looked out the window at the view of the alley behind her apartment building. She could see a couple of strait cats eating the garbage that was spilled out of the trashcans. There was broken glass, crack pipes, blunts and trash every where and the town drunks were posted up at the end of the alley drinking Wild Irish Rose at 8 am in the morning.

She stood there looking out of the window and thinking to herself, just a little while longer and I will be out of this place for good. I will be happy when that day comes.

The thoughts filled her head but in six months, she would be moving out for good, that in it self was enough to make LaShay endure the rest of the time she had left in her pitiful involvement.

Navy Seals: The New Breed

Winter 2008

Apparently, four African American women, three Caucasian women and two Hispanic woman applied for the Navy Seal Program three years ago and were turned down solely because they where females.

Now with the new law in place, Frankie Rose Jackson, Bobbie Lynn Ray and Rosalina Santiago could now pursue their dreams of becoming Seals. All of the girl's fathers where ex-marines stationed on Paradise Island together and each ran their household like it were boot camp.

The girls never had a chance, because being born girls didn't stop their fathers from training them like they were boys. Frankie's father had her running ever since she could walk, and by the time she was in High School, she was on the swim team, the track team and in the weight training class. Frankie's father Frank Jackson was in the Marines for 25 years before he retired. Frankie was born that following year and her daddy wanted a son, but when he saw her little angelic face, he fell deeply in love with his baby girl. Frankie was a very smart woman and she had received several science awards while she was still attending high school at Princess Anne. She was so smart, that she once won $5,000 dollars towards college at a science fair in Greensboro. Frankie was drop-dead gorgeous, with caramel colored skin, greenish-brown eyes and curly jet-black hair.

It was Frankie's first day on campus, and she was excited! Frankie's plans were to pledge Delta as soon as they held a rush. Bobbie Lynn Ray and Rosalina Santiago where the only girls in their families, and they grew up with the same training as Frankie. You could say that they all were military brats. Rosalina Santiago was straight out of Spanish Harlem New York, so that girl was tough. She had long curly brown hair, thick lips, small dark brown eyes, and a beautiful set of white teeth. Rosalina started boxing at fourteen years old and she always boxed boys; she didn't want to fight girls.

After college, Frankie wanted to become a Navy Seal so she applied for the BUD training program. At that time, women could not be in the BUD program, but times had changed and there were now over 200 women that were in training to become Navy Seals.

Frankie always dreamed of becoming a Navy Seal, her father was a drill sergeant and he was one of the top ranking Seal Commanders. He would take Frankie on the base in Virginia and Florida so she could see the Seals train. She loved watching them, and she would practice swimming everyday with her dad and the squad leader. Frankie graduated from Duke University with a BS degree in Chemistry and she was accepted in the Bud Training program under the Officer Candidate School as a Tadpole (pre-trainee to become a Navy Seal) in July 2011.

Bobbie Lynn and Rosalina were both accepted in the Officer Candidate School too. Bobbie Lynn graduated from Duke with a degree in Chemical Engineering. Rosalina graduated from Chapel Hill with a degree in Criminal Justices and Physics.

The women where loving the attention. Frankie loved men and Lord knew she had her share in high school and college.

The first day was exhausting for Frankie; she spent the entire day getting shots and uniforms. Finally, it was TAPS and the whole company was exhausted and needed to get some sleep, because the next day was the beginning of training and it was going to be a bitch.

"Ladies and Gentlemen, get some rest, because you are going to need it. Reveille is at 0430, and then we will see what you are made of." With that said, the Drill Sergeant shut off the lights and walked out of the barracks.

Frankie fell fast asleep and started to dream. She had always had sex three or four times a day, and thirteen weeks with none was already starting to get to her. Before she left for training, she thought she had indulged herself in all the sexual activities that she would need to sustain her until she got out of training. Frankie started to dream about the night before she went to BUD training camp. She had two of her girlfriends and four guys over the house and they all had engaged in a sexual game. Frankie was not one to discriminate against male or female, if she found you sexually attractive, then that was her only concern.

Coming Soon

That evening at her house, they started playing nude twister, a game that Frankie loved and was quite good at it. Frankie's rules were different than anyone that she had ever played with.

"Left foot red, right foot yellow," one of the girls said, as she spun the wheel. Frankie had her foot underneath Seth's and the girl called out again, "Right hand on the blue and left hand on the green." Now Frankie's mouth was right between Seth's ass, and his nuts where hanging along with his dick. Frankie stuck out her tongue and started licking Seth's balls. Just when he was about to come, the girl called out "Right foot on yellow!" Frankie moved in the direction where her right foot landed on the yellow circle, and Seth was about to bust when she stopped.

As the girls got information in front of their barracks, the Drill Sergeant yelled at them the entire time. Once everyone was out of the barracks, with information and standing at attention, Drill Sergeant Gates (the Gates of Hell), started calling 'cadence' as the girls marched towards the chow hall for breakfast.

The Academic training courses were beginning, so the girls were headed over to the "C" Building for class. The course included training on engineering, military indoctrination, Naval history, navigation, seamanship, damage control, Naval leadership, Naval administration and military law.

The Fear of Falling In Love

Falling in love is bitter sweet, especially when the right one sweeps you off your feet. In the beginning you can't seem to stay away, you have to see 'em every single day.

Soon the newest begins to wear off and you're not sure if it's worth the cost, the cost of opening up your mouth and letting your lips say, "I love you and with me I want you to stay."

You can feel it in your heart but still you allow fear to keep you apart. What would your crew say if they knew, how would this effect your rep, so you must go on and let this be your best kept, best kept secret that you will never share only when you're alone and in the mirror you stare.

Looking at your own reflection as you think how I could've let myself go there, I don't fall in love, that's for punks.

What could have happen along the way was I slippin on my game? Please someone explain – explain to me this love trick. I'm falling in love – hell I'm already there, the only thing that is keeping me from letting go is FEAR – it's painless once you just let go, so I've heard – falling in love – LOVE, that four letter word.

RAIN DROPS

The sound of the rain falling, fingers tapping on the counter top, hot water boiling on the stove, wrapping up next to a cozy lit fire, being alone,

Is it to soon to call you, is it to soon to be this close, what happens if we kiss, will it stop there?

I can see your face as I stare out my window, like tears rolling down your beautiful brown skin the rain touches me. My body begins to get wet and my skin begins to shiver.

It's the touch of the rain soft drops falling, falling on my head, spinning around in a fantasy world the raindrops turn into sparkles of pearls.

You place your hand on my shoulder and I began to move, with the sound of the raindrops as my grove. I see your face everything is so clear. I hear the rain whispering sweetly in my ear. I reach out to touch you, but then you're gone.

The raindrops turn into teardrops running down my face. I open my eyes to try to refocus on life. I see the rain drops as the softness of your touch. I see the tear drops as the seriousness of your heart.

This is what I see in the rain today, I see you. I see me. I see life in a different way, thanks to the rain for all it has told, may it continue to show me new things, the raindrops falling against my windowpane.